PITFALL

PITFALL

TERRY KIRK

WINNIPEG

Pitfall

This book is a work of fiction. Names, characters, businesses, organizations, places, events, and incidents either are the product of the author's imagination or are used fictitiously.

Copyright © 2025 Terry Kirk

Design and layout by Lucas c Pauls and M. C. Joudrey.

Published by At Bay Press June 2025.

At Bay Press is an independent Publishing House that values and supports copyright. Copyright is imperative to the growth and support of human creativity, diversity and diverse voices, freedom of expression, culture, and an informed society. You've purchased this authorized edition and in doing so have supported this intellectual property and its human author. You have respected intellectual property laws by not reproducing, scanning or distributing any part of it by any means without permission. You are helping our Press to continue to publish books for all. Thank you. No part of this book may be used or reproduced in any manner for the purpose of training artificial intelligence technologies or systems. In accordance with Article 4(3) of the Digital Single Market Directive 2019/790, At Bay Press expressly reserves this work from the text and data mining exception.

No portion of this work may be reproduced without express written permission from At Bay Press.

Library and Archives Canada cataloguing in publication is available upon request.

ISBN 978-1-998779-70-3

Printed and bound in Canada.

This book is printed on acid free paper that is 100% recycled ancient forest friendly (100% post-consumer recycled).

First Edition

10 9 8 7 6 5 4 3 2

atbaypress.com

We acknowledge the support of the Canada Council for the Arts.

With the generous support of the Manitoba Arts Council.

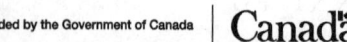

For
AREN FYFE WILSON

PART ONE

THE PIT

*Blessed are the young,
for they shall inherit the national debt.*

HERBERT HOOVER,
President of the United States (1929–1933)

1
THE PIT

The lavish lobby of the Chicago Board of Trade was bustling with men in overcoats and fedoras. Heads turned as Frank Cork, thirty-two and still brimming with youth, strode under the goddesses of industry and agriculture perched above its front door. Every trader in town knew that Frank had made a killing selling wheat futures on the city's commodities exchange. His fast fortune came with all the trimmings: his sprawling modernist home, late-model car, and even the right to swagger a bit at as he stepped off the elevator, tall and dapper-looking, onto the ninth floor at Duttons.

Dorothea, the receptionist, greeted him from behind a sleek, black console adorned with a single chrome letter—D for Dutton & Co., Chicago's leading commodities brokerage firm. With her pulled-back hair, taut eyebrows, and tightly tucked-in shirt, she was as polished as her desk.

Frank paused only long enough to scoop up the Friday edition of the *Chicago Tribune,* dated October 25, 1929, then walked purposefully along the partners floor with Rosie, his sixty-five-pound Irish Setter. Frank's wife, Katrina, claimed she was allergic to the breed, although he had a hunch it meant, "You look after the hound." Either way, Rosie was always in tow. "Here comes Duttons' head trader with his goddam dog," he once overheard his bank manager say.

In Frank's corner office, Rosie settled in by the windows overlooking the Chicago River, and Frank scanned the business news, picked up his call sheet, and began working through his names. His script seldom varied: "Hey, so-and-so. Frank here. Wheat's down two cents. It's a great time to buy. Can I put you down for thirty units?" His clients were busy entrepreneurs and professional men who usually gave him the green light; his calls may have been rote, but the trades he made on their behalf were large enough to move wheat prices most days. During his ten years as a trader, Frank had witnessed a breathtaking expansion of America's economy: stock markets created millionaires like tom cats siring kittens.

At 9:30 a.m. sharp, Frank's intern, Lewis Montgomery, stepped in. He was a handsome devil, as poised as a cadet. After a false start at West Point, the young man had graduated with the same double degrees in agriculture and economics as Frank. Every spring, Frank poached the program's top grads; this year, he'd acquired Lewis.

Shoulder to shoulder, the two athletic men spanned the breadth of the red-carpeted hallway as they set out on their rounds. Stopping at each door, Frank did the talking, and Lewis took notes. Their final stop was the office of the managing partner, James Dutton III, known to all as Mr. D. Frank began their ritual visit in his usual way: "Morning, sir. Any orders for the pit?"

"Well, butter my butt and call me a biscuit," Mr. D said.

Frank ignored the man's homespun humor, which was as affected as his southern drawl. The same could be said of Mr. D's attire—the buttoned waistcoat over a bulging belly, the dangling pocket watch, the spectacles, and a bowtie with scarlet polka dots that matched his face.

"We're here for your trading orders, sir," Frank repeated his request.

Mr. D rose to his full height, midway between Frank's naval and his chest, and made a show of stretching his arms and letting out a gaping yawn like an intern recovering from an all-nighter at his desk. Frank rolled his eyes on the sly, and Lewis suppressed a snicker; everybody knew that Mr. D always knocked off work by four.

"It's a great day to be a trader, Son, as easy as dipping your rod and worm into a pond of hungry fish," Mr. D gloated, handing over his order sheet with the self-importance of a man who'd just signed the Treaty of Versailles.

Frank snatched the paper and scanned the names. Only ten, yet they were a who's who of America's wealthiest rural families. "I'll catch you a big one, sir. A trophy fish for mounting on your wall," he said, flashing his most winning smile. But their chitter-chatter was all a charade; they both knew there would be no wins today.

Their morning rounds were done, and Frank and Lewis descended to the pit.

WHEN THE CHICAGO BOARD OF Trade opened its nine-story tower in 1883, it was dubbed America's boldest building. Decades later, the trading pit in the Great Hall still took Frank's breath away. Its stained-glass skylight rose to eighty feet and filled the room with dimpled light. There were granite columns, a frescoed ceiling, soaring windows, and full-length curtains that kept peering eyes and shards of sunlight off the board. In the center of it all was the amphitheater that gave the pit its tell-tale name. It was open for trading between

10 a.m. and noon and 1 and 3 p.m., and only those who paid handsomely for a seat on the Board of Trade were allowed in.

Frank stood at the back of the pit waiting for the opening gong, buffing his cufflinks along the sharp creases of his suit pants, trying to stay calm. Most traders had their good-luck charms: some dangled their grandfathers' pocket watches, others fiddled with their favorite pens. Frank had his cufflinks. They were a gift from Katrina five years ago when he was named head trader—Celtic wheat sheaves etched into gold and, if it ever came to that, a bit of money right there on his cuffs.

Across the front of the room ran the board—a giant slab of slate covering the entire height and width of that towering wall. A labyrinth of metal scaffolding stood between the traders and the board, and a dozen clerks, chalk in hand, scurried along the catwalks, scaled the ladders linking one level to the next, and scribbled the bids and answer prices as fast as they humanly could. The placement of the numbers on the board determined where traders stood: the pork bids were tracked down low in the center, so the pork men huddled mid-hall, and the wheat bids were recorded high on the left, so Frank and the wheat men stood at the back, craning their necks. Lewis stood in the raised gallery with the interns.

The room was awash with brawny athletic men who had wrestled their way through college, as he had. Many sported noses reshaped by an illegal right hook, and all wore the unstructured white jackets required by traders in the pit. Not many lasted long; turnover was through the roof. The few who succeeded knew how to out-yell their colleagues and elbow their way to the front of the room. The stench of their sweat and adrenalin filled the pit during trading hours and lingered long after markets closed.

At precisely 10 a.m., the gong pealed throughout the Great Hall. Frank loved that moment, even lived for it, his colleagues would say. Since reading about the Pamplona bullfights in *The Sun Also Rises,* by the Chicago sensation Ernest Hemingway, he imagined a bull bounding into the arena, the matador's cape flashing red, and the crowds erupting. Most days, he cast himself as the fearless matador; this morning, he felt like the ill-fated bull.

Instantly, Frank began bellowing the orders he'd collected on the ninth, and others barked back. Their calls and responses sent the clerks climbing and reaching, chalk debris falling like fairy dust into traders' hair. When prices rose, half the pit roared in victory, and the other half wailed in pain. But prices were falling, and the pressure was sky-high.

No one saw it that day, but Frank Cork was coming undone.

2
THE PARKWAY

On Monday morning, Frank slid his cufflinks into the sleeves of his crisp white shirt, combed a slick of brilliantine into his hair, and took a quick look in the mirror. Dorothea liked to say he looked like Gary Cooper, but when his skin turned coppery during the summer months, strangers told him he was a dead ringer for his dog. He retrieved the gift he'd bought for Katrina's birthday—a set of fine-tipped sable paint brushes in a soft leather pouch that she'd been longing for—and bolted down the stairs.

She was in the kitchen, standing at the counter with the morning papers and a coffee, still in her robe. Lengths of creamy-white silk curved around her seductive hips and tumbled to the floor. By God, he thought, Wally Caldwell better come through; one quick look at Katrina and he could think of better ways to start his day. He was pitching the city official over breakfast at the Parkway Hotel; Caldwell was spearheading a massive city-wide project to build new schools and had large sums of public money to invest until projects were underway. If things went as planned, Frank would be leaving the Parkway by 8 a.m. with Wally Caldwell's school board check in hand.

Frank slipped the gift to Katrina, leaned in, and whispered in her ear: "Thirty-two today and almost as beautiful as the day I met you." It was perfect, he thought, until she snickered, and he realized his mistake. *Almost* as beautiful. If his mother had been there, she would have smacked him across the head and called him a thick Mick like his father—all mouth and no brain. Some days, he had to remind himself that he was the city's top trader.

They'd made the climb together, he and Katrina, two poor kids from Chicago's South Side. He'd seen her across the pews at St. Stanislaus Kostka Parish Church—he was half-Irish and half-Polish, and she was Polish like his mom. As teens, they both won scholarships to the University of Chicago during the Great War. He studied agriculture and economics, and she earned a philosophy degree—ethics or aesthetics, he was never quite sure. He learned to line up his facts like a balance sheet; she preferred the soft corners of literature and ideas. They were married in 1919, a month after graduation. Ten years and two children later, Katrina had hardly changed—those Slavic cheekbones, that flawless skin. He was the one with the wear-and-tear lines cropping up at the corners of his eyes.

Franny and Robbie, fair-haired bunnies at eight and six, bounded into the kitchen with homemade birthday cards. Katrina donned her tortoiseshell glasses, swept up a handful of flaxen curls, clipped in a pin, and transformed herself from wife to mom. He couldn't have loved her more. But it was time for goodbyes—gentle embraces, rollicking hugs, and four sets of matching green eyes like shamrocks in the snow.

"We'll celebrate tonight," he hollered over his shoulder as he headed out the door.

"Thank you for the brushes, my love. I'll be here," she called back.

IN THE GARAGE, FRANK PILED into his 1929 roadster, the Hudson Super Six Cabriolet in jade and moss green. Katrina had selected the colors, which were a bit showy for his taste. The Parkway, Chicago's landmark hotel, was located in uptown Chicago by the zoo, between his home in the posh village of Glencoe north of the city and his office in the Loop, Chicago's downtown. Caldwell had set up the meeting, and the location made sense. Instead, what puzzled Frank as he drove toward Lincoln Park West was why a clever man like Wally Caldwell would even consider choosing him to invest the city's millions.

He'd never pretended to be the smartest or hardest-working trader in his firm; he'd paid his way through university on a wrestling scholarship, after all. No, the hallways of Duttons were lined with wiser men than him, although none had been quite so lucky. He wasn't born lucky, like some. In fact, Katrina said his childhood was so fraught with misery that he'd deserved the break. He wasn't sure he merited much of anything, but he'd hitched his wagon to wheat futures and had one helluva ride. Food products like pork, milk, and especially wheat, had fed the troops during the war and fueled eye-popping post-war returns.

FRANK PULLED INTO THE PARKWAY, Chicago's answer to the finest hotels in New York. Not even the Plaza, with its charming horse-drawn carriages and views over Central Park, could compete with the stunning vistas from the Parkway across Lake Michigan. He handed his keys to the valet and slipped him a few coins to keep an eye on Rosie. The hotel appeared to be stone-cold quiet that day. The St. Valentine's Day Massacre must have terrified the tourists away.

A few months earlier, on February 14th, rival gangs—Sicilians versus Irishmen—had blasted their way to infamy around the corner on North Clark Street, fighting for control of the billion-dollar contraband liquor trade spawned by Prohibition. Al Capone versus Bugs Moran—even the names made him shudder. The Sicilians had lined up the Irishmen against a brick wall at the Clark Street warehouse and slaughtered them, seven in all. The entire city was still reeling from the carnage. According to the papers, the Irish kingpin, Bugs Moran, lived in an apartment right upstairs but had missed his date with destiny by showing up at the warehouse late.

Stepping into the hotel's casual eatery, the Chat Room, Frank peered around. He imagined Moran's men taking the bullets while their boss lingered over bacon and eggs. There was no sign of anyone who might go by the name Bugs Moran, but Wally Caldwell was there. Frank ordered the Continental and took a pass on the bacon and eggs.

"Futures are simple instruments," he told the school board executive, "like a wager or a bet." His job as a trader, Frank said, was to predict the price of a product on a future date. If the product sells at his price on his date, his clients make money; if not, the bet is lost. Some people choose to wager on horses, others on grain. At that practiced point, Frank put down his napkin and looked Wally Caldwell in the eye: "Wheat's a safe bet."

"The world's gotta eat," Wally Caldwell replied.

Frank almost bolted upright. Those few words were music to his ears. It was a proven fact that whenever a prospect said them, his work was done. He sat back, tucked into his Danish pastry, and let Wally Caldwell say his piece.

"Bank stocks and railway shares are nice additions to any portfolio, but everyone needs flour and bread," Caldwell said.

Frank nodded as if to say, "How true," and dabbed at the corners of his mouth for any pastry flakes. By the time the waiter had taken their plates, he was slipping Wally Caldwell's check into the breast pocket of his pinstripe suit.

WHEN THE VALET BROUGHT HIS car around, Rosie's snout was sticking out the passenger window. He'd named her not only for her auburn coat but also as a tribute to Red Fyfe, his favorite wheat. The hardy grain had transformed the Canadian Prairies from vacant lands into fields of gold and spawned the modern hybrids like Marquis. Still, a loaf crafted from Red Fife was a thing apart. Mmmm, he could taste it, smell it, the dense crust and nutty flavor enwrapped in its reddish-brown crust.

The valet was hovering. He tipped the man and slid behind the wheel of his Hudson. It was not quite 8 a.m., meaning he had enough time to swing by the infamous warehouse for a quick look and still make it downtown in time for his daily catch-up with his best friend, Bobby. Wait a sec. Turning onto North Clark Street, there was trouble ahead. Thirty feet from his car, a white van was idling on the side of the road. A crew was loading crates, and the man standing watch looked like a prototype for the gangsters plastered across the *Daily News*. Sweet Jesus, here he was, one block from the Parkway yet smack in the crime-ridden underbelly of the city. Why was he always pushing things one step too far?

He threw the Hudson into reverse, slamming to a stop as a black sedan veered around the corner and blocked his path. He manhandled his roadster back into gear, swerved around the van, then throttled that engine with everything it had. *Rat-a-tat-tat-tat*. Dammit, the Hudson was backfiring. Wait, it wasn't the engine; it was a gunshot—no, a machine gun, the bullets blasting in a spray barely a car length from his head. His ears rang, and the shattering noise inside his head drowned out every other sound, even the wailing of his dog as she dove for cover under the front seat. Fear and confusion reigned from his head to his feet.

The driver in the black sedan had been shot but wasn't giving up the fight. The gangster car thrust forward, right up Frank's arse. In his rearview mirror, Frank caught a glimpse of the man at the wheel, fighting for his last breath, blood oozing from his head, the horn blaring, the car swerving, the shooter and his weapon coming into view. The face of the shooter filled his mirror; it was ghastly and unforgettable, with a long, livid scar above the eye. Hail Mary, full of grace, the evil snout of the man's weapon was whirling his way: he had a split second to avoid the fate of the driver in the black sedan. Frank cranked the steering wheel hand over hand, and the Hudson lurched around the corner onto West Dickens Street. Lake Shore Drive was moments away.

Frank careened into the southbound lane and, for the first time, welcomed the onslaught of morning traffic. He was alive; he'd beaten the shooter. His heartbeat began to normalize, and Rosie returned to her seat, trembling. Had the black sedan crashed to a violent end along West Dickens Street? Was the white van on his tail? Had the shooter seen his face? What did it mean for his future and family to have come eye-to-eye with the violent men who were terrorizing his city? He took up his usual route, passing Navy Pier, crossing the Chicago River, entering the Loop, and coming to a stop behind the Board of Trade Building at the corner of LaSalle and Jackson streets.

Hector, the parking attendant, greeted him as always, decked out in white gloves, a red serge jacket with gold braid on its sleeves, and a matching cap. The only visible flesh was on the young man's earnest-looking face, which was as black as his shoes. "She's a real showstopper," Hector said, letting out the kind of whistle men reserved for broads and cars. "Sorry to see wheat's down this morning, sir."

Most days, Frank enjoyed the market banter with Hector. The kid had moxie, networking with traders in the parking garage. If he weren't Black, he would have been given a shot in the mail room by one of the firms. But today, Hector's whistles felt grim: the last thing Frank needed was a reminder that his car was hardly discreet. Had he been followed? He peered up and down the side streets, checking for the scar-faced shooter or the white van, but there was nothing unusual in sight. He shook off his anxiety, strode under the goddesses, through the Great Hall, and into the office of the president, Robert MacNamara. Bobby. It was 9 a.m., and only one hour to go until the opening gong would kickstart the flow of winners and losers for the day. The receptionist handed him a coffee in his regular mug.

"Mr. MacNamara will see you now," she said.

FRANK'S BEST FRIEND HAD A face as welcoming as a hound, with large jowls, a permanent five o'clock shadow, and a suit too tight for his roly-poly frame. "Wheat's down," Bobby said, sounding as downcast as the grain.

Frank resisted the snide reply that the parking attendant had already said as much. But in Chicago, market-watchers could talk about wheat all day. It was a leading stock market indicator: when wheat was up, stock markets were up, but when wheat fell, trouble was on its way.

"Yeh, it was flyin' as high as the Cubs all summer long," Frank said. "Then the weather turned cool, wheat fell, and the Cubs lost the World Series." He was still smarting from the three-run fluke that had cost his team the 1929 season.

He'd put money on the game, along with every other trader in town.

Frank and Bobby met at UChicago, completing the same double degree. Their wartime service was researching how to pack the most calories into a soldier's belly for the least cost—trench rations, the army called them, although soldiers called them "trench rats." They were an instant fit, him and Bobby, like dollars and cents. Frank had even named his children for the friendship: Frances and Robert. Franny and Robbie.

After graduation, they'd started in the industry together—Bobby downstairs at the Board, bringing order and integrity to a dog-eat-dog world, and him upstairs at Duttons, putting his flippant mouth to work seeking rapid riches and market glory.

"It's not like you to be late," Bobby chided. "Must have been one helluva client."

"Bee's knees," was as much as he was prepared to say about his breakfast at the Parkway and visit to North Clark Street. Catching gangsters in the act was one thing, but gossiping about it was a sure path to an early grave. No one squealed in this town. The St. Valentine's Day Massacre erupted in broad daylight, yet months later, there hadn't been a single arrest. The authorities couldn't even agree whether the shooters were mobsters or cops. The *Tribune* claimed two police officers were among the killers, while the *Daily News* reported they were mafia men posing as cops. Either way, the sneaky bastards were probably looking for his Hudson right now.

He took his usual seat on this side of Bobby's desk. Was that dried blood under his fingernails? He had a faint recollection of furiously scratching the back of his neck all the way down Lake Shore Drive. He buried his nails in his lap and shifted in his chair until he had a clear line of sight from Bobby's window to the parking garage. He half-listened while keeping his eyes peeled outside. Their meeting would wrap up soon, as it always did, with Frank citing the pressures of clients and the morning bell. But Bobby rose first, startling him and bringing their visit to an abrupt close.

"There's something we have to discuss," Bobby said.

"Go for it," he fired back, standing to meet Bobby eye to eye, one face chiseled and the other round.

"No. Not here, not now," Bobby said. "I'll be at the university at noon for your speech. We'll talk then."

Their friendship was a professional minefield—the city's top trader and the head of the Board of Trade. It created visions of backroom shenanigans and secret deals, although things didn't actually work that way. As the industry watchdog, Bobby was not the type to simply roll over when slipped a treat; Frank knew this because he'd tried. Yet here they were, best friends, with nobody else around.

What was it that Bobby had to say that couldn't be said here and now?

3
THE PODIUM

Frank chucked his sweat-drenched shirt inside the sleek, ebony armoire in his office and skimmed the invitation to ensure he had the details right.

> Department of Economics, University of Chicago
> 12:30 p.m., Monday, October 28, 1929
> Keynote Speaker: Francis Cork, Head Trader, Dutton & Co.

It was tight. He was due at the Hyde Park campus in half an hour and still hadn't prepared his remarks. Would he drive? He'd read about gangsters planting bombs in their enemies' cars, yet he wasn't prepared to kowtow to this pack of curs; too much of his childhood had been overshadowed by fear.

He pulled on a fresh shirt from the supply in his drawer and buzzed Dorothea. "Ask Hector to bring the Hudson around. And tell him to leave it running."

What could he possibly say to this luncheon crowd? He cracked open his daily briefing binder and ran his finger down the closing prices in international wheat markets. The Big Six: Antwerp, Lyon...six cities in all, including Chicago. Everywhere, wheat was down. But moaning about stock-market gloom was out of the question. Many investors made their fortunes buying low. Even gamblers rallied around the underdog: it was the prospect of a breakaway horse that lured the crowds to Arlington Park.

Damn, it was time to go. He'd have to wing it. He donned his suit jacket and overcoat, decided to leave Rosie asleep in his office, and headed down to the street. Sweet relief, neither Hector nor the Hudson had been blown to smithereens. Had he set the young man up to take his fall? After handing him the usual loose change, Frank added a bill from his pocket.

On campus, Frank parked in the lot outside Rockefeller Chapel. It should be safe; these mobsters were God-fearing Catholics, after all. Still, it felt like a close shave when a group of divinity students glided by. He sprinted across the rugby field, making it to the podium just in time to stand relaxed and smiling at the microphone. The coterie of local academics and businessmen sized him up: good posture, good suit, good hair. These were the things that mattered in a luncheon speech: men in short socks wielded very little influence, he'd found.

The mood in the room was smug. In New York, gold and steel stocks were being beaten down, but in Chicago, agricultural commodities were holding their own. Wally Caldwell was right: the world's gotta eat. Reporters were lined up across the back of the lecture hall, and bulbs flashed as he began his remarks.

"It's a pleasure to be back on campus. On my way into the hall, I ran into two distinguished academics—former professors of mine. When I told them I'd be sharing my insights on laissez-faire economics, one of the laureates said, 'Yes, we were just laughing about that.'"

He waited for the tittering to settle, then turned to the subject at hand. Oozing with emotion, he spoke of the long run of giddy commodity prices that had made many in the room rich. "Food staples may not dominate the headlines of *The Wall Street Journal*, but they've brought new-found prosperity to our city," he boomed and was emboldened by the warm applause. With each sentence, Frank moved his audience closer to his mark—from commodities to grain, to the tall, reedy blonde with the plump berries and feathery spikes. Wheat.

He could almost feel the crowd lusting for his money and his grain. He led them back to the sweltering days that spring when the price of wheat, like the weather, had reached a record high—$1.62 per bushel. He sipped from his water glass and wiped his brow as if the heat was engulfing the hall. Then he moved them forward to the cool summer evenings on the shores of Lake Michigan when wheat prices and the temperature dipped: "$1.60, $1.50, $1.40..."

Frank paused and locked eyes with the men with money, one by one. After that dramatic effect had run its course, he outstretched his arms to embrace the room and bellowed, "Buy low, sell high. There's never been a better time to invest."

A voice from the back of the room shouted, "Bravo!" and another hollered, "Bull." It was a vaunted word among market men that signaled growth and gains, and Frank deftly turned the insult on its head: "I admire your confidence, sir." The crowd howled, and the heckler went quiet.

After touching on the importance of free markets and small governments, Frank lowered his voice and added, "Our people are our strength. This city is a beacon for newcomers from around the world; some are even standing for public office. Please join me and give them our support."

The audience gasped, sucking up every ounce of oxygen in the room. Was Frank Cork siding with the Czech immigrant running against the city's long-standing mayor? As if on cue, Frank plucked a newspaper clipping from his breast pocket. "Here's what the *Chicago Tribune* has to say about Mayor William Thompson, known to all of us as Big Bill: 'Thompson has meant filth, corruption, obscenity, idiocy and bankruptcy. He has given the city an international reputation for moronic buffoonery, barbaric crime, triumphant hoodlumism, unchecked graft...and made Chicago a byword for the collapse of American civilization.'"

Not an ounce of doubt was left in the room: Frank Cork was using the podium to declare war on Chicago's mob-boss mayor. The clutch of reporters lifted their pens and dropped their heads in unison like a set of ten pins going down in a strike. One angry listener stormed out of the room, and everyone else sat on their hands. "You thick Mick," he could almost hear his mother say. He stepped out of the spotlight and carved his way through the hall. A stranger with a chest as wide as a map of Ulster stepped out and blocked his path. When the man snarled, "Eejit," Frank could have sworn it was his father.

If he hadn't just trashed the most powerful man in the city, he'd be accepting a speaker's gift from Bobby on stage; instead, he found Bobby waiting for him behind the coat rack.

AT ROCKEFELLER CHAPEL, FRANK AND Bobby stood shivering beside the Hudson. This was where their friendship had begun—on campus. They'd spent long, liquid afternoons in its speakeasies and "blind pigs," drinking from bottles in brown paper bags. These days, they sipped their Bourbon in crystal glasses over ice, although neither the law nor their friendship had changed.

"What's up?" Frank asked.

"There's been a complaint," Bobby said.

Frank waited while Bobby weighed whether to cross the line that kept Board executives and traders at arm's length. He could almost hear Bobby wavering between "should he" and "shouldn't he," like a child plucking the petals off a daisy. The pit would be re-opening for afternoon trading soon, and Frank was growing impatient.

"Just gimme the facts, then I can decide how to fudge them." He immediately wished he could take it back; he'd been flip enough for one day.

"There's going to be an investigation...by the Board...into wheat futures," Bobby laid it out, drip by drip.

"An investigation?" They both knew that any probe into wheat futures would lead to new regulations with more teeth: in Canada, the instruments were already illegal. "Who's complaining?"

"Let's just say it's the largest wheat shipper in the world."

He began running through the major growers in the American wheat belt: Idaho, Kansas, Montana, Oklahoma, Wyoming, New Mexico—"Prices are volatile," Bobby added. "Farmers are looking for someone to blame and we're an easy target. Who's going to defend traders?"

"I thought that was your job," Frank fumed.

"You're churning. At least, that's what they say. Driving prices up and down, collecting fees with every move like some kind of bump-and-grind dancer working for tips."

He'd never understood Bobby's fascination with girlie shows; if his friend had spent less time in the hoochie-coochie clubs along Polk Street, he might have found himself a wife.

"Everything I do is legal. And sanctioned by the Board of Trade. Who are these sniveling whiners, anyway? Do they have a name?" It was his second try at securing the identity of the complainant; three times and Bobby would declare him out.

Silence. Frank admired his friend for that—thinking before speaking. He'd have to try it someday. He reached into his busy breast pocket and handed Bobby his notebook and fountain pen. Bobby took the hint, scribbled a few words, and passed them back.

"Look, Bobby," he said, feigning disinterest in what his friend had written, "I've been lucky. More than I ever imagined. But I'm learning that luck and bull markets have a lot in common; at some point, they both run out."

They shared a wry smile. Then Bobby turned to leave, and Frank checked his notebook with the speed of a stock market index changing from up to down. There were five words in all. *Yuri Dyachenko. Saskatchewan Wheat Pool.*

BY 1:30, FRANK WAS BACK in the pit. The trainees in the gallery were behaving like back-slapping boys, except for Lewis, who was studying the board. Frank signaled to meet him outside the Great Hall and handed over Wally Caldwell's school board check. "Add it to our trading pool. Let's get that money working today."

Lewis nodded, and Frank gave him Bobby's note.

"Who the hell is Yuri Dyachenko?" Lewis asked.

Hearing the name out loud for the first time, Frank felt the blood rise from his neck to his cheeks. God save him from becoming a red-faced blowhard like Mr. D.

"Do you know what I like about Rosie?" he asked.

"No, sir."

"She's a setter, not a mutt like me."

"Polish and Irish, I believe." Lewis had been at the firm since the spring and knew these things. "You, sir. Not the dog."

Frank ignored the wit and focused on containing his fury, which was rising like steam in a locomotive's stack. "My mother was *Za chlebem*—Polish for people with no bread. The hungry. And my father came from potato-famine immigrants, which is the kindest thing you could say about the man. But they're both one generation off the farm."

On the other side of the wall, "Buy, buy, buy" orders were thumping away. Lewis stood at ease, and Frank paced and vented: "Me, out to hurt farmers? *Ha*. That's the last thing we do. Our pricing information helps farmers make planting decisions, bargain for better rates, and gain access to international markets. Sure, trading wheat futures has made me rich. And one day, it will make you rich too. But over my dead body will some double-dealing dilettante at the Saskatchewan Wheat Pool drag my name through the mud," Frank said, crashing his fist against the door to the pit.

"I'm on it," Lewis said. "By the way, sir, who wrote the note?"

Now was not the time to tell his intern that the president of the Board of Trade had tipped him off on a confidential cross-border investigation into their firm. Besides, Frank had only one person on his mind—Yuri Dyachenko.

"Dig up everything you can on the sonofabitch, and meet me back here at 3 p.m."

4
THE DRAKE

By the time the closing bell rang in the pit, Frank was hankering for sunlight and fresh air—not that the sky was very bright nor the air very alluring by late afternoon in Chicago at the end of October. He and Lewis picked up Rosie in the office, then hoofed it up the Magnificent Mile to the Fountain Court in the Drake Hotel, Frank's regular watering hole. By God, it was gorgeous, and teaming as always with clients and colleagues after trading closed for the day. But as they entered the rococo dining room, a wave of angst rolled over him. The St. Valentine's Day Massacre had been sensational for its timing; however, a hit at the Fountain Court on the city's top trader would attract top marks for panache. He could see it as clear as a picture: bloody bits of his body splattering the Carrera marble floor while the water in the elaborate fountain that gave the room its name turned red.

He reined in his imagination and slipped the maître d' a tip to secure his table.

They wended their way among the white linens—Frank Cork with his dog and his protégé. Some rose from their chairs, others gave a soft salute, and one called out, "What's up with wheat today?"

"Up" was hardly the right word. "It's a great time to invest. Give me a call," he said with a smile.

Their table was perfect, overlooking the lake yet hidden behind a wall of palms. They settled in for a late lunch in high-back chairs upholstered in crimson and cream. Frank kick-started their discussion with the numbers: "Wheat dropped three cents this morning and another two cents this afternoon."

Lewis let out a low whistle. "That's a 3 percent drop in a single day."

"If it falls in foreign markets overnight, we'll have to change course tomorrow. Check with me in the morning before you start your calls."

There were no industry trendlines for a freefall like this. The best Frank could do was grasp at truisms in an effort to forecast what lay ahead. "Things happen in threes," he said, "when the sun, the moon, and the stars align." Lewis flinched, and Frank realized he sounded more like a two-bit fortune teller than a market sage. And yet a trio of long-simmering events was coming to a perilous boil as they spoke.

"First," he told Lewis, "soldiers flooded home after the war, women decided to keep their jobs, and the glut of workers kept wages low. Second, America went on a post-war shopping spree: radios, cars, washing machines. Spending went through the roof. And third—"

"Third," Lewis jumped in, "low wages and high spending drove debt levels to new highs. But where's it all heading?"

"Nowhere good, Lewis. Nowhere good."

They grew quiet and took in the view. A tanker was chugging into the harbor, a rusty red slab under a dense canopy of smoke. Frank daydreamed about sailing by the Drake in the spring in his sleek, black sloop. When the waiter came by, they both ordered the daily special: thick slices of rare beef on toasted sourdough bread, with pickles and hand-cut fries on the side. Lewis rubbed his belly, although it was a stretch to call it that: his athletic frame was as trim as his crew-cut hair.

Tucking into their sandwiches, they gossiped about on-the-take traders, the crime engulfing their city, and the mendacious mayor. The gutter was always an amusing place to spend some time.

When the plates were cleared, Lewis pulled a brown envelope from one of the black leather briefcases the firm issued to its interns each year. Frank sliced it open with his dinner knife with more vigor than required. Inside was a single page with headings and bullet points that looked as well-organized as Lewis himself. The memo began with an overview of the Saskatchewan Wheat Pool. Technically, it was the Saskatchewan Co-operative Wheat Producers Ltd., but everyone called it "the Pool." No wonder: "Saskatchewan" was a mouthful.

Lewis's note said it was derived from the Cree word for swift current, *Kisiskâciwan*, which was pronounced like Saskatchewan but with a "ki" sound upfront: *ki-suh-ska-chuh-wn*. Frank said it a few times. You never knew when it might come up in conversation. Chicago, for example, was the Algonquin word for "striped skunk," which he had found useful to mention to the mayor more than once.

Admittedly, the Province region merited a big word: it was the size of Texas. More importantly, the Pool had six million acres under management and produced 25 percent of all the wheat traded internationally. Jeezuz.

He glanced up at Lewis, feeling sick. Bobby had warned him that he was up against the world's biggest wheat exporter, but now it had a name, a size, a place.

"Let me guess," Frank said. "The purpose of the Pool is to insulate its grain from market forces."

"That's right. Farmers register their land in return for a guaranteed price for their grain."

"But fixed prices are the bane of our business," Frank spewed. "Who wants to wager on the price of wheat when it's already been announced by the Pool?"

"No one," Lewis said. "But the Pool has declared war on wheat futures, and it's coming after you."

"I'm being framed," Frank erupted. Men at the surrounding tables stirred, which didn't temper Frank's tirade one bit. He'd always tried to be affable, yet his list of enemies was growing by the day.

Lewis reassured the waiter they would behave, and Frank resumed reading Lewis's memo, going straight to the section on Yuri Dyachenko. As the head of the Pool's international desk, Dyachenko was its point man for cross-border trade. The Ukrainian—which made him a Russian, according to some—was sent to Canada by his family as a youth to escape poverty and oppression, only to find more trouble ahead than behind. He spent his first pitiful winter in a soddy, a lean-to covered in damp earth. "What an unthinkable housing solution for such a charming name," Frank said with a grimace. The next part was even more bleak. When the Great War broke out, Dyachenko was registered by Canada as an "enemy alien," conscripted into its army, and placed under military surveillance for six years. "Imagine the shame," Frank sighed. If the man wasn't accusing him of manipulating wheat markets and threatening his career, he might have felt sorry for the prick.

Frank pulled out his pen and showed hints of a smile as he underlined key terms: *Russian immigrant, enemy alien, military surveillance.* Were there any more vilified words in America? His industry was not about to yield to a campaign by this foreign interloper, and nor would his firm. Duttons was the largest broker on the Chicago grain exchange, and he was its head trader. They'd stamp out this man. He flipped to the final paragraph—Next Steps—and inhaled Lewis's bold advice: "Warn the Pool that retaliatory steps will be taken."

Immediately below was the phone number for Yuri Dyachenko's boss.

THE LAKE WAS DAZZLING IN the window, and Frank felt good: he was emboldened by the memo, hours had safely passed since his run-in with the mob, and his cufflinks sparkled in the sunlight.

Outside the Drake, Rosie sat on the curb, Frank bought the afternoon edition of the *Daily News,* and the doorman hailed them a Checker cab. In the back seat of the cab, he thumbed through Chicago's most widely read newspaper. Across the top of the City Page ran the headline, "Super Trader Frank Cork Yanks Support for Mayor," and staring back at him was yours truly, arms spread wide at the podium, embracing the tony crowd.

The article was overstated: he hadn't quite counseled all the bigwigs in Chicago to switch their votes from ayes to nays. But the nuances didn't matter; he knew there would be consequences for having said anything at all.

5
THE PRESS

After his late lunch, Frank bustled into the firm with Rosie and Lewis in tow. He stopped at reception to ask Dorothea to pick up long-stemmed roses and a birthday card for Katrina, and Lewis lingered, as he was inclined to do when Dorothea was at the front desk.

In his office, Frank hurled the news rag into his wastebasket and made the call to the top dog at the Saskatchewan Wheat Pool. "Did you really expect Americans to cede to the demands of a weasel with the wartime record of Yuri Dyachenko?"

The sound of the man clearing his throat pushed its way across the line from Regina, Saskatchewan, to Chicago, Illinois. Frank forged ahead: "The head of your international desk was registered as an enemy alien of your country for six consecutive years, and you didn't know? Shall I send you a copy?"

Frank filled the silence with his firm's plans to retaliate, which included suing the Pool for slander, boycotting its grain, and a few lurid threats he'd perfected as a wrestler when squaring off before a match. By the time the call was done, the Wheat Pool executive had apologized three times. These Canadians were a puzzling lot. During Frank's ten years as a trader, he'd never heard an *American* businessman say, "I'm sorry."

Moments after he'd squelched the cross-border fight, Frank's intercom issued its irritating buzz, and Dorothea's voice broke through: "I have the mayor's office on the line."

Before anyone had even spoken, he knew, as if hot air were blasting from his receiver and pumping up the temperature in his office by a degree or two, that it was no minion; it was Big Bill himself.

"I'm trying to manage the worst crime wave in this city's history," the mayor huffed. "We've got gang warfare on our streets. Sicilians are slaying Irishmen in broad daylight. As if that's not enough, I've gotta read in the *Daily News* that Frank Cork is letting his big mouth flap in the autumn breeze."

Frank had worked on this man's campaign two years ago and could attest that the city's top official had more in common with a steamroller than a mayor.

Big Bill revved up his powerful engine: "My contacts at the Board of Trade tell me your industry is under attack from powerful foreign interests. And your best friend Bobby has teed you up to take the fall."

Frank's angst about having gone too far in his lunchtime remarks vanished: it was time for his city to get out from under the thumb of this mayor.

"I've got nothing against traders," Big Bill continued, his voice barreling down a well-traveled road from menacing to mean, "although it's never been clear to me what you leeches actually do. I can shut down your industry in sixty seconds flat. No more commodities trading in this town."

The mayor was on an unstoppable roll. It was time to push back; you can't give a bully too much rope. "I don't think you'd find that very popular, sir," he said. "Chicago is the commodities capital of the world. Voters in this city like to trade."

The mayor did not respond well to the challenge. "You will regret taking me on, Frank Cork."

Slam. The line went cold. Dorothea buzzed again. "I have CPD—the Chicago Police Department—on the line."

A Sergeant Thompson introduced himself. Really? A cop with the same last name as the mayor?

"You had breakfast with one Wally Caldwell this morning," the mayor's namesake declared. Like half the city's police force, the copper had a Chicago take on an Irish brogue. "Mr. Caldwell tells us you're his broker. You both left the Parkway Hotel at eight this morning."

"What's the purpose of your call?" One thing he'd learned as a wrestler was that offense is always better than defense.

"We've received a report of a shooting on North Clark Street."

"Anyone killed?"

"No, the shots struck the car."

That was a relief. No one was dead. He covered the mouthpiece and exhaled.

"Did you see anything? You were in the vicinity at the time," Sergeant Thompson pressed.

The cord on Frank's phone was just long enough to allow him to pace the length of his desk. Back and forth he went, maintaining a poker face, even with no one in the room. "Mr. Caldwell and I finished breakfast around eight, then I drove to the Loop for a meeting with the president of the Board of Trade. I'm sure Mr. MacNamara will confirm that." But for the omissions, all of it was true.

"You saw nothing?"

The cop had cornered him. "Correct," he lied. "But good luck."

During the fraction of a second when the receiver hung suspended between its cradle and his ear, Frank heard Sergeant

Thompson's tell-tale lilt: "We'll be sending someone by."

Frank circled up his narrow spiral staircase toward the upper reaches of the bookshelves lining his back wall. On the landing, he'd added a wet bar up by the WXYZs. Some of his favorite authors were there: Evelyn Waugh, Max Weber, Thomas Wolfe...He poured a shot of Kentucky Bourbon—Old Fitzgerald, Whisper of Wheat—into a crystal tumbler and carried it back down the winding stairs. He nosed it, swirled it, and admired the long, slim "legs" clinging to his leaded glass. Ah, liquid gold, his favorite among wheat's many gifts.

Stretching out on his couch, Frank let his mind return to the shooter—the man with the livid scar. All his life, he'd been plagued by menacing men: his father, Mr. D, now gangsters, the mayor, maybe even the police. Where could he turn? Weren't citizens supposed to look to their elected officials for help? Clearly, the purveyor of that principle hadn't met the mayor of Chicago or the governor of Illinois: Big Bill and Len Small. Big and Small—even their names sounded more like a Laurel and Hardy act than leading statesmen.

Frank knew a thing or two about both men: it was a toss-up which was the more corrupt. Big Bill's connections to the mob were so flagrant that one of his political cronies had affixed his campaign posters to a crime boss's hearse as it wended its way to the cemetery from the church. It was hard to imagine a more crooked politician, yet the governor took corruption to a whole new level. Small was indicted twice while in office: first, for stealing millions from the state's treasury, and second, for ordering a hit on one of his jurors during the governor's embezzlement trial. The governor's campaigns were no holds barred: he sold pardons and paroles to raise campaign funds and used the Ku Klux Klan to get out the vote. True, there was a new man in the governor's mansion these days, but in Frank's experience, there was no chance of any Illinois governor helping him stand up to Chicago's mayor.

He must have drifted off. The sun had moved around to his westerly windows and was waking him as gently as a nudge from his wife. Katrina—she was all he'd ever wanted in life. Frank glanced at the large Roman numerals on his desk clock. They were just the right size for viewing from his couch. Damn, was it really after six already? He'd promised her he wouldn't be late and still had the hour-long drive to Glencoe ahead.

He stopped by reception to pick up the flowers and the card. Dorothea tucked in some birthday candles for Katrina and stepped from behind her desk to give Rosie her end-of-day pat.

"You've had a busy day, Mr. Cork," she said.

"Never too busy for a nap."

Dorothea tittered. Her looks bordered on severe, yet she giggled like a schoolgirl at almost anything he said.

Hector handed over the keys to the Hudson, and Frank opted for the shoreline route home. He anticipated the views of Lake Michigan washing over him and the stresses of the city disappearing behind his back; instead, the aftermath of the North Clark Street clash kept playing in his head. Not only had he witnessed a gangland shooting, but he'd lied to the police. What if the doorman at the Parkway had seen him turn right, not left? Or tenants in the rooming houses along North Clark Street had watched from the windows as his Hudson careened past the van?

He slowed as he entered the village of Glencoe. Behind the groomed hedges, fathers lobbed softballs with their boys, and on the sidewalks, girls played hopscotch and waved as the dog in the posh green car rolled by. Frank turned into the driveway of his own sweeping spread and entered his house from the garage. Franny and Robby leaped on him, whooping "Daddy"—his favorite word. The housekeeper hollered, "Bath time," and Rosie herded the children upstairs. Katrina was at her easel, hands covered in paint, and the canvas was awash in bold dabs and slashes, as complex and confident as the woman wielding the brush.

"What's it called?" he asked.

"*Torn Apart*," she said.

Under her smock, her dress fell long and loose below the knees, the color of a ripe plum. It was the flapper look she'd told him once. Personally, he preferred the clothes she'd worn during the war when dresses had curves instead of lines. But Katrina added all the right contours, even to this shapeless style. She unclipped her hair, and a cascade of soft curls tumbled down her back. He encircled his hands around her waist and apologized for being late. She moved closer, and he skimmed the tips of his fingers along her collarbone, dipping them into her jugular notch as if testing the warm surface of a summer lake before plunging in.

But ardent hugs and gentle touches were not the only things that passed between them; they had their differences, too. He liked the literal lines of Winslow Homer, the great American landscape painter; she preferred the curious figures of the modernist Marc Chagall. He loved the baseball stadium in Wrigley Field; she was partial to the Chicago Art Institute in Grant Park. In short, she was smart, sensual, and serene, and he was not. Overall, though, their marriage had grown richer, and they had too.

Katrina made them highballs, he gave her the roses and the card, and they carried their drinks into the sunroom overlooking the pool. Billowy, white curtains framed the French doors onto the patio, and the moon softly lit the room. Franny and Robbie came down for kisses in their pajamas before the housekeeper settled them into their beds.

In the dining room over dinner, Katrina caught him up. "Franny's been bumped up a year in tennis; she's playing with the nine-year-olds. I have to hustle to return her serves."

His eyes twinkled at the vision of Katrina and Franny duking it out in their all-whites.

"And Robbie's joined the chess club," she said.

He whistled, impressed; Robbie was learning chess at six. Frank couldn't have felt prouder of his kids.

She carried the plates to the kitchen and emerged with a warm cake; he lit the candles, and she made a wish. She asked about his speech, and he confessed that his runaway mouth had gotten the better of him. When she wanted to know more, he leaned in and kissed her instead.

Her birthday, he decided, was not the time to tell her that a stranger named Yuri Dyachenko was hell-bent on destroying his career or that he'd come face-to-face with a scar-faced shooter who was probably looking for him. But when they'd finished celebrating as lovers do, and Katrina had collapsed into a deep sleep, Frank crept to their bedroom window and stood watch.

6
CRASH

When Frank awoke, he resolved to set aside his fears and reclaim his life. Yes, crime was rampant on the streets of his city, but he'd done nothing wrong. He hugged his kids and kissed his wife goodbye. When she ran her hands slowly down the inseam of his pants, he knew that all would be right with the world.

The drive downtown was business as usual, too—windy and sixty-five degrees Fahrenheit. At the parking garage, he assuaged his conscience by spending a few extra minutes with Hector, who thanked him for the large tip and said he'd add it to his portfolio. Hector had money in the market? Impressive.

In the lobby, Frank faced a choice: Should he drop by Bobby's for their morning chat as he'd been doing for nine years, or was it time to accept that battle lines had been drawn? He made the wrong choice. A chill had settled over the president's office. There was no coffee on offer in his special mug and no sign that Bobby was even in. He'd been betrayed by his best friend. Frank mustered his dignity, returned to the lobby, and rode the elevator upstairs.

ON TUESDAY, OCTOBER 29, 1929, Frank Cork stood in his usual spot at the back of the Great Hall of the Chicago Board of Trade, buffing his cufflinks back and forth and waiting for the opening gong. The mood was grim. The previous week, the London Stock Exchange had gone into crisis, albeit for reasons of its own. But the loss of billions by Brits had chastened American investors, too. By Thursday, the New York Stock Exchange had plummeted 11 percent, and on Monday, it nose-dived another 13.

At 10 a.m., the gong pierced through the trading pit like a starter's gun. The race was on. Within seconds, the room erupted in panic. The sell-off was frantic and furious—every speculator in America was trying to dump their stock before the market tanked. Traders were sweating and screaming, "Sell, sell, sell." Neither the stock market ticker nor the men climbing ladders and scribbling the trades on the big board with chalk could keep pace. With no tracking of the bids, the entire marketplace was trading blind.

Men began moving in and out of the room, swapping updates. One bereft trader told Frank he was just off the phone with New York: the NYSE was in free fall again. The losses on America's largest stock exchange had hit $30 billion; it was the steepest decline in the value of stocks since America launched its first stock exchange in Philadelphia in 1790. But there was more: Goldman Sachs, the country's premier trading firm, had lost almost half its clients' money. And some stocks couldn't attract a single purchaser at any price; their market values had dropped to nil.

Frank listened, his eyes never leaving the top left corner of the board where wheat futures were tracked. From the back of the pit, he watched as the price of wheat crumbled to thirty-nine cents from $1.05. In less than an hour, his entire fortune was wiped out. It was the largest sell-off of shares in a single day. With Frank's fortune went his clients' trading accounts and the Wally Caldwell funds to finance Chicago's public schools.

Pandemonium broke out in the pit. Hearts were pounding, bodies crashing, white trading jackets being hurled to the floor as traders fled the Great Hall; not even the Corinthian columns and eighty-foot skylight could contain the din. The carnage felt biblical in scale. It was Sodom and Gomorrah. No, it was the Great Flood. The collapse of wheat was sending waves of destruction from the gilded offices of the Chicago Board of Trade to the wheatfields of the world.

PART TWO

WINTER WHEAT

*Winter wheat plants must survive
the many stresses of winter.
However, as long as the crown remains alive,
new roots and leaves can be regenerated.*

— *Winter Wheat Growers Manual*,
University of Saskatchewan

7
THE PENTHOUSE

Lewis hauled Rosie and a pumpkin down the slick stairs of the 'L,' the city's elevated train, battling both sleet and rain. Among his many roles as Frank's intern, one was caring for the dog if Frank was delayed. Usually, that meant filling her water bowl or taking her across to the park, but when Frank hadn't shown up the day after the Crash, Lewis had taken Rosie to his flat that night. Now, it had been two days since he'd heard from Frank, and here he was, hauling the soggy redhead back and forth on the 'L.'

Lewis rode the elevator to the eighth, shed his wet clothes, and hoofed it up the back staircase to the ninth. "It's a day early, but Happy Halloween," he said, presenting Dorothea with the pumpkin.

"It looks just like you," she laughed.

Given the jack-o-lantern's witless smile, he wasn't sure whether to say thank you or feel crushed. But he stood close enough to take in her perfume and became lost in its warm, worldly smell.

"Chanel N° 5," she said.

Determined not to swoon, he groaned instead: "Of all the days to be summoned to the managing partner's office."

A puddle was gathering under his shoes. After more than

six months on the job, it was his first scheduled meeting with James Dutton III. There were legions of stories about the managing partner dazzling worldly investors in the boardroom, then dashing out to bid on pork hocks with a group of hog farmers down the hall. Duplicitous Mr. D—the man could do a pirouette that would make Charlie Chaplin proud. Which version would show up today?

Lewis ducked into the client washroom that was out of bounds for associates and interns, ran one of the fancy hand towels through his hair, and strode across the firm. Ricco, Mr. D's executive assistant, was stationed outside the inner sanctum like Saint Peter at the Pearly Gates.

"Next time it's raining, try an umbrella," Ricco taunted him.

Between his Portuguese accent and spending too much time with Mr. D, Ricco sounded like a cross between Rudolph Valentino and the Broncho Kid. Lewis cut short their usual game of who has the more important boss, and Ricco showed him in.

The managing partner's office was exquisite, although less impressive than Frank's: Mr. D controlled the firm's budget, but Frank brought in the bucks. There was nothing nuanced about the hierarchy in a brokerage firm; the better office went to Frank. Lewis waited with all the decorum of a West Point recruit until Mr. D kickstarted the meeting: "I've had a visit from Mrs. Cork. That woman's as pretty as a pumpkin and twice as smart."

Mr. D might be the only man in America who would summon up an autumn vegetable to describe Katrina Cork. Lewis decided not to dignify the remark.

"Look, son, where is Frank?"

"Sorry, sir, I haven't seen him—"

"If you can't run with the big dogs, stay under the porch."

"How did things go with Mrs. Cork, sir?"

"She sashayed in here uninvited, all legs and long lashes like a doe in a riflescope. She practically ordered me to produce her husband. Such a fuss over a grown man not coming home. Every trader in the city avoided their families last night—other than me and you, Son. In any event, grab yourself a spade and shovel and go find Frank."

"Yes, sir," he said, turning to leave.

"And Lewis, you'll need some privacy. Use Frank's office... until he's back." Mr. D stood and placed his palm firmly on the small of Lewis's back like a square dancer doing the do-si-do. With an allemande left, Lewis was out the door.

He brushed past Ricco and used the back stairs to lug his things from the eighth to the ninth floor. If only his mother could see him now, in a penthouse office with a pet. Granted, it was only for a few days: his boss just needed a post-Crash break. Who wouldn't? Lewis had hit a few rough patches of his own. As a kid, he'd never aspired to be a military man. He'd chosen West Point for the free education, although eight years of mandatory service was payment enough. However, when rumors began circulating about the "hazing" rituals for recruits, Lewis decided no one was going to hang him head-down from a pier. Instead, he'd come up with a scheme. Fellow students were invited to place bets on stock market prices, which was something Lewis had an uncanny knack for, even as a teen. Would IBM discount its stock to $100 or hold firm at $122? If Lewis lost, he sprung for a round of beers; but if the others lost, they had to swear off administering any initiation rites on him. Lewis had won every bet.

Alas, the army brass uncovered his scheme. Lewis was suspended and required to withdraw at the end of the year, signaling the end of Lewis's military career. Still, he'd dodged the hazing ritual and found his true calling—wagering on stocks.

One university degree later, here he was on the ninth. He'd been in Frank's office dozens of times but never on his own. It was a goddam shrine. There were paintings of Frank's family and photos of Frank shaking hands with the mayor, playing golf with the governor, and selling wheat futures to the president of the United States. There was even a photo of Frank in his one-piece Black Tom leotard that wrestlers wear, winning a trophy for some boom-boom-boom three-strike sequence, he supposed.

Walking the halls, he felt as out of place as an immigrant at a country club. But after a tour of the entire floor, there wasn't a single partner in sight. Where was everyone? He asked Ricco, who insisted on knowing what "his people" were doing at all times.

"The associates are processing Buy orders for the few clients who still think the market might rally, and the partners are consoling themselves at Berghoff's down the street," Ricco said.

Lewis was not up for either activity. He shut the door and stretched out on Frank's couch. It may have been the dizzying height of Frank's ceiling, or the smell of Bourbon imbued in the buttery grain of Frank's couch, but for the first time in his professional life, he napped.

WHEN THE LATE-MORNING SUN MOVED from one office window to the next, Lewis stirred and sprung off the couch. What a disaster if one of the partners showed up and found him prone before lunch. He reflected on his assignment and whether to feel abused or elated. On the one hand, he'd landed his first mandate for the managing partner, but instead of showcasing his hard-earned skills, he was wasting his time searching for someone who'd taken a few days off. On the other hand, here he was, the first intern in the firm's history working on the ninth.

Lewis tackled Frank's in-basket first, hoping there might be a letter explaining the man's whereabouts. No such luck. His first call would be to Frank's wife, Mrs. Cork. He reached for Frank's Montblanc pen—it was the size of a large cigar, and its gold nib looked like it belonged in a museum of fine arts—then fished out his red Parker instead. It had brought him luck during his university exams, and he needed it to work its magic one more time. Magic—that's what it would take to make money in this market, especially with Frank gone. He stuck his oversized feet up on his boss's zebrawood desk, rolled his Parker in his fingertips, dialed the Cork residence, and waited for the missus to pick up.

Mrs. Cork didn't mince her words. "I suppose you're calling for that reptile, Mr. D."

"All of us here at the firm are concerned about your husband. And about you, Mrs. Cork."

Ye gods, he sounded fifty, not twenty-three. What tone should he take with his boss's wife? And in these circumstances? Christ, the family dog was living with him. He'd only met her a couple of times, once at the office Christmas party—she was intoxicating—and a second time at their home. Frank had asked him to deliver some papers to Glencoe for signing, and she'd invited him in. He'd declined, of course. But then Frank had insisted, and next thing you know, she was giving him a tour of the ground floor. What he'd give for that eat-in kitchen overlooking the backyard pool. Whisky sodas with the boss in his study came next. He'd never forget the walls—lined with books—and the drapes matched the chairs. What a room. What a wife.

She hadn't replied to his opening volley, so Lewis tried again. "Is this a convenient time for you?"

"No, there is nothing convenient about any of this."

She was right. It was a stupid question.

"Please. Call me Katrina," she relented.

This time, her voice drew him in, as warm as Frank's whisky. What was it called? Whisper of Wheat.

He must have disrupted her as she sipped her morning coffee in the kitchen by the pool, draped in some alluring robe. She would have bustled down the hall to pick up the phone—ivory silk cascading over beautiful breasts and bountiful hips. His mind wandered. He was slipping it from her shoulders and letting it tumble into a soft puddle around her bare toes. They shimmied into the shallow end, naked, descending deeper and deeper until he was fully immersed in the warm, wet turquoise of Katrina and the pool.

"My husband never came home last night," she said. "When I woke up this morning, I was bombarded by news of traders throwing themselves out of their office windows."

He yanked his feet off Frank's desk, and his mind snapped back to the here and now. The only water in sight was the mean-spirited rain, promising another soggy, wet Halloween tomorrow.

"I understand you drove into town to meet with Mr. D. How did that go?" He wasn't ready to call her Katrina yet.

"I don't drive. Besides, Frank's car isn't here. I called a cab."

He made a mental note to check up on the Hudson. Was it still in the parking garage?

"As for the visit, Ricco made a ridiculous fuss, gushing all over me and calling me the wife of the firm's top biller. I'm not sure I'm the wife of anyone anymore."

He didn't tell her that Ricco gushed over everyone.

"Does that man ever give anyone a straight answer?" she asked.

He wasn't sure whether she was talking about Ricco or Mr. D—both of them fit the bill.

"How that cad got to be managing partner, I'll never know. He assured me Frank would be back soon and brayed some truism like, 'There's no slack in that boy's rope.'"

Lewis stifled a guffaw.

Frank's wife was releasing two days' worth of pent-up anxiety into the phone. "Does anyone actually believe that James Dutton III grew up 'eatin' possum and rustlin' squealing pigs?' Then he winked at me, and I winced back. It didn't stop him from walking around to my side of the desk and rubbing his grubby little hands up and down my back. He found it suave. I found it smarmy."

Was the managing partner making unwelcome passes at Katrina Cork or trying to steer the firm with strength and compassion through difficult times? He was willing to give her the final word on that.

"Don't worry," she said. "I know how to separate that man's wheat from his chaff."

They giggled, and he was pleased that he'd made her feel better, at least for now.

"Katrina,"—there, he'd said it—"I'm sure your husband will be back in a few days. Until then, we'd like to keep the police out of this. Can we agree on that?"

She didn't commit. Did Frank's wife know more than she was letting on?

8
THE TRAIN

Frank staggered from the trading pit into the lobby of the Board of Trade, under the stone goddesses, and into the chilly Chicago air. Like the market, Frank had crashed. Stunned, punch-drunk, he had a notion he'd been shot—one bullet to his head and another through his heart. A decade's worth of gains had violently disappeared. How could he go home to Katrina? All he'd ever been was the breadwinner, and now he'd failed spectacularly at that. Not only had he destroyed his family's finances, but he'd exposed Katrina and his children to the threat of violent retaliation from the city's most ruthless men. As long as he was in the city, his family was at risk. The only emotion Frank could muster was fear—fear of the chaos that lay behind and the hopelessness that loomed ahead. His starched collar felt like a chokehold around his neck, and he ripped loose his tie. Forcing himself to move forward, he had only one thought in mind: *Get out of town now.*

Head down, shoulders rounded against the barrage of humans spilling out of office towers into the streets, he made it to the river. Men in fine suits were skulking near the trusses of the Clark Street Bridge. Would they jump to that cruel death? Would he? He reeled and headed down Wells to West Harrison Street and Grand Central Station.

By the time Frank arrived at the foot of the terminal's looming clock tower, the hot sweat he'd earned in the pit had turned clammy and cold. Newspaper hawkers were yelling, "Extra! Extra! Read all about it. Black Tuesday. Market Crash." He stumbled past the ticket desk into the train shed. The dim light from its glass roof was no match for the billows of grimy smoke and steam: he could barely make out the trains, let alone whatever lay ahead. A conductor shouted, "All aboard." And Frank Cork fell into line like a lemming walking off a cliff.

FRANK'S FLIGHT FROM THE CHAOTIC streets of Chicago stretched through the day of the Crash and well into the following day. The fog in the train shed seemed to have taken up residence in his head. A single word kept repeating itself—*Crash*. It was as loud and decisive as the opening bell.

Flattened by shame, Frank drifted between somnolence and stupor. During one long stretch, he was in the river battling the current and grasping for Katrina's hand; during the next, he was fleeing a firestorm of bullets in his car. A man with a grotesque scar haunted him relentlessly from the train's window while assassins stormed down the aisle. Amplifying the terrifying images were voices, too. His father and mother mocked him—"You're not good enough for Katrina. Not smart enough to be a trader"—and he slunk lower in his seat like a man hiding even from himself. In rare moments of lucidity, he heard the names of cities and towns called out as his train tracked northwest: Minneapolis, Fargo, Minot. Hour after hour passed: light became dark, and day became night. His wristwatch had stopped ticking hours ago. He was as wiped out as the stock market—immobilized, ruined, bereft. Hunger came and went.

The conductor boomed, "Canada-US Border." Canada? He bolted upright in his seat. It was the man's peaked cap he saw first, then the flash of gold buttons as the conductor advanced up the aisle, pausing row by row, demanding tickets, and inspecting the bits of paper with great officialdom. Had he bought a ticket? He patted himself down. Nothing. Why had no one asked for one until now? The conductor was closing in, just a few rows ahead. He rifled through his wallet and reached into every nook and cranny of his suit. He counted his pocket change—enough for a phone call, maybe a cab, but not for train fare from Chicago to Canada. The conductor had the face of a dull book, but he'd read about the burly, burned-out cops the railways were hiring to clobber hobos with billy clubs and hurl them from moving trains.

What to do? He was entering a foreign country without a ticket and barely a penny to his name. Dressed to the nines in his LaSalle Street suit, there wasn't a soul who'd believe he was broke. Would they yank out his cufflinks before heaving him onto that treeless terrain? He buried the brazen gold chunks deep inside the pocket of his pants. The train was slowing as it neared the longest international border in the world. The doors were opening, and a new crew coming on—Canadians, he supposed. He had no bags, not even a coat. He'd make a run for it. Hold on. Stay calm, walk slowly, he told himself. Then he summoned all the authority he could muster and stepped through the doors and onto the platform. By God, it was cold.

Frank Cork looked around as if he were a regular in the one-horse town. It was growing dark, maybe 5 p.m., dusk, but light enough to make out the haughty-looking building beside the station. Was it customs? The border police? He wanted nothing to do with either. Turning away, he caught a glimpse of his smudged reflection in the window—a disheveled man with tired eyes and a day's worth of coppery stubble. But wait, what was that movement behind him? Steps ahead, there was a car, a black Buick, maybe a cab. He snatched open the passenger door and jumped in.

It wasn't that Frank Cork decided to go to the wheatfields that day; rather, it took him a thousand miles to get off the train.

"Where to?" the driver asked.

INTERNATIONAL STREET. THAT'S WHAT IT said on the street sign. It seemed a bit over the top in a town that made the village of Glencoe look big.

"I'm new here. Just off the train," Frank said to his driver while casting about for clues as to where he was.

"That's Portal, North Dakota, and this is North Portal, Saskatchewan," his driver said, tipping his head one way, then the other.

He wound his watch and set it to Saskatchewan time. He felt like Gulliver among the Lilliputians—a stranger in a strange land.

"You've landed smack on the border," the man said. "I'm heading for Gainsborough, down in the province's southeast corner, just over an hour's drive."

Frank didn't quite say yes, but the car moved forward all the same. He'd already combed through his pockets on the train and knew there wasn't enough to cover the hour-plus fare. He'd have to deal with all that soon enough, but for now, he was safe.

"In from Minneapolis?" the driver asked, checking out his client's big-city attire.

"No, Chicago."

"I see. Amazing service, the Soo-Dominion Line. Direct from Chicago to Moose Jaw five days a week. You must have left yesterday around noon. It would take about thirty hours to get to Portal."

Really? Where the hell was Moose Jaw, and why did it merit a high-speed train from Chicago every business day?

"It's the first time I've heard of it stopping in Portal, though," his driver said. It sounded more like a question than a fact. "Usually, it slows at the border for a crew change, then barrels on to Moose Jaw."

"You betcha," Frank said, having nothing to add to the conversation.

The driver had the good grace not to bat an eye.

Nevertheless, Frank felt he owed the man some sort of explanation. "I'm here doing research...on wheat."

It wasn't a bad alibi. Better than researching lumber—there wasn't a tree in sight. And it was safer than admitting he sold wheat futures for a living. Every Chicago trader knew that, in Canada, their industry was both illegal and reviled.

Yet Frank didn't stop there. "I'm writing a book," he added. Damn. Why hadn't he drawn the line at research? He'd never so much as written an annual report. Sure, he had dabbled with the idea of creating a storybook for his kids. During his childhood, his father was always making up stories—Irish tales full of death and dying and faeries and famine. "The Chronicles of Conor Cork," his father used to call them, as if a dignified title might convince you that his yarns contained a shred of truth.

They started well, his father's tales, with a rhyming couplet to get you going: "Once upon a time on a legendary savannah, lived none other than the fae Morgana." By the end of the first line, you had a hero, a setting, and sometimes the plot. But they never ended well. Before his father had finished his tale, their apartment was in chaos. Folktales, regrettably, became intrinsically linked with wooden spoons and leather belts.

"My wife likes to read," the man at the wheel said, making it clear he had no interest in discussing books.

Frank welcomed the reprieve. "Nice cab," he said.

"She's a 1911 Buick. General Motors' first closed-body car. With a 4-cylinder engine to boot."

"*Vroom.*"

"Ha. You can say that again. I'm Will. Will Howard."

"Francis Cork. Call me Frank."

He immediately regretted blurting out his name. He should have made up some literary alias, like Bob Cratchit or Moby Dick. He wasn't very good at this pretending to be someone else; he decided to size up his driver instead. Pretzeled behind the wheel, Will Howard was the tallest man he'd ever seen; the Buick could barely contain his legs. The man was about his age, but under his punched-down, worn-out leather hat, his face was crisscrossed with the lines of a wind-whipped prairie. Will Howard and his decades-old Buick—they looked like a matched set with their weather-beaten surfaces and imposing frames.

The men settled into the drive. Will reached into his breast pocket, removed a pouch, pinched a clump of tobacco, rolled it into a ball, and stuffed it into his mouth. Frank looked away. Watching Will chew his wad had an air of intimacy about it that was as disconcerting as walking in on your parents in the throes of an intimate act. For more than an hour, the scenery never changed: the Buick trekked due east across endless miles of flat, indistinguishable land. The road system was a giant grid. Township roads ran east-west and range roads north-south. Frank was too alert to sleep, too tired to talk, and too spent to muster any rage; all he could feel was remorse, guilt, sadness, and shame.

When signs of a town finally appeared, Will broke the silence: "Where are you staying?"

"At the local hotel," he lied.

"It's closed," Will replied, turning off Highway 18 onto Railway Avenue, Gainsborough, Saskatchewan. A clutch of stores clung to two sides of a single street stretching alongside the tracks. Pedestrians were plunging their boots into a deep, viscous stew of horse manure and sawdust as they made their way among the shops. The Buick rolled past a cobbler, tanner, blacksmith, butcher, general store, and a lumber yard tucked well back from the road with a big-toothed beaver on its sign, skipping to work in a pair of dungarees; it was the only whimsical touch in sight.

"Where do people stay?" His anxiety was back, mingling with fatigue.

"That's an excellent question. You're actually our first visitor since it closed. There's the hotel now." Will invited him to look at where he might have stayed.

"THE DO – I – ION," the sign read, like a word in a half-finished crossword puzzle, two of the consonants obscured by prairie dust.

"The Dominion," Will announced.

If the signage wasn't enough to deter guests, the chain running across the stairs did the trick.

"The hotel owner got himself into trouble last week renting the rooms by the hour. The girls upstairs moved on, and out came the chain."

Frank was relieved to have been spared the local bawdy house. On the ground floor, men were strolling in and staggering out, as dusty as the sign. Was Will going to deposit him here, penniless and exhausted?

"The bar seems to be thriving," he said.

"Yep. She's a real cash cow. Your Prohibition has been good for us. Americans pour across the border for drinks."

Given Frank's experience elbowing his way into the Drake after markets closed, he guessed the Dominion attracted more of a trickle than a pour. Will took another pinch from his pouch. The acrid juices in his hard-working mouth created a stench that was both intriguing and vile. The closed-body Buick had the wherewithal to lock out the prairie weather while locking in everything else. His question hung in the air, as trenchant as the smell. Where was he going to stay?

Will advanced the Buick slowly along the strip, passing the post office, two churches, and a few dozen homes, all clad in weathered boards, their windows as opaque as the wood. Saturated in taupes and grays, the very color of the town proclaimed the intemperance of the weather and the impermanence of those arriving somewhere new. Every structure seemed to proclaim, "This is for now. We'll be building something better soon." A lone brick house stood out, a Georgian, perched back from the street with a gas lantern glowering in the end-of-day light like a carny announcing its occupant had money to burn.

"The doctor's house," was all Will said, then declared they'd reached the end of town. An awkward silence followed. Will added tentatively, "There's an outbuilding on the farm. The odd itinerant stays there when they're passing through."

Frank squirmed. Was he really about to accept shelter from a man who'd picked him up in a cab?

"It's empty now. You'd be welcome to stay the night." Will was feeding him the offer one spoonful at a time. "We take in boarders, my wife and me, if you're stuck here for a spell. It's mostly grain cars that pass through here. There's a train to Moose Jaw next week, and from there, you can take the Soo-Dominion Line back to Chicago. I'm sure you've got that all worked out."

No train for a week? He couldn't possibly stay here for seven days. He should never have left North Portal, although he wasn't planning to board a train without a ticket anytime soon.

"Yes, thank you," he heard himself say. "I'd be pleased to stay a night or two."

When they passed the Gainsborough train station, Will pointed the Buick north. "We're ten minutes up the range road."

Frank relaxed ever so slightly, knowing he had a bed for the night, and Will told him about the Howard farm. He started way back.

"The Canadian Prairies are the northern part of the Great Plains, which are down in your neck of the woods. People say they've been around since the ice age."

Will's telling of the tale brought to mind the renowned conductor of Chicago's Symphony Orchestra. The steering wheel was forgotten as Will waved his arms about like a maestro.

"The mighty run-off charged down from the peaks of the Appalachians and the Rockies like opposing cavalries and collided in the middle. *Crash*," he yelled, smacking his hands together like cymbals.

"When the water dried up, we got this incredible flatland, crisscrossed by rivers running north to the Arctic and south to the Gulf of Mexico. I'm sure you know them—the Mackenzie, the Missouri, the Mississippi . . ."

Despite his fatigue, Frank imagined it all—the majestic mountains, the powerful run-off, and the mighty waters splitting as if Moses were parting the Red Sea. Then, all around him, through the dusky light and steamed-up passenger window, there they were.

The wheatfields.

FRANK'S FIRST REACTION WAS CRUSHING disappointment. There was no Red Fyfe; there were no fields of gold. It was the end of October, and the harvest was done. Last season's plants lay in long lines of pale stubble, and the new growth was barely visible between the rows. But when the sun began its long act of setting over that boundless plain, the Prairies became infinite and glorious, ablaze in pinks and orange with a final flourish in mauve. In that instant, he knew with the certainty of a man seeing his features reflected in the face of his infant child that his fate was no longer his own. His future, like his past, was inextricably tied to this grain; whether they rose or faltered, they would do so as one. And then it was dark, and the prospect of intractable ruin hit him like a blow to the gut. Creeping nausea followed waves of hunger; he hadn't eaten in two days.

"Welcome to the Prairies," Will said.

9
HECTOR

It was Halloween and Lewis Montgomery's first day going directly to the ninth floor. It came with many advantages, including first dibs on the coffee and pastries and seeing Dorothea the moment he stepped off the elevator. At Frank's sleek desk, he killed a bit of time making a note to pay the Corks' phone bill and call Katrina every second day. But it was time to extend his search beyond Frank's office. Had Frank left the Hudson behind or fled the city by car?

Lewis grabbed Rosie and headed for the LaSalle Street parking garage. An attendant stood guard over a pegboard laden with keys. Lewis had seen the young man a few times when he was coming and going with Frank over the past year. They eyed each other furtively—same age, same city, one white, one Black, one in the penthouse, the other in the garage.

"Lewis Montgomery," Lewis introduced himself.

"Hector Ray," the attendant said, stooping to give Rosie a pat.

"Mr. Cork left the Hudson with you for a couple of days?"

"The car's here all right, but not Mr. Cork."

"When was the last time you saw him?"

"Just before the Crash. He arrived late, which was unheard of. You could set your clock by that man. He was upset, practically shaking. At lunch, his office told me to bring the car around to LaSalle Street and keep it running. I've never done that before. When Mr. Cork came down, he seemed agitated, which was also a first, and gave me a very large tip."

It hadn't occurred to Lewis to tip the man. Was it demeaning? Or required?

"Anything else?"

"Yessir. Some wise guy came snooping around in the afternoon, asking about a green car. He was a Wop with a wicked scar above his eye. I wasn't about to lie to a man like that. I told him we had a few green cars, but not one word more. The next morning, Mr. Cork dropped off the Hudson at the usual time, and I haven't seen him since."

"Could you deliver it to Mr. Cork's home in Glencoe?"

"Now, sir? How would I get back?"

It was a good question. "I suppose you'd take a cab."

"There ain't no cab in this city that's gonna give me a ride, sir."

Hector might be right about that; Lewis really didn't know. "We'll both go. And I'll call us a cab to get back." It was a dumb idea. If he were going, he didn't need Hector, too.

"Yessir," Hector said, excited. "So long as I'm back by 3 p.m. when the pit closes and everybody wants their cars."

It would have been fun to drive the Hudson: at West Point, the military vehicles had been the highlight of that God-awful year—the Harley-Davidson motorbikes, Dodge half-tons, and Nash Quad off-road jeeps. But it was too late to ask Hector to hand over the keys. Besides, it was timely to see what was going on in the city in the wake of the Crash. He reached for the driver's door at the exact moment that Hector, like a chauffeur, swung open the back door for him. They exchanged uncertain looks. Then he slid into the passenger seat, and Hector took the wheel. The end result? They were side-by-side on the Hudson's bench seat.

LaSalle Street was teeming with people. There were frenzied line-ups outside the brokerage houses—men looking to buy stocks on the cheap. Others were banging on banks' doors, frantic to withdraw any cash amid warnings of collapse. The Hudson exited the financial district and wended its way through a warren of desperate-looking streets. Men without jobs stood on the street corners, shivering, with nowhere to go and nothing to do.

On the street corners, hawkers yelled, "HOOVER SAYS NO RELIEF FUNDS FOR THE POOR." Although Lewis found the President's remarks callous, he knew the editorials would be heralding the cold-blooded policies as common sense.

Hector signaled a right turn onto Route 42 toward Glencoe, and Lewis exclaimed, "Wait, it's Halloween. I'd better bring something for Katrina...er, Mrs. Cork and the children. Flowers, no, a pumpkin. Is there a greengrocer nearby?"

The car swerved as Hector descended into a part of the city that he knew, but Lewis did not. The Black and white neighborhoods of Chicago were as distinct as the squares on a chessboard, and nobody crossed the lines. A memory came flooding back from when he was twelve, maybe thirteen—the Chicago race riots. It was the smell he remembered most: the stench of the fire in the Black Belt. Even blocks away, the smoke had filled his family's flat, leaving a grey haze the color of gravestones on his bedroom walls. Five days of fires and rioting left two dozen Blacks dead, hundreds injured, and thousands without homes. A decade later, not much had changed.

It had been a mistake asking Hector to detour: there was no sneaking around in Frank's flashy car. They dodged the profanities, raised fists, and menacing faces of racism that were moving pack-like toward them. In a snap, Hector decided to forego the greengrocer and made a beeline for the highway.

AS THE CITY AND ITS chaos disappeared behind them, Lewis took a crack at trading stories with Hector about their growing-up years. Lewis had once asked his mother about his own roots. "White trash," she'd said. Ever since, he'd avoided conversations with anyone with maternal ancestors or a double-barreled last name. But Hector wasn't opening up, not even when Lewis regaled him with stories about his God-awful year in the army. So, Lewis tried a different approach, prattling on about William Levi Dawson, the only Black lawyer in Chicago, and how Frank was thinking about supporting a possible bid by Dawson to secure a seat in Congress. Hector kept his eyes on the road.

Lewis rang the doorbell empty-handed at the Cork's house, and Katrina appeared. Even in these tragic circumstances, she radiated intelligence, beauty, and everything Lewis wanted in a woman. His breath quickened and his cheeks grew warm. She invited him in, and by God, he wanted to say yes. But Hector was waiting in the Hudson and, weighing whether to wave him in or leave him in the car, neither seemed ideal. Katrina took in the situation: she thanked him for bringing the car, handed him the garage key, and called a cab.

By the time Hector parked the Hudson, and as Lewis returned the keys to Katrina, a Checker taxi pulled into her drive. The cabbie looked ready to throw it into reverse at the prospect of picking up the unlikely pair and a large red dog, but Lewis waved the fare under the driver's nose, and they were on their way.

Immediately, Lewis gushed about Katrina—that skin, those eyes, that hair. Hector reciprocated with a few of the virtues of his sweetheart, Maisie. Gone was the tense exchange of two strangers trying to find common ground: they'd found it. Minutes later, though, Hector was moving from matters of the heart to cotton markets. For two years, he'd been investing every spare cent on the New York Cotton Exchange. It was in his blood, he said. His family had worked in the fields dating back to emancipation in 1865. He, too, had spent his school holidays picking cotton until his family moved from Georgia to Chicago a couple of years back.

Lewis knew nothing about cotton. Five years earlier, the Chicago Board of Trade had allowed trading in cotton futures, but Duttons had taken a pass because New York and New Orleans had cornered the market. Nevertheless, he tracked cotton in his briefing binders and once heard Frank ruminate about adding it to their mix. With wheat markets beaten to the ground, Lewis thought it might be the right time.

"You must have some not-so-busy hours in the parking garage."

"It's quiet most of the time, other than first thing in the morning and end of day, and a trickle at noon."

"What do you do the rest of the time?"

"I read."

"Could you disappear for a few hours? From my window on the eighth floor, you can see cars coming in and out of the garage. You might be able to rip down the back stairs if a car rolled in during off-hours."

"What would I do on the eighth floor?"

He could see Hector was trying not to sound too excited. "I'd have to smooth it out with the other interns, but you could take my chair for now. I'm working from Frank's desk these days. I think others will go along—no one had an easy start in this business—but God help us if Mr. D finds out."

"What would I do?" Hector persisted.

"For one week, you'd read—soak up anything you can find on cotton futures and commodity exchanges. In week two, you'll get to work. I have to prepare the goddam briefing binders for Frank every day, even when he's not around. I'll show you how, and then they're all yours."

It was time to address the elephant in the room. "I can't pay you," Lewis said. "But you can keep whatever you make at the garage, and I'll top it up with one square meal a day—the most exquisite food you've ever eaten. I'll bring it to you after the pit has closed and the partners have gone home. I'll even throw in a dessert to take home to your sweetheart. You'll never have another lonely night."

"It's a creative idea, but I can't afford to put my job at risk."

Lewis stifled a smile: Hector was playing hard to get. "Trading is a risky business. If you don't have the stomach for it, you should stay in the parking garage. By the way, this is risky for me, too."

Hector paused as if weighing the odds, then nodded yes.

"Oh, one last thing," Lewis added, "and this is important. The moment Frank shows up, all bets are off. And God knows he could stroll in here tomorrow looking as pleased with himself as a Cheshire cat."

"That sounds like Mr. Cork," Hector said. "As clever as the green-eyed cat that led poor Alice down the rabbit hole."

Lewis laughed heartily, and with that, their deal was done.

THEY WERE BACK AT THE parking garage before three. Lewis decided tips weren't condescending. They were how the man got paid. They shook hands and confirmed they'd meet here at 4 p.m. tomorrow, and he'd introduce Hector to the eighth floor. Before leaving the parking garage, Lewis peered into the dark corners for anything untoward. There were no corpses nor any other sign of Frank.

Making his way to Duttons, Lewis almost kicked himself. My God, what had he done? His boss leaves town, and he commits to smuggling the parking attendant into the firm and scoffing food from the partners' dining room. He'd gone too far. Still, it would cost the firm nothing, and who knows, maybe Hector could take over the binders for a spell while educating Lewis about cotton.

At his desk, his empty daybook taunted him. Where was Frank? Not even the man's wife knew. He tackled the bookshelves, flipping open the covers and shaking the pages upside down: there must be a little black book, a train ticket, maybe a receipt. His search came up empty, and it was time to head home. He clipped Rosie's lead on her collar, and after a twenty-minute ride on the 'L,' they were climbing the narrow steps to his flat. Although it was in the northernmost reaches of downtown Chicago, the apartment was the same as the one he'd grown up in.

That night, not a single caller knocked at his door. Who wants to go trick-or-treating above a store? He picked up the novel on his bedside table, *The Great Gatsby*, by F. Scott Fitzgerald.

He was puzzled by Jay Gatsby's obsession with Daisy. Of all the women Gatsby could attract, why was he fixated on another man's wife?

10
THE HOWARD FARM

The Howard farm sat within a few miles of the borders dividing Saskatchewan from Manitoba and Canada from the United States. When Will pulled into the yard and unfurled himself from behind the wheel of his cab, Frank got the full measure of the man—the lanky build and straw-colored hair poking out from under his hat. If wheat were a person, it would be Will.

Three rag-a-muffin kids dashed out to greet them in the moonlight: Willard, Olive, and June, six, four, and two. Frank watched them latch onto Will's legs for the ride to the farmhouse door. The scene made him miss his own children so intensely, it was a struggle to stay composed. Will's wife, roundly pregnant and as short as her husband was tall, waited at the door.

"Laura-Jean, meet Frank Cork," Will said, winking at her with the smug look of a hunter who's bagged big game.

He had anticipated a long-suffering wife living in the grips of Will's tobacco habit—the stained hands, the spitting and chewing, the smell. But no, this was a woman not only smitten with her husband but the ruler of their roost.

Outside, the Howard farmhouse was a pragmatic structure aligned with the linear qualities of the Prairies: the road grid, the railway tracks, the quarter sections, the endless plain. It was a twenty-by-twenty-foot house on a forty-by-forty-acre lot; even the nail heads were square. Inside, there was a single room with a woodstove in the middle. At four hundred square feet, it was the same size as his office. Everything appeared handmade—the braided rugs, the beds, the linens, the kitchen table, and rough-hewn benches in lieu of chairs. His eyes landed on what appeared to be the only exception, a blanket that looked like it had been purchased at a dry goods store. It was the color of unwashed sheep, with four wide bands of once-vibrant hues: red, yellow, green, and indigo.

"It's a Hudson Bay blanket. My wedding gift from my father," Laura-Jean said. She invited him to feel the quality of the wool, and he obliged.

"Will tells me you're an author, Mr. Cork. Tell us more."

He hadn't been on a job interview, well, ever. Duttons had recruited him right out of university. But he could see where this was going. Soon, she'd be asking whether he could afford the rent. Whatever sum she had in mind was more than he could pay. He was a beggar now—not a boarder nor a guest.

"I grew up Irish-Polish-Catholic. Over time, the hyphens disappeared. I'm simply American now. What about you?"

She wasn't about to let him change the subject yet. "Any family? Are you married?"

"My parents grew up poor in Chicago. They married young and had me by the time they were eighteen. I was my mother's only child. A blessing, I suppose."

She caressed her belly. "It's hard to imagine that."

Frank fell silent. He had just walked out on his firm. How would he survive without a penny to his name, let alone fend for Katrina and the kids? He'd had no time to construct a resumé for Will's wife. He set down the blanket and caught sight of a newspaper on the rocking chair, the *Regina Leader-Post*. Beneath the elaborate masthead was a single word in colossal type: "CRASH."

She followed his gaze. "Will brings the paper home from town most days. Did you leave your suitcase in the car?"

"A pencil and a notebook are all we writers need." He was discovering an untapped capacity for white lies.

Her left eyebrow rose in a skeptical arch, "Even our itinerants travel with a rucksack."

"It was a last-minute opportunity. I grabbed it." He sensed that an understanding had passed between them. He suspected that the newspaper headline, only five letters, had told the tale.

"There are a few cast-offs in your quarters," she said. "Help yourself." As he turned to leave, Laura-Jean added, "I must say, Mr. Cork, you look like a character straight out of East Egg."

Was she testing his alibi? "You're a Fitzgerald fan," he replied.

"We don't get a lot of books coming our way, but we hear the reviews on the radio. I was intrigued by the story of Gatsby, a covetous, commercial man who meets a tragic end." She was peering into his soul. He was tired and inclined to say something flip, but the need to sing for his supper constrained his tongue. Instead, he smiled weakly back.

Will picked up two kerosene lanterns, and Frank followed him past the garden to the edge of the wheatfield, a hundred paces from the house. Will introduced him to Queenie the cow, paused to let her lick the tobacco juices from his yellow fingers, and said goodnight.

FRANK'S QUARTERS WERE A BARE-BONES outbuilding suitable for storing tools and best described as a shed. He stood at its only window and saw the small blue flame bob to the outhouse, then back to the house. A moment later, the lanterns in the Howard farmhouse were snuffed out. He checked his watch; it was only 8 p.m. What was he going to do until it was time for bed? The potbelly stove in the corner looked welcoming, and he considered lighting a fire. On closer inspection, its black cast iron body was covered in rust. There were only a couple of lumps in the coal bin, and curiously, its pipe vented through the back wall rather than up and out the roof. Freezing as it was in the shed, he took a pass on lighting the thing.

The bed was a metal frame with a mattress that looked handmade. The six-foot sack was made of a rough, striped fabric—ticking, he remembered his mother calling it—stuffed with chicken feathers and tufted with bits of yarn. A tick mattress. Even saying it set his neck on fire. He'd had the itch since he was a kid. He'd consulted a doctor once, who said it was just a bad habit and all in his head. No, it's on my neck, he'd replied, and lived with the nagging disorder ever since.

There was nothing to do but retire for the night. He curled up cannonball-style under the quilt, which was a meager version of the bed, and waited for the warmth to return to his limbs and his itch to settle. Queenie stood on the other side of his thin wall, her gentle moos the only sound.

There was a window beside his bed, and when he lifted his head ever so slightly, it offered a view outside his shed. The moon had come out from the clouds, and he had an uninterrupted view of the distant line dividing the endless wheatfield from the luminous sky. He marveled at the beauty until, finally, he grew warm, then sleepy. His hot breath collided with the cold glass to create a frosted veil that looked like a curtain had been drawn for the night.

"*Noca noc*," his mother might have said—night night, in Polish—if only she'd been that kind of mom. Instead, Laura-

Jean's words about Jay Gatsby kept running through his head. "He's a covetous, commercial man who meets a tragic end," she'd said.

Was she talking about him?

WAKING THAT FIRST MORNING INCOGNITO on the Prairies, Frank could hardly get out of bed. The rush of adrenalin that had triggered his flight instinct for a thousand miles had stopped dead. He peered out the small window beside his bed. Until yesterday, he'd never seen a wheatfield; now he was living in one. The farmhands were already at work, some reaping the last of the autumn harvest, others planting the new crop of winter wheat before the first frost. By mid-March, the soil would release the seedlings from its brumal grip, and the survivors would send up new shoots to meet the sun. But that was months away. He'd be long gone by then.

He straggled out from under his comforter, squeezed his feet into his Chicago shoes, and tried lighting the small stove. Rummaging for kindling, he couldn't find a stick of wood inside or out. He settled for a lump of coal, but the downdraught filled his shed with smoke. Giving up on the stove, he foraged instead for something to wear. Among the items others had left behind, he found an oversized pair of dungarees that he secured at the waist with a jute cord and a jacket fashioned from the same twill as his bed. He traded his dazzling shoes for a pair of boots someone had declared too worn to wear to the next farm—his outfit was done. He looked like a member of a chain gang. No, wait…He looked like Will.

After storing his cufflinks deep in the pockets of his suit pants and stowing his Chicago finery beneath his bed, Frank's morning got underway in the outhouse. It had a star-shaped window in its door for light and air and an Eaton's catalog for wiping. He skipped over the ladies' underwear section and went right to plumbing: there is nothing more enticing than a toilet when doing your business on a frigid board. Washing his hands and face required cracking the glaze of ice in the pitcher and dousing himself with water that was colder than an Eskimo fart; he'd shave in the kitchen. He exited through the swinging door and glanced at the thermometer affixed to the outhouse wall. It measured not only the temperature but how sorry he should feel for himself as he fought his way across the gusty farmyard to the house. Whether it was the sloppy boots or shapeless pants, his gait had changed from a stride to a shuffle.

Laura-Jean was baking. Carrot muffins for Halloween, she said. He couldn't face food yet—certainly nothing orange. After two days, his hunger had become more of a constant than a pang. At Duttons, his mornings began in the firm's pantry with banter about the price of wheat, but in the Howards' kitchen, everyone offered their insights on the weather as they filed past the woodstove.

"Chillier than usual this morning," Laura-Jean said, pouring him a coffee from the blackened pot.

"Hurrah, there's snow," little Willard called out, rummaging for a scarf.

"Pretty strong winds from the west," Will said, helping himself to a muffin.

It was Frank's turn. "Sixteen degrees Fahrenheit." He announced the temperature with as much aplomb as a broadcaster reporting whether the Dow was up or down. Everyone was impressed. He'd passed his first test.

There was little doubt that the weather merited mention on the windswept central plain, far from the moderating effects of any ocean. Temperatures veered wildly, Will said, citing highs and lows in his lifetime of a murderous 45 degrees below in winter and a punishing 114 on the hottest summer days. Frank swore that when he made it home, he'd never complain about the Chicago weather again.

Laura-Jean had moved from the muffins to the potatoes, and Frank couldn't help feeling queasy as she gouged out their eyes. She handed him a paring knife, and he scraped at the skin and listened to her story about her family leaving prosperous lives in Ontario for adventure on the western frontier.

"Did they find it?" he asked.

"Adventure is a relative thing," she said. She told him she'd lost her sister to the Spanish Flu and her mother to a stroke, although everyone called it a broken heart. She married Will and became a mother barely out of her teens. Her only surviving sister, Mary, had married a brute of a man and moved to Oak Lake, two hundred and fifty miles away. Laura-Jean had visited when Mary's first child, Maurice, was born that spring: she'd found her sister melancholic.

"What about your father? Is he still around?"

"My father is the local doctor. He lives in town."

Frank remembered the doctor's house and found it hard to envisage Laura-Jean growing up in such opulence.

"Dr. John Fyfe," she said.

"Fyfe!" he exclaimed. That made two: his trusty wheat and host's maiden name. One more "fife," and he'd have a trifecta. Surely, there would be luck in that.

FRANK WORKED ALONGSIDE LAURA-JEAN ALL morning, helping with her endless chores while fantasizing about Chicago abuzz with talk of the Crash. If he were there, not here, he'd be weighing in with the press instead of peeling potatoes. "What happened to wheat?" reporters would be asking. "Was there more carnage to come?" Markets were shaped by the answers to such questions, consuming information the way forest fires consumed trees—no empathy, no soft underbelly, no forgiving heart. He was desperate for news.

Laura-Jean turned on the radio, a large brown box on a rudimentary shelf that Will must have built. It looked like it weighed fifty pounds. Given there was no electricity on the Howard farm, it must have one helluva battery. An announcer crooned, "This is CJGX."

"GX stands for grain exchange," Laura-Jean explained. "The station went on the air two years ago, and Will managed to get us a radio at an auction and a license to listen. It's been our lifeline to the world ever since," she said, tugging at her wedding ring.

He was incredulous. "You have a radio station run by a grain exchange?" It seemed as unlikely as discovering a Bourbon convention in the basement of St. Stanislaus church.

"It's on every day, starting at 8 a.m., offering up music, radio plays, and book reviews. It even plays recordings of live opera from the Met. It's as if you were right there, in Manhattan. And, of course, we get more information about the price of grain than any reasonable person would want to know."

Frank felt sick. Yuri Dyachenko and his allies controlled what was broadcast into the kitchens of every wheat grower on the Canadian Prairies. How could he ever stand up to such a powerful opponent? He had to hand it to them—controlling a radio station was a brilliant idea. Chicago was the epicenter of global wheat markets. Yet, all he seemed to hear about were gangland murders, while here, wheat prices were being announced within minutes. He strove to look nonchalant while taking in every word: there had been a slight rebound since Black Tuesday, but prices were almost 70 percent below their springtime high.

It was a relief to have news, although with it came flashbacks to the Crash. Sure, he'd expected a steep decline and had tried to hedge, but no one had foreseen this level of ruin—well, perhaps a handful of speculators worldwide. His practice of trading on margin had been a triumphant strategy for ten years. Borrowing funds to top up his trades by typically 50 percent had allowed him to invest an extra fifty on every hundred bucks. However, when the market collapsed, it meant he'd not only emptied his trading account but run up a staggering debt. Nothing was one thing, but less than nothing was worse.

Laura-Jean was giving him a funny look, and he realized, to his embarrassment, he was violently stabbing the potatoes. Dammit, he was supposed to be a writer, not a hard-bitten trader responding to stock market news.

As if on cue, she piped up, "Will tells me you're writing a book."

Her voice dripped with skepticism. He'd already surmised she was nobody's fool—he'd arrived in a corporate suit that cost more than a suite at the Parkway Hotel. She must have raised that arched eyebrow of hers and thought: "A writer? Hardly." He'd have to make up an answer on the quick; fortunately, traders were good at that.

"Yes, thank you for asking. It's a story about…wheat. It takes place…on a prairie." He skated and stalled, then found his stride. "On a legendary prairie in an ancient mythical land."

Frank reached back to when he was six or seven, and his father was charming him with one of his stories. He pictured the scene at their kitchen table as if it were yesterday—his father with a paddy cap on his head, a newspaper on his lap, a stubby in his left hand, a pencil in his right, and an ashtray full of cigarette butts precariously close to the table's edge.

Back then, when there was still some Conor Cork left in him, his old man eked out a living betting on the bangtails at the track. He had a head for numbers, you had to give him that. Frank would wait patiently while he muttered about whether to put his five on Baby Juniper or Byerly Turk and worked out the odds on the back of his broadsheet. Then, at some point, between too many pints and passed out, his father would lift his head, put down his pencil, and tell the kind of folktale that Irishmen have been known to tell.

What was that tale about a prairie? Or was it a plain? The one with the dark title…"The Ravaging"…That was it! "The Ravaging of the Plain of Ré." Or, was it Ri?

"It's called 'The Kingdom.'"

But wait. He'd have to adapt the Irish version his father told to win over his skeptical hosts. What was the Cree name for this region that Lewis cited in his memo? It started with a K. That was all he could remember.

"The Kingdom of Céyh," Frank said. It sounded like a "K," but he pictured a "C"—his father had often reminded him there are no Ks in the Irish alphabet. And he'd add a fada over the 'e' for good luck. The Kingdom of Céyh," he said again, and this time, the particulars of his father's grand tale came rushing back. How could a half-starved child ever forget a tale about an entire kingdom being wiped out by famine and drought?

Frank recited the opening line from memory: "Once upon a time, on a legendary prairie in an ancient mythical land, lived a King and his seven sons."

He glanced at Laura-Jean. She seemed intrigued. He had passed his first test as a writer. He thanked her for her hospitality and made a dash for his shed.

ON THE HOWARD FARM, THE Halloween meal that night comprised the last of the autumn produce from their garden: potatoes, carrots, turnips, and Brussels sprouts. They ate pumpkin pie for dessert made with blackstrap molasses that had turned it to the color of the rusted-out potbelly stove in his shed, but it had an old-fashioned goodness, that pie, drizzled with warm cream, compliments of Queenie the cow.

In Glencoe, he would have been donning a costume to head out into the night with his kids. Who would he have dressed up as this year? A tinman with no heart, a scarecrow with no brain, or a lion wracked by fear? He felt like all three—heartless, stupid, and scared. Katrina would be telling their children he was away on business and so sorry to miss Halloween. She'd be turning out the lights to signal that there were no treats to be had at the Cork's house this year and leading Franny and Robbie into the chilly Halloween night. But in Glencoe, mothers didn't take their children door to door. Fathers did.

And that's when it would hit her: her husband wasn't missing.

He was gone.

11
GONE

Ricco was hassling Lewis on the line. The rivalry between Frank and Mr. D—the head trader and the managing partner—infected the young men who worked for them. Ricco hollered, "Mr. D runs a brokerage firm. He can't be fielding calls about your boss. If he'd wanted to waste his time talking to the press all day, he'd have run for Congress."

Lewis laughed off the lecture, but Ricco was all business. "What are we planning to say about Frank's disappearance?"

We? The whole mess had landed on his plate.

"Write it up," Ricco commanded. "Bring it to me for sign-off, then stick to the script." Ricco's Valentino ways included a slight lisp, which didn't stop him from using expressions like "thtick to the thcript."

Lewis half-listened while skimming the newspapers spread out on Frank's desk. There was one headline he couldn't resist reading aloud. "Last seen near exchange, tearing ticker tape to bits." You could laugh or cry at the pathetic image of yet another investor losing his sanity along with his savings. Lewis welled up, but Ricco laughed and carried on.

"What about Mrs. Cork? Are you handling her?"

"Yes." If only, he thought.

"And what are you planning to say about Frank?"

"I won't be telling reporters that he was last seen tearing up ticker tapes at the Board of Trade. Gimme a break, Ricco. I can handle it."

DURING THE NEXT HOUR, LEWIS fielded a dozen calls from Frank's clients, several politicians, and the press. Clients were demanding their money back; the governor's mansion and mayor's office wanted to know what was happening to the price of wheat; and reporters were chasing rumors that the acclaimed trader had killed himself. Now, he had the *Daily News* on the line. Had Frank Cork been wiped out? Had the LaSalle Street Legend thrown himself off the Clark Street Bridge? Lewis had no idea, but he had to admit it made for a compelling story.

Mid-morning, he sauntered down the hall to see Mr. D. He simply ignored Ricco, and before he'd taken a seat, Mr. D yelled, "Send him in."

Lewis launched into his plan for finding Frank. "Dorothea is now routing all his calls to me, including clients, politicians, and the press." Hector's name never crossed his lips.

"Bless your pea-pickin' little heart. What's our script, son?"

"Yes, Mr. Cork saw the Crash coming. No, he did not jump off a bridge. Yes, we do know where he is. And no, we are not disclosing his whereabouts at this time."

"That dills my pickle, son. And what if those nosy parkers want details?"

"These are unprecedented times, and Mr. Cork is undertaking extensive economic research in the field. We are committed to having our clients back on top of the market in the shortest possible time."

"Heehaw. I'm as happy as an ol' dawg chewin' on a catfish head. By the way, where *is* Frank?"

"I'm working on it, sir. That's going to take a bit more time."

LEWIS WASN'T KEEN TO LIE to the press, the governor, or the mayor—although, in his limited experience, they were all pretty practiced at it themselves. Back at his own end of the hall, he wondered why Frank, the wizard of wheat, had been wiped out while other traders dodged the crisis. According to the *Daily News,* some traders like Jesse Livermore had not only avoided the Crash but made a killing on it. That brilliant son-of-a-bitch had shorted the San Francisco earthquake in 1906, making him one of the richest men in the world. Now, the millionaire had done it again: he'd shorted the Crash. Why Jesse Livermore and not Frank?

Lewis had the eighth floor send up Frank's trading records. Surely, they would tell the tale. They read like a three-act play, written in numbers instead of words.

Act One lasted nine years, featuring routine borrowing and exhilarating returns. A fast-paced Act Two followed, coinciding with this year's spring market when wheat had risen to $1.62. The play had reached its climax: from such a dizzying height, there was nowhere to go but down. Act Three was sheer tragedy. It started in September when Frank began hedging his bets with minerals and steel, and it reached its sorry conclusion on October 29th, 1929. That was the day the color of the ink changed from black to red. All of Frank's investments crashed: minerals, metals, even grain. In all, it was an agonizing piece of theater—a startling rise and a sudden fall, like a prima ballerina leaping to new heights then tumbling off the stage.

Lewis closed his eyes and reflected on how that dark third act must have played out for Frank. Within minutes of the Crash, the eighth floor would have reported Frank's losses to

Mr. D, placed a freeze on Frank's trading account, and shut down the head trader's access to the firm's seat on the Board of Trade. Both Frank and his wealth had disappeared as if they were one.

WITH HIS NEW UNDERSTANDING OF Frank's bleak financial outlook, Lewis decided to inquire at the hotels and inns. Given the state of Frank's bank account, he started with the dives. It wasn't easy outmaneuvering the folks who pick up the phones at reception desks. He played the parts of a concerned friend, a debt collector, and even an insurance adjuster but kept getting the same reply: We have no such guest here.

By mid-day, he decided to take his search on the road: he'd grown too comfortable padding around Frank's office in sock feet. He called Katrina about borrowing Frank's Hudson for the day, and she insisted on joining him. How could he refuse? An hour and a half later, they were pulling up to the Drake Hotel.

His approach would have been to speak in hushed tones to the concierge with a tip in hand, but Katrina wasn't about to slink around. Every set of eyes in the place swiveled as she strode through the lobby to the check-in desk, looking like a million bucks. Her full-length fur coat hung open over tailored slacks, black pumps, and a cashmere sweater as perky as a pair of cone-shaped paper cups; even her handbag, which was large enough to carry army rations for a week, looked elegant. Everyone stared. He was supposed to be managing the press, not fanning the flames of a story that he'd been assigned to douse. Imagine the scandal if they were caught in a photo at the city's poshest hotel—Duttons' intern with the missing head trader's wife.

At the check-in desk, Katrina got right to her point. "I'm looking for my husband," she said.

The desk clerk seemed practiced at handling women of a certain station in life asking that precise question in that very way. "We have no such gentleman staying with us," he said curtly to Lewis, then turned to Katrina, gushing with charm, "But we'd welcome you and your husband as our guests at any time."

It was clear in that instant that they could visit hotels all day, but there wasn't a desk manager in Chicago who was going to tell Katrina whether her husband was staying upstairs. Lewis proposed they try the Parkway and to let him have a go at it this time.

THE VALET AT THE PARKWAY flashed a knowing smile as the Hudson wheeled up the stunning entryway. But opening the car door, the man in uniform was startled to find the unlikely pair. Lewis slipped the valet a dollar, left the car running, and told Katrina he'd be right back.

In the lobby, men the size of refrigerators were standing by the elevators and in the corners like potted plants. In other cities, this kind of security detail would signal the arrival of a monarch or movie star. But in Chicago, it meant the mob. He parked himself at reception, peeled off another crisp bill, and launched into a lie.

"I'm here from the office of Robert McNamara, President, Chicago Board of Trade," Lewis said. "One of the city's top traders is missing, and the Board would like his whereabouts handled discreetly. I'm sure many of your clients value discretion," Lewis said, making a show of casting his eyes disparagingly toward the potted plants. "We have reason to believe Frank Cork is staying here."

The manager fussed over the registry for what seemed like an eternity. "Mr. Cork was here for breakfast on the 28th."

It lined up with what Hector had said: Frank had arrived late on the day prior to the Crash, as nervous as a cat. Then, a wise guy with a scar showed up. Had something happened to Frank between the Parkway and the parking garage? Twenty-four hours later, Frank was gone. His financial records painted a picture of a man fleeing his losses, but was there something else going on? Who was the man with the scar?

Frank's trading records also revealed he was heavily indebted. The Chicago mob was into everything these days, but loan-sharking was still its bread and butter, and wait... wasn't Al Capone widely known as Scarface? My God, what was Frank up to? Anyone would have fled if they owed those men money.

"No luck," he told Katrina when he returned to the car, and they drove home in silence.

AT 3:30 P.M. THAT DAY, November 1st, Lewis wandered down to the eighth. He'd decided on a no-fuss approach to Hector's arrival. The young man had donned civvies, revealing a slight build under all that red serge. His hair was tightly cropped hair, and he wore spectacles as he poured through the fine print in the newspapers splayed across his desk. Other than his complexion, he looked much like the other analysts, researchers, and aspiring traders who populated the eighth floor.

Lewis did the rounds, chatting up each of his colleagues and looking interested in their answers, then got to the point: "I've found someone who knows a thing or two about cotton. It's quiet around here these days and a good time to take another look at the crop. Meet Hector Ray. He'll be working part-time for a few hours a day. He'll work from my desk until Frank's back. I know I can count on you to give him the usual hard time."

Lewis busied himself at a filing cabinet as a few trickled over to greet his recruit. Usually, new colleagues were greeted with vigorous physicality—handshakes that left knuckles in arthritic knots and backslaps that necessitated long soaks in a hot bath. There was none of that. Had he done the wrong thing? No, but he'd certainly have to try some new approaches. "Gather around," he commanded, then manhandled Hector himself. Then he headed upstairs, leaving Hector to sink or swim.

THE PANTRY, WHICH WAS TUCKED in behind the partners' dining room, was a glorious place. It had floor-to-ceiling cupboards and a fridge full of the world's most spectacular foods—deviled eggs, pomegranates, and glazed ham. Lewis was a frequent visitor and, while distracting the staff with light-hearted barbs, he piled up a plate for Hector befitting the cover of a gastronomy magazine. Then he added a piece of honey cake for Hector's gal. At five o'clock, he ran it down to Hector who, to his surprise, was not doggedly reading alone in the corner but holding court among a rapt group of associates. "Humans have been putting cotton to work for more than seven thousand years," Hector was saying. Lewis set the food offerings on his old desk and disappeared. Keen as he was to have Frank back, Lewis hoped that Hector's moment of glory would last at least a few days.

At six o'clock, Lewis buzzed Dorothea. She was done for the day, she said. But, yes, she'd join him for a sandwich in the pantry. Although her company was only so-so, she more than made up for it with her good looks. He walked her to the "L" and felt an almost irrepressible urge to kiss her. But if Dorothea told Ricco, that gossip would have a field day spreading rumors about the office romance. He resisted and, in a burst of unspent energy, returned to the office for one more search. This time, he even ran his hands under the couch. Nothing. There was no spent revolver, no suicide note, not even a dust ball. How does a man simply disappear? He sat at Frank's desk and listed every possible option, organized it from most likely to least, and circled number one.

Was Frank dead?

12
DECEPTIONS

After the Halloween meal, Frank walked with Will in the yard. It was time to bring the conversation around to money. Will lifted the hood on the Buick and tinkered a bit in the moonlight, and Frank plunked down on the running board. It was an exceptional place to perch. Low to the ground, all he could see was wheat. The ancient grain predated the story of Genesis by thousands of years. He looked past the alternating rows of old stubble and new spikes and conjured a vision of the fields in full display. In fifteen years of Sundays at St. Stanislaus church, he'd never experienced the presence of God, but he felt it here. "When did you buy your cab?"

"I didn't," Will said. "My dad won it in a card game. And I won it from him. I was sixteen."

"I didn't know you played cards."

"I don't, but I did at the time. Winning the cab was a great note to go out on."

Will sure could talk, and he was happy to listen. It was easier than making up stories about a mythical king.

"It became my new best friend," Will said. "Out went Huck, and in came the Buick."

"Who's Huck?"

Will held out his yellowed fingers to Queenie, and she

wandered over for a lick. Will tucked a blade of autumn grass between his teeth and a wad of tobacco into his cheek. Chew-and-a-chaw. Spit. Chew-and-a-chaw. Frank listened to the time-worn rhythm of Will's busy mouth, and Will told him about Huck.

"My father scooped me up like a deck of cards when I was five," Will said. "We traveled from town to town—Anamoose, Gwinner, and Kulm. I discovered Huck behind the bar in the Anamoose Diner. The barmaid helped me parse the sentences and learn the words. I can still recite the dialogue between Huck and Tom and Aunt Polly and Pap Finn."

So, Huck was an imaginary friend, the beloved title character in *Adventures of Huckleberry Finn*. Men in capital markets didn't talk this way. Frank and Bobby had been best friends for a decade, yet he couldn't recall a single conversation about relationships, made-up or real. No, he and Bobby talked about whether wheat was trending up or down and who was the better team, the Redskins or the Cubs.

"Where was your mother?" he asked. Was he really asking this stranger about his mother? He never even talked about his own.

"I didn't see her much as a child," Will said.

"But you won the Buick and a forty-acre parcel of land."

"No, I got one hundred and sixty acres—a quarter section—for free. I staked my claim, built the house, and planted forty acres in wheat. That was the deal. All across Saskatchewan, hundreds of thousands of quarter sections were handed out to immigrants and locals who were willing to settle the land. People flocked here: it was the promised land. But don't ask me about growing wheat. I was brought up on One-Eyed Jacks and Suicide Kings."

Frank laughed out loud for the first time since he'd fled

Chicago. His nostrils flared and took in the aroma of a wheatfield in the autumn air. There were hints of warm, nutty toast like a buttery chardonnay and vague undertones of lightly fermented wet grass like a Sauvignon Blanc, maybe a Sancerre. He wanted to swirl it in a glass, nose it, sip it, and remember it when he got home.

"But how do you make ends meet?" Frank asked, moving the conversation toward the subject at hand.

"In every direction, there are families who traveled halfway around the world to work this land. So, I reap, and my neighbor sows."

Frank understood. He'd spent his most blissful hours as a trader feet-up after markets closed while overseas markets were still at work, driving up the price of his grain. Yes, he knew all about reaping while others sowed. Still, could the Howards really survive on a share of the revenues from this farm?

As if reading his thoughts, Will said, "Tomorrow, we'll head into town. I'll show you other ways of getting by."

FRANK AWOKE ONLY MILDLY CURIOUS about Will's livelihood—they'd ruled out farming and poker—but was wildly excited about heading into town. He'd call Katrina and speak to the kids. There would be a phone at the post office, and the telephone service at his home would still be intact; the bastards wouldn't have cut off his line yet. He'd call her collect—or send a telegraph at least.

But as his warm toes hit the icy floor, he had second thoughts. Of course, he wanted to speak to her, but what would he say? He'd utterly failed her. Their home would soon be repossessed. All he'd ever wanted was to protect her. Yet if she knew where he was, she'd have to lie to the many interlopers that would soon be snooping about—the police, the press, maybe the man with the scar. Katrina was hopeless at lying; it was one of the things he treasured about her most. No, the less she knew, the better. He'd tell her that he was alive, but nothing more.

He crossed the bracing field to the throne, plunked himself down on the frigid board, and changed his mind again. There was nothing he wouldn't do to provide for his family, and the life insurance he'd bought for them was the only money in sight. He might even fake his death to trigger that policy or actually do the deed by throwing himself in front of a train. But if he told her he was alive and she collected the life insurance money, she could be indicted for fraud. No, he'd have to get word to her through somebody else. But who? There weren't a lot of options. His mother? Most days, she hardly knew who *she* was, let alone her son. And he could hardly ask Lewis to keep such a secret from his firm (the kid was just getting started in life), which left Bobby.

Will stood waiting beside the Buick, clearly keen to get started on this adventure, whatever it was. The man had only one gear—slow—but no one could have climbed behind the wheel of that car any faster.

In town, Frank asked Will to drop him at the Gainsborough post office and placed a collect call.

"Mr. MacNamara, please," he said.

The receptionist at the Board of Trade picked up. "May I tell him who's calling?"

"Yes, it's Mr. Dyachenko of the Saskatchewan Wheat Pool," he lied. He pictured her entering it into the call log, puzzling over how to spell the key words. Mr. David Chenko? Of Sascatchuan? He couldn't care less how she wrote it as long as there was no record of a call from Frank Cork.

Bobby came on the line. "Yes, Mr. Dyachenko. What can I do for you, sir?"

"It's Frank. Listen up. We'll be no more than thirty seconds here. I told your front desk that it was the Wheat Pool. So, if anyone asks, you're going to say that Dimwit Dyachenko was checking out grain elevators along the Canada-US border and called you collect. You spoke briefly and hung up. But Bobby, you never heard from me. Are we agreed?"

"Frank—"

"Bobby, I'm fine. But my luck has run out. The Crash. What a disaster. And I've had a brush with the mob. There was a shooting. I saw those grizzly mobsters and they saw me. I was in the car; it's the only two-toned green Hudson in town. I told Katrina we should have gone with the black. The best thing I can do for my family is to disappear, at least until I can come up with a plan. I need to find a way to earn some serious money fast. And get these men off my back."

"But Frank—"

"I expect to be back in a few weeks. But give me, say, six months, max. If I'm not back by then, you can do what you gotta do. I fudged the name of the caller, but the phone records will show where I'm calling from. But not now, Bobby. The wheatfield is my only refuge. I won't be phoning you again."

"Frank—"

"Gimme your word, Bobby. You say nothing—not to the firm, not to the police, not to Katrina."

"Katrina? Frank, you gotta call Katrina, or I will."

"No. There will be lots of people snooping around, including insurers. I don't want Katrina lying to officials; she's no good at it anyway. It's going to be hard on everyone, I know, but you have to trust me on this. I'm going to save my family if it's the last thing I do."

Silence.

"And Bobby. One last thing. Any investigation into the trading practices or me or my firm will *not* be moving forward." He wasn't certain that the Wheat Pool had bowed to his threats, but he was damned sure that Yuri Dyachenko was in no position to ruin his life.

"Take care of yourself, Frank," Bobby said, hanging up.

He felt like a prisoner who'd used up his only call.

FRANK WAS SURPRISED WHEN WILL soared past the turnoff to the Howard farm. Within ten minutes, a sign announced MANITOBA, and Highway18 became the 13. He would pay careful attention to Will's route, mapping out the main arteries and the back roads in his mind. Without a cent to his name, there would be no easy path home. He had to be open to every option: riding the rails, flagging down a trucker, even stealing a car.

Will was never quiet for long. "Beware that in Manitoba, they flip their clocks around like damn fools. You'd never catch a Saskatchewan farmer agreeing to that, creating chaos for the livestock and grain. Over here, people are always missing the train."

It took a moment to cotton on that Will was bent out of shape about Daylight Saving Time. It was useful information all the same, the kind of detail that might matter if he were plotting an escape. Having barely poked their noses into the province, Will turned south on the 256. Yet another long, flat stretch of road lay ahead. While the wide-open prairie unfurled in the passenger window like a silent film, Will layered on the script.

"When I got the Buick, cars were as rare as hills, so I put her to work. Our first beat was picking up settlers at the train station and driving them to their new land. It was always a dramatic moment. Some were elated, bounding out of the Buick to plant a stake or fall to their knees in prayer. Others were despondent; they'd gone to bed dreaming of the Garden of Eden but awoke eye-to-eye with the serpent instead of Eve."

He could picture these world-weary settlers who'd journeyed the equivalent of forty nights and days. They would be Russians fleeing revolutionary violence and Poles arriving exhausted from peasant farms as his mother's family had. They must have collapsed with relief at the sight of towering Will and his breakthrough Buick and been enchanted by his stories of the Prairies, whether they spoke English or not.

"When the war hit, the newcomers stopped coming, and I had to start over again. Soon, I was picking up enlisted men at their homes and driving them to the train. It was gut-wrenching in a different way, seeing them ship out as excited boys and return home as burned-out men—if they made it back at all."

There was no doubt that Will had put his car to work, but where was this story heading? The war was a decade ago now. How was Will making ends meet now? Frank was counting off the minutes as they traveled down the 256 South. It had been thirty minutes—about twenty miles. As if on cue, Will announced the international border. Frank looked around and saw absolutely nothing of consequence on this uninterrupted plain—no fences, no guards, not even a flag.

"Perfect timing," Will said. "I'm meeting my clients here at ten."

Clients? What clients? Will pulled to the side of the road and stopped the car, explaining that they were just north of the border, by a foot at most. It seemed as fanciful as Will's old friend Huck. They got out and sat on the running board. Chewing on blades of grass, the fresh air was as welcome as an outhouse breeze. They must look like a couple of hayseeds from a Buster Keaton flick, Frank thought.

Will continued the story of his car, job by job: "When the war wound down, America Prohibition arrived in the nick of time. The Buick and I were back in business again."

Frank looked around. There were no signs of clients. In fact, there were no signs of anything at all.

"My supplier—"

"You have a supplier? I thought we were meeting clients?"

"Yes, I meet my clients here every morning, five days a week. But they're often late. I also have a supplier. He lives in Wapella, an hour north." Will was tilling his tobacco, bringing the moist stuff to the top. "I call him the Wapellan. In this business, people prefer to be discreet."

"What business are we talking about, Will?"

"It's pretty straightforward for a smart guy like you, being an author and all. Gainsborough is wet, and America is dry."

Was Will challenging his author alibi? If so, it was tit for tat; he was coming to see that Will's taxi business was also a front.

"Wait," Will said, "here comes Shorty and the boys now. Careful, they'll be packing, and they're not always easy."

Two menacing black vehicles appeared in a cloud of dust. What had Will got him into? He'd fled Chicago to get away from wise guys like these.

"There's a Steamer and a Hup," Will said.

"What?"

"The cars—a Stanley Steamer and a Hupmobile."

It was easy to pick out the Steamer: it was hissing like a prehistoric beast. He'd seen dozens of photos of Capone's Town Sedan, painted up in black and green to pass itself off as a CPD cop car. No wonder the good citizens of Chicago were wary of the police; you never knew who was behind the wheel. But these vehicles were all about standing out. A pair of gangsters got out and moved their way, one short and the other looking as clever as a flat tire.

Frank leaped from the sideboard into the Buick, leaving one of his oversized boots behind. He buried his head below the dash and peeked up. The barrels of two 12-gauge shotguns were staring him in the face. "Forgive me, Father, for I have sinned . . ." He repeated it three times, faster than the Holy Sacrament had ever been said before.

Will stepped between the artillery and the Buick, as cool as a jungle cat. The men lowered their weapons, and Will moseyed around to the Buick's trunk. From Frank's vantage point below the dash, he had a clear line of sight to the faces of these men. The scar-faced shooter from North Clark Street was not among them, but they were cut from the same cloth— same fedoras, trench coats, and baggy cuffed pants spilling over their spiffy shoes.

Will was unloading wooden crates from the rear. They were wooden slat boxes with hammered-on tops with "WHISKY" written in block letters along the sides, exactly like the cases of Old Fitz Frank had been buying from the pharmacist on LaSalle Street for years. Will hauled them two at a time to just shy of the gangsters' cars. Frank ventured out from his hiding spot for a better look, and the penny dropped. Will's fixation with a border that he alone could see was about skirting the Prohibition laws. Will sold liquor in Canada, not the US.

There were no introductions to Shorty or the flat tire that day. Frank watched from the car while the men sampled the product with Will over cigarettes. Then Shorty slipped Will an envelope, and the mobsters disappeared the way they'd come—under a veil of dust and steam. Will folded himself back into the Buick one long limb at a time, then pointed his vehicle north. The big man's hands shook as he tucked the envelope into his breast pocket and reached for his pouch. Strands of tobacco fell to the floor, and dollops of perspiration flowed down Will's forehead, unchallenged by the cold.

Doing business with these men took nerves of steel and a blind compulsion to support your family. He had the latter, but nerves of steel? He was already starting to scratch. Mr. D was right: making money during the past decade had been as easy as dipping his rod into a pond of hungry fish.

Was he ready to swim with the sharks?

13
DEAD ENDS

Lewis swilled his mentor's Bourbon as he considered option one. Was Frank dead? If so, there were only two scenarios: Frank had done the deed himself, or someone else had done him in. Chicago had earned the nickname Murder City for a reason: its homicide rate was twenty-four times the national average. Had a loan shark gone too far when collecting an unpaid debt? Perhaps. But Frank's profile didn't square with the murder victims Lewis read about in the daily news. Post-Crash, LaSalle Street men were far more likely to hurl themselves out a window than get pushed. He decided to tackle suicide first.

Looking around, he couldn't help asking himself why anyone with this office would possibly kill themselves. If life got really tough, you could simply shut the ruby-red curtains, give Dorothea a buzz, and spend some quality time on the couch. But he immediately chastised himself: Don't be facetious. Suicide is serious stuff. He knew nothing about it. In South Side, you spent your entire life fighting to survive. You didn't have to kill yourself; you could always count on someone getting to you first.

The mere thought of Frank dangling from a rafter or blowing his head to smithereens was revolting. Lewis leaned back on the hind legs of Frank's chair, propped his feet up on Frank's desk, and tossed his pen in the air. He sent his Parker higher and higher, adding somersaults at the top of the toss and dive-bombs at the bottom, snatching it in the nick of time before the nib collided with the flawless surface of Frank's art deco desk. The riskier the toss, the clearer his thoughts became. Frank Cork had everything the whole world wanted. Sure, he'd had a setback, but he also had a family that loved him, and he could always make the money back. Suicide? Not likely. Besides, there was no dead body and no note.

Playing with his pen was only getting him so far. He wasn't about to borrow the Hudson from Katrina again. Instead, an hour later, he was driving to Frank's yacht club in a Hertz Drive-Ur-Self Model T. The boats were up in their cradles in the yard, covered with a dusting of frost. He and Rosie combed the grounds and peered into the clubhouse windows. The dance floor and billiards room were spectacular, and he fancied himself sipping gin and tonics on the wrap-around porch in the spring. But there was no sign of Frank.

He made the rounds of every hospital in Chicago, providing elaborate descriptions in case Frank had been admitted under a false name or delivered in parts under no name at all. He snuck peeks into patients' rooms, and the smells alone made him thankful to be a trader, not a nurse. His last stop was the morgue. It came as a grim surprise to learn that Mrs. Cork had been there, too.

After dropping the car back at the Drive-Ur-Self, he realized he'd been focusing too much on the *where* of it all: *where* was Frank instead of *who*. Could it be that he didn't know the man as well as he'd thought? They'd spent five days a week in the pit together for a year. But Duttons' head trader was an icon, which made him—what was the word?—aloof. As the firm's rainmaker, Frank kept his relationships guarded so partners couldn't poach. He had to admit that he had no idea what Frank's marriage was really like or how brutal his childhood had been.

He paced the corridors of the firm. There wasn't a partner in sight. His oxfords pinched—surely, feet weren't meant to be crammed into wingtip shoes twelve hours a day. There were also things, of course, that he and Frank had in common. They'd both grown up in poverty in South Side, and they both loved the pit. They'd had the same education at the same university, albeit ten years apart, and certainly had the same taste in women. Some might say they were cut from the same cloth: Frank would never have hired him if it hadn't been the case. And if there was one sure thing he knew about himself, it was that he'd never cash in his chips. Never. No matter how bleak life got, he'd fight with every ounce of his being to survive, and he was willing to bet his last dollar that Frank Cork would, too.

Packing up his things to head home, Lewis realized that for all his banging on doors, phone calls, and tips paid to strangers, he was no further ahead. Frank had been missing for the best part of a week, and he didn't have a clue where the man was. But before he struck suicide off his list, he'd check with the people who knew him best whether Frank might have killed himself.

IN THE MORNING, LEWIS CALLED down to the Board office and asked for Mr. MacNamara. The receptionist put him briefly on hold, then told him the busy executive was free. What a surprise—last week, the head of a dog kennel wouldn't have returned his call, and now, the president of Chicago's most prestigious institution was inviting him to come on down.

When Lewis entered Bobby MacNamara's office, they were both taken aback. The Board executive was, well, plumper than Lewis anticipated and had the look of a man who never cussed. Traders were sweaty, muscular men with language choices that would make a sailor blush. Opposites attract, Lewis thought. Admittedly, he came with his own set of surprises: he was rougher around the edges than the typical Duttons' intern—more military, less prep. Nevertheless, "Call me Bobby," the powerful executive said.

"Where were you on Black Tuesday, sir?" Lewis asked. Everyone around town was asking that.

"I was right here," Bobby said, pointing at his desk, "shouldering the weight of the biggest economic crisis in this city's history."

"I bet," he said, picturing the man in a captain's hat on the upper deck as his ship went down.

"During these troubled times," Bobby said, "the Board must be as reliable as the opening bell, as stalwart as the statuary above its door."

Lewis smiled wanly at best, and Bobby yanked himself down from those lofty heights and resorted to another age-old trick—flattery. "Frank raves about you. Says you're the best intern he's ever had."

Lewis knew better. Frank didn't rave about anything, least of all about his intern to the president of the Board of Trade.

With his flattery falling on deaf ears, Bobby took to bragging about the Board instead. Good on him—no one else was singing its praises in the wake of the Crash. Certainly not those who had witnessed it first-hand, as he had. The stench of the panicked sell-off was still in his nostrils, and the memory of traders fleeing the pit en masse was seared into his brain.

Lewis cut him short. "Bobby, where is Frank?

"You're asking me? I thought you were managing that. I invited you here because I assumed you had some news."

"No, sir, I'm the intern. You're his best friend."

"Frank will be licking his wounds for a bit, that's all. He's had a big blow. Any news on your end?"

"Nothing." He was here to ask Bobby about suicide. He had to frame the question in his head before he could say it out loud. But Bobby, despite his measured pace, beat him to it.

"Lewis, there are men in our industry jumping to their death these days, especially in New York. But Frank is not the type to do that. His mouth gets him into trouble enough."

BACK UPSTAIRS, LEWIS FLIPPED THROUGH the *Tribune*. Graphic photos and lurid stories of gangland murders had become the daily fare, and crime writers like Jake Lingle were the toast of the town. Yet, Bobby didn't seem worried about his best friend at all. The man had been clear on the subject of suicide—Frank would never kill himself. He wondered what Katrina would have to say about that. It was time to ask her and to buy himself more time. He wasn't expecting either topic to go well.

Katrina picked up on the third ring. He'd conjured up an image of her breezing down the hallway to pick up the phone, but there was nothing breezy about Katrina that day.

"Bobby just called," she stormed. "He claims you don't know a thing about my husband's whereabouts. You haven't moved the yardstick one inch."

How dare Bobby accuse him of doing nothing. That man's only handiwork had been stirring up trouble with Frank's wife. But Bobby was quickly forgotten. On the other end of the line, he heard short gasps for air, the type of sound that was often paired with shoulders heaving and eyes welling up with tears. His heart ached for her. She had moved from fury to tears in two seconds flat.

"I guess Bobby and Frank are pretty close?" he asked. Questions, he'd learned, could have a calming effect; they left the other person feeling in control, able to decide what they were willing to say.

"They certainly go way back," she replied, composed again. "We were a triangle at university—Frank, the golden boy, was always on top, and Bobby and I propped him up from the corners. But, Lewis, I've had enough of this. You're all talk and no action. I'm done."

New sounds were coming across the line—Katrina huffing and blowing, angry again. "I made it through Halloween," she said, "but I won't be spending Thanksgiving or Christmas like this. I should have called the police a week ago. You talked me out of it, Lewis," she moaned. Then the dam burst. "There's no more money," she bawled.

What could he say? It was certainly not the time for probing questions about her husband's possible suicide. So, he resorted to breathing instead: loud and fast at first, matching her breath for breath, then rhythmic and quiet, in and out, as if they were one. "I need you, Lewis," she said, barely audible. "These are untraveled roads. You are my sole companion, my guide."

Untraveled roads, all right. Was she sad and looking for comfort, or was it something else? Lewis decided to focus on his goals for the call. "We continue to feel confident at the firm that we'll find him." He was rolling his Parker in his fingertips to steady his nerves. He put down the pen and leaned into the call. "We are trying to resolve this matter internally. Discreetly. None of us want to wake up to a headline with the word 'suicide' next to your husband's name—"

"Suicide," she repeated, aghast. "That's absurd. Frank is a fighter. He would never kill himself."

He took it as a clear no. "Did he have any enemies? We all have a few." A pair of West Point cadets came to mind.

"Enemies? Are you shuffling me from suicide to murder?"

The conversation was a minefield, just as he'd predicted. "Please. We can't find him without your help."

"The mayor," she snapped.

Pow! When she made up her mind, there was no pussyfooting around.

"Big Bill was furious when Frank announced he was changing his vote. I'm not sure Frank actually said that. It doesn't sound like Frank. He would have said something vague and mildly facetious like, 'Change is inevitable, except from a vending machine.' But the papers claimed he said it, and I guess that's what counts."

She paused, and he let the silence hang, giving her time to think.

"And Mr. D," she added, naming enemy number two. "It's a love-hate thing. Initially, Mr. D was the father Frank never had. But Frank outgrew him, becoming a better trader than James Dutton III will ever be. So, here we are, with Frank lost—or worse—and with you, Lewis, trying to find him. Does that arrogant SOB even care whether my husband is alive?"

Lewis took stock of his agenda. No to suicide, but yes to enemies: the mayor and Mr. D. Now, he had to buy himself more time. "You mentioned Christmas. That sounds like a good milestone. Can you give us until then?"

She whimpered something between a yes and a breath. He seized it. "Thank you, Katrina. I'll call you in two days. We'll hope for some news by then."

He opened his daybook, struck a line through suicide, and

moved down his list to scenario two. *Murder*. He circled it slowly, then added three names beside it: Scarface, Mr. D, and Big Bill Thompson, the mayor.

14
THE WAPELLAN

On their way back from the drop, Will proposed the Dominion for lunch. The steps were crowded with hungry farm laborers desperate for wages, although there were no pennies per bushel to be earned these days. Inside, a dozen men in dirty trousers and worn hats stood along the bar at the back of the busy room, each with a boot on the brass foot rail and the other on the wide-plank floor. Each had one elbow propped on the bar, and the other engaged in throwing back shots.

Frank followed him toward the cluster of round tables up front by the windows, where locals were eating toasted club sandwiches and drinking chilled beers. For a moment, he envied their camaraderie, co-ops, and collectives, their worker movements, and even their Wheat Pool. As a trader, he'd had partners and friends in the pit, but they were seldom pulling together on the same team. No, Frank's world was populated by winners and losers, and his victories came at others' expense. For the moment, Will Howard was the closest thing Frank had to a friend.

Why had he tied himself so firmly to the yoke of financial success? How had he accorded money with the stature to drive him from his family and flatten him with shame? And he wasn't the only investor or trader feeling this way. Stories were circulating in the press about clients and colleagues plummeting from their office windows, and he'd seen for himself the desperate-looking men lurking in the shadows of the Clark Street Bridge. He had understood their plight and the desperation that drove them to that bleak solution.

The waiter set down their lunch, and the smell of warm bread and frothy beer brought his mind back to the here and now. He pushed back his chair and stood. Then, he cast his eyes around the room as if he were at the lectern again, raised his glass, and shouted: "To Red Fife."

There was a chorus of clinking glasses, and he was moved by the fellowship he felt with these men.

WHEN THEY WERE WELL INTO their sandwiches, Frank turned to Will: "Tell me about this man in Wapella...your supplier." He liked the heft of the word. It sounded like a man who might have money.

Will wove the story of the Wapellan at his own pace. Canada briefly banned liquor during the Great War, then kicked the political football to the provinces to decide. The provinces were just as canny and booted the choice down to cities and towns: wet, dry, or damp. Frank knew a bit about Prohibition—banning booze had not been good for wheat—but this notion of a "damp" town was something new. Will said it was a typical Canadian compromise, sitting between "no booze allowed" and "drink whatever you please." No wonder Canadians had half a dozen political parties at any given time.

"Gainsborough is wet," Will continued, "which means we can make it, drink it, even sleep with it so long as we don't sell it in the US. And we've got everything we need to make whisky—water, yeast, and grain. A couple of brothers from

Wapella, the Bronfman boys, built the first stills in Saskatchewan and a handful of warehouses. Boozoriums, they call them. Crazy name, but the company has done pretty well. Seagram's—you may have heard of it."

Frank smiled at the understatement by a man who thrived on hyperbole. Yes, he'd heard of Seagram's: since its humble roots in Saskatchewan, it had become one of the largest distributors of alcoholic beverages in the world. American Prohibition killed any competition from US firms and gave the company a free ride. But all this talk of whisky was making him yearn for an Old Fitz—that bracing burn, that throaty massage.

But Will's story wasn't done. Riding on their success on the Prairies, the Bronfmans moved their business to Montreal, and the Wapellan bought up their stills and boozoriums for a song. The purchase included a license to sell spirits to other provinces; however, the real money was in sales to the US. Next thing you know, Will had his Gainsborough run. Given the Prohibition situation in the US, everything was done on the quiet, Will said.

Frank took stock of what he'd learned. His new friend Will had a supplier with a still in Wapella and a warehouse in Gainsborough, behind the train station by the creek. It sounded like a sure scheme to make some cash on the quick. He hadn't felt so excited since landing his first job in the pit.

"I'd love to see the still," Frank volleyed, expecting to be rebuffed.

"Sure," Will said.

The server came by with the bill. Their toasted clubhouse sandwiches and pitcher of beer came to twenty-five cents; the coffee was on the house. In Chicago, Frank was always the one reaching for his wallet, but he kept his hands under the table, and Will picked up the tab.

IN THE MORNING, FRANK AND Will traveled a hundred miles northwest to Wapella.

"There's a Wapella not far from Chicago, too," Frank observed to pass the time.

"There are only so many good names to go around," Will said. "When my dad was a kid, Gainsborough was in the Northwest Territories and was called Antler. Antler, NWT. But there's a town named Antler twenty miles south of here in North Dakota—Antler, ND. So, our forefathers decided to rename our town and came up with Gainsborough, like the British port city, although there's not a ship in sight. Then, when I was a kid, Canada acquired the Northwest Territories. The southern part became the province of Saskatchewan, and Antler, NWT became Gainsborough, Saskatchewan, one blessed name at a time."

Interesting as that was, Frank brought the conversation back around to bootlegging. "If we worked as partners, I could double your volumes and cover half your expenses. I'd pay you room and board and hold onto a bit of the money for myself. What if we tried it for a month?"

Will jumped at the idea and pushed for two months. Frank held firm. Even a month seemed like an impossibly long time. When they shook hands, Frank sighed with relief. He had his room and board covered and the prospects of a ticket home. It was a start.

AT NOON, WILL ANNOUNCED THEY were at the still. He'd pulled the Buick to a stop at a grain elevator jutting up from the flatlands like the Neolithic rocks at Stonehenge. What had that famous French architect called these structures? The first fruits of the industrial age. This one showed signs of having been painted once, auburn remnants clinging to muted greys.

There was no security at the still; it was as inconspicuous as the Canada-US border. They simply walked in. Will led the way up the ladder to the second floor—the headhouse, he called it. And there was the whisky, hidden behind a season's worth of grain.

The headhouse was as cold as the Prairies. A trap door in its corrugated roof was propped open with a hoe, letting the fumes out and the skylight in. Under the trap sat the stiller. The man was a far cry from a chemist in a lab coat; he wore a buffalo hide around his shoulders and a Stetson on his head. He smelled like he hadn't washed since Prohibition came into effect.

"Meet Stets," Will said. "The man won both his hat and his nickname in a brawl with a Mounty."

Frank looked confused, and Will explained that Mounties were cops who rode around on horses. All the while, Stets beamed, showing off two rows of brown stubs where most people had teeth. Years of sampling the product could do that to a man, Frank supposed.

Will gave him the tour, explaining that the still was comprised of three zones. In zone one, fermenting, the grain, yeast, and water were mixed into a potent mash that smelled like warm bread and wet nappies. In zone two, production, the musky liquid was boiled, purified, and reduced to a fraction of its volume as it moved from chamber to chamber and into a collection container to cool. Finally, in zone three, the hooch was bottled and stored.

It seemed straightforward enough until Stets piped in. Given his teeth situation, Stets didn't really talk; he wheezed. Still, he managed to explain his process: "I make my tails cut early, and my heads cut late. I also leave the hearts in my tails." It made wheat futures sound like a cinch.

Will translated. "Heads are the earliest version of the product in its rawest form—ethyl alcohol. Tails are the pungent distillate that's been boiled off, and hearts are what's left, the good stuff. Stets' recipe is 45 percent alcohol, otherwise known as ninety-proof."

Frank gasped, "So that's it? What about the oak barrels, storage cellars, honeyed flavor, and amber hues?"

"No, no, no," Stets waved the questions away. "We're making bootleg whisky here, not Single malt Scotch. I add a shot of sulfuric acid at the end, which gives it a bit of age. For color and flavor, I blowtorch some wood chips and toss them in. Fifteen minutes except for Sundays, when I go to church, and they soak all day."

They'd reached zone three, the storage space. Will announced that there were three thousand bottles in inventory, to which Stets added a few hundred every day. A pair of packers placed them into the crates that he'd seen Will load into the Steamer and the Hup and delivered them to the warehouses. The Wapellan owned five of them, one every fifty miles or so along the US border. Will received four crates a day, five days a week, fifty weeks a year. Frank did the math: four crates a day at $6 per crate was $24 per day, two-thirds payable to the Wapellan and one-third to Will. So, Will made $8 per day, five days a week—$2,000 a year.

Frank decided they could increase the price tenfold. At twelve bottles per crate, Will was selling his whisky to the mobsters at $.50 per bottle. In Chicago, Frank was paying $15 per bottle for Old Fitz; Prohibition had tripled the price. The mob would be re-selling Will's whisky for $10 per bottle and $120 per case. Frank explained the margins to Will, and they settled on a path for bringing their prices in line with going rates. Still, while Frank's share would be better than penury, even the increased prices wouldn't make a dent in his mortgage or trading account any time soon.

"Could you double your production for the Gainsborough warehouse?" Frank asked Stets.

"Sure. I can distill it if you can sell it," Stets said.

Will looked at Frank and nodded yes.

But Frank wasn't done. "Is this the biggest operation around?"

"Gawd no," Stets said. "That'd be Moose Jaw. Down in the tunnels under the town."

Right, Moose Jaw. If he hadn't bailed off the train at the border, he'd be in Moose Jaw now. Frank thanked Stets for his time and told him he'd been impressed by both the still and the stiller.

THE MOMENT THEY WERE BACK in the Buick, Frank exclaimed, "Let's go to Moose Jaw."

"Sure, but not now. We've got a run to make in the morning," Will said, setting out for home.

From the passenger seat, Frank reflected on his first week on the Prairies. He had a new partner and a small business venture underway, but two issues were leaving him cold. One, his clients were America's largest organized crime ring, and two, he hadn't met the supplier.

"I'd like to meet the Wapellan," Frank said.

But Will said nothing and kept his eyes fixed on the road.

Had Will invented the man?

15
THE MAYOR

An entire month had elapsed since the Crash, and trading wheat futures in Chicago had ground to a halt. Not only had the city's top trader disappeared, but investors had vanished, too. If anyone had money to burn, they weren't wagering it on wheat.

Lewis was relieved to have his Frank file to work on since there wasn't much else to do. Hector had settled in on the associates' floor, hung on to his job in the garage, and taken over the binders. He'd also prepared a roadmap on how the firm might add corn to its offerings and pitched Lewis on it one late night when all the other associates had gone home. Hector wouldn't be the first trader to rise up from the mail room, but he might be the first Black.

MONEY-WISE, LEWIS WAS HAVING HIS own problems. Interns were paid breadcrumbs until they got their own book of business and earned commissions on their trades. It was enough to sustain his apartment, which was a big word for such a small space, and get back and forth on the "L." Beyond that, he ate his meals in the firm's pantry and helped himself to Frank's whisky when he needed a drink. His suit, which he purchased with his first paycheck, was almost as frayed as he felt. But at least he was showing up; many of the partners had given up on commuting into the city at all.

All this spare time allowed Lewis to dig through Frank's bookshelves. They were a treasure trove of industry know-how that no one taught you at school. The Department of Agriculture's 1929 Annual Report reminded him why he had spurned the government recruiters on campus. One of its mealy-mouthed findings read: "There is an inability to justify the wide daily fluctuations in wheat prices with the laws of supply and demand." Ha. Why didn't they just spit it out? Traders must be churning the price of wheat to make more money for themselves.

Lewis was shocked to discover the number of interests and agencies poking their fingers into traders' pots. There must have been a dozen—farm groups, agricultural lobbies, even the Saskatchewan Wheat Pool. If traders didn't defend their practices, who would? For the first time, he understood that courting politicians was part of Frank's job, and in Chicago, that meant the governor and the mayor. Lewis found a file with their biographies on an upper shelf that could only be reached from the bar. The governor's fact sheet read like a political thriller. The man stood accused of selling pardons and paroles to white slavers. White slavers? Did America still have those? In Illinois? The mayor's file was also bursting with clippings on his countless connections to the mob. His public welfare commissioner was charged with operating a kickback scheme. Recently, a beat reporter from the *Tribune* had written a stage play about the corruption. With a single word, the title said it all—*Chicago*. The play was an instant hit on Broadway.

Had Frank been murdered by Chicago's mob boss mayor? His last visit to Bobby had turned up nothing, but he'd try again. He'd grown comfortable talking about murder and suicide; before joining Duttons, he'd never even heard the word "corpse."

Bobby's assistant took him through, and Lewis plunged right in: "Frank got out the vote for the mayor in the last campaign. So, when did things turn sour?"

"When Frank shifted his support to the man's rival," Bobby said, heaving a sigh as if to say, *Do I have to spell out everything for this kid?*

"There must be a whack of municipal contracts at stake," Lewis replied, counting the zeros in his head—roads, highways, a new airport, sanitation systems, hospitals, schools. "Was Frank's support for someone other than Big Bill really enough to get him popped?"

"Frank is very influential in this city—from South Side, where he grew up, to the posh northern village that he now calls home. He's half-Irish and half-Polish, so he packs a punch among the Irish voters who have determined the outcome of elections in this city for a generation. But he's also a player among the Poles and other emerging groups of ethnic voters. Above all, Frank opens doors—and wallets—up and down LaSalle Street. So, when he turned his luncheon speech at the university into an election soapbox, some felt he should have spent more time talking about markets and less time on the mayor."

"It was only for a moment at the end," Lewis challenged the president of the Board of Trade. Bobby gave him that irritated look again, and Lewis decided to stick to questions. "But why did Frank say anything at all?"

"Because traders and their long-standing practices are under siege. Politicians are being pressured by farm groups and others to impose new constraints, and Frank is the only person in the entire industry with the balls to fight back. And mark my words, he'll pay the price."

"But murder?" Lewis persisted.

Bobby showed him the door.

ON SUNDAY AFTERNOON, LEWIS WENT to his childhood home in South Side. His father was "long gone," as his mother liked to say. He wasn't sure what she meant by "gone," but he hadn't seen the man in years. By the time he'd walked the block from the "L" to his mother's flat, he felt both frightened and sad. Empty bottles and paper bags littered the streets, and homeless men loitered outside the jazz clubs that buzzed with sensual energy at night but were lifeless caverns by day. Tax dollars aimed at improving people's lives were diverted to the mob. His mother insisted he bring Rosie, implying that the dog was the closest thing to a grandchild she might ever have. She served up fried pork, fried yams, and fried bread, and sent him home with enough leftovers to last the week.

ON MONDAY MORNING, BOBBY CALLED to say there was something he'd forgotten to tell him. "The Chicago police dropped by to confirm that Frank was with me the morning before the Crash. Apparently, there was a gangland shooting early that morning, and a witness spotted the Hudson at the scene."

"The Hudson? Is Katrina safe?" Lewis's anxiety level went through the roof. "When Frank disappeared, he left the Hudson downtown in the parking garage. I didn't think it should sit there running up fees, so I drove it to Glencoe. But maybe Frank intended to leave it in the city, away from his family. Bloody hell, what have I done?"

"Assuming the story is correct, and Frank saw these criminals in action, they'll be looking for him—not his car. So long as Frank is gone, Katrina should be fine."

Bobby's story jived with Hector's account. "Is that why he fled? He's protecting Katrina from a bunch of goons?"

Bobby's shocking report had altered the focus of Lewis's search in thirty seconds flat. Lewis thanked him and hung up, but he couldn't help wondering how Bobby had forgotten a call from the police about Frank being a witness to a gangland crime.

The file on the mayor sat open on his desk. Was it a coincidence, or was Bobby under Big Bill's thumb like everybody else?

16
THE MOB

In the morning, Frank and Will drove to the Gainsborough warehouse to pick up their share of the output from Wapella. The barebones building bore an uncanny resemblance to the site of the massacre on North Clark Street, and once again, the face of the shooter came flashing back. Frank found the crates buried behind rusted-out carburetors and stovepipes and loaded them into Will's car. He hadn't done such heavy lifting since swinging his long-nose golf club on the eighteenth hole.

It might have been exciting, this first run, but for the pitiable fact that two crates a day would not deliver a path back to his life. If he were going to make running rum worth his while, he'd have to upgrade to Moose Jaw. He kicked some scrap metal out of the way and made another decision, too. He needed an alias to sell whisky to the mob. If anyone reported his activities to the Board of Trade, he'd never be allowed to trade securities again. And that was not the only reason for an alias. Capone's men would have tracked down the owner of the green car. They'd have his name, and he wasn't about to use it here.

He ran his alias idea by Will: "I usually make up a new identity when doing research for a book. Otherwise, the moment you tell people you're a writer, they insist on being the feature character in your book. Why don't I say I'm a farmer—"

"Shorty would find that ridiculous, and so would I," Will said.

"Well, they won't buy whisky from me if I'm a lawyer or a cop. How about insurance? James Gordon, traveling salesman." He forced out a guffaw as if he couldn't possibly know anything about finance or insurance.

Will was delighted by the intrigue. And so, it was settled: for trips to the border, James Gordon it was.

At the drop site, there wasn't a soul in sight. They were mid-way between the two Antlers, Will said, Antler, ND, and the former Antler, NWT. Then the heavy artillery wheeled up. It was the Steamer and the Hup, but this time three men got out. They looked like a human bar chart—three blocks of flesh, high, low, and wide.

"It's Shorty and Wally Whacker," whispered Will, "and I don't know the new guy. There's been no turn-over on this side of the border since the Bronfman's sold to my Wapellan, but the gangsters come and go."

Shorty's fedora soared eight inches above the rim, and even with platforms on his shoes, his trench coat almost hit the ground. Wally Whacker looked as clever as a flat tire. He was clearly no relation to Charlie Wacker, chairman of the Chicago Planning Commission, president of Wacker and Birk Brewing, and one of Frank's favorite clients. There was even a street named after Charlie—Wacker Drive. But this Whacker, the one pointing a handgun at him, probably spelled his name with an "h" like whack—if he spelled it at all. Still, Whacker and Wacker. He couldn't imagine a third whacker in his life anytime soon, but two felt lucky.

"G'day, gentlemen," Will said. "This is my partner, Mr.

James Gordon. You've often asked me to double your quantities, and Mr. Gordon will be seeing to that."

"Jimmie Gawdini," Shorty said. The diminutive was surprising given that Frank was six feet tall and didn't look remotely Italian. By God, he was scared. His neck was on fire, and he couldn't possibly scratch. He reminded himself that he'd once sold wheat futures to Herbert Hoover; selling whisky to Shorty should be a cinch. But how to get started? Saying "Hi Shorty" didn't feel quite right. Sometimes it was better to keep your mouth shut and look stupid than open it and remove all doubt. Wally Whacker was even less approachable: the man's sunglasses were as opaque as his gloves.

Frank and Will unloaded the crates, and everyone sampled the product, passing the bottle around, taking a swig, and swilling it in their mouths while using body parts ranging from bulging eyes to a karate chop across the throat to rank the experience. These were men of few words. After the tasting circle, out came the cigarettes. Shorty lined up five in his mouth, from the left side of his mouth to the right, lit them all with his shiny brass handheld lighter, and handed them out. Everyone smoked for a bit, struggling to keep them going in the prairie wind. When the bar charts grew bored with that, they introduced their weapons with so much adoration and respect you'd think they were reciting a blessing at their sons' bar mitzvahs.

Whacker presented his lethal-looking, thirty-four-inch Thompson 1928 sub-machine gun. "Tommy" could fire seven-hundred reps per minute, Whacker bragged.

"Chopper" was up next—Shorty's Smith and Wesson. It looked as compact and deadly as Shorty himself and could de-limb a man in a heartbeat.

Finally, the new guy showed off his twins—"Organ," a

Remington pump-action shotgun, and "Piano," a long-range Colt. The sound of it firing was music to his ears, the lug said. Nevertheless, Frank greeted each armament with the dignity it deserved, and the mobsters gleamed like fathers of the bride.

When the cigarettes burned out and the circle of men had ground the butts into the dirt, Shorty announced that the whisky had earned a passing grade. It was time for Frank to make his move: "I'd like to double the volume and triple the price per crate."

Shorty grunted and Frank took it as a yes.

Frank and Will inched the loot forward while staying on their side of the invisible border, and the gangsters hauled it the final few feet to their cars.

Jimmie Gawdini had run his first rum run.

AT THE DOMINION, FRANK AND Will ate their first official partners' lunch. There wasn't much of an agenda; Frank considered asking Will whether their clients might invest in a futures contract but decided to keep the thought under wraps. So, they ate lunch, drank beer, and got caught up on the grain news, like everybody else. They skimmed the *Leader-Post* while CJGX ran through the latest dismal numbers.

When the waitress brought coffee, Will launched into the ins and outs of selling Canadian whisky to the Yanks. By the time he was done, Will had woven in every possible word for his product: panther piss, pinch-bottle, poteen, hooch, moonshine, demon rum, rotgut, bathtub gin, giggle juice, and more. Frank learned that the industry, too, had many tags, from bootlegging to rumrunning.

Technically, Will said, bootleggers smuggled their goods over land and rumrunners by water.

"Bootleggers," he explained, "were named after soldiers in

the Civil War who shoved bottles down their boots and snuck them into camp. Nothing very glamorous about that," Will said. "But rumrunners, they're cut from a different cloth. My favorite is Bill McCoy—the famous Captain McCoy and his fleet of pirate ships. He controlled the most lucrative run of all, from the Bimini Islands in the Bahamas to Miami. Until he was caught," Will said.

"Where are these other lucrative runs?" Frank asked, trying not to sound too interested.

"There are two of them, both from Canada to the US—Montreal to New York down the eastern seaboard, and Windsor to Detroit across Lake Erie. Those are 'the big three.' My run—the Two Antlers—is more of a one-man show."

Frank smiled, and Will corrected himself. "Two-man, at the moment."

Will added that he fancied himself a rumrunner, although he didn't so much as cross the Gainsborough Creek, which you could step over during a drought.

"I've adapted many of McCoy's techniques," Will said. "McCoy never moved his cargo onto US territory, keeping his pirate ships just offshore and engaging US-based gangs to pay off the customs and port officials and bring the bottles to shore. Likewise, I always stay within spitting distance of the American frontier."

"Smart," Frank said.

"McCoy also resisted adding fake labels and watering down his goods, which was commonplace among smugglers, and his products became known as 'the real McCoy.'"

Admittedly, there was nothing misleading about Will's labels: seven large white letters—WHISKY—on a field of black. No fake luxe brands or false claims, and no mention that Stets created the amber color with a blow torch and the whiff of maturity with sulfuric acid drops.

"I also think of my products," Will said, "as the real McCoy."

Frank raised his mug: "To the Two Antlers."

As he threw back his drink, Frank also chugged down his misgivings about joining an industry whose heroes were marauding pirates and licentious soldiers.

JUST WHEN FRANK WAS CERTAIN he could never be surprised by Will again, his new partner did exactly that. "When I was a cop—"

Frank bolted forward. "A cop?"

"It didn't last long. My boss complained that I spent too much time at the Dominion showing off my gunslinger tricks. I was pretty good at twirling my pistol around my trigger finger."

"Your boss? You mean the sheriff?"

"The sergeant. There are no sheriffs on the Prairies. We have Mounties here. He said I was better suited to the other side of the law. Perhaps he was right. I keep him in whisky, and he keeps me out of trouble."

Frank added bribing police sergeants to his list of concerns about his new venture. When they reached the farm, Will pulled a bottle from the cargo space under the driver's seat: "Take it for your room and get to know our product, partner."

HIS ROOM, HIS QUARTERS, HIS suite—Frank had heard them all now; it was a shed. But as soon as they arrived at the farm, that's where he went. He took a swig from the bottle. Agh, it tasted like something you might administer on a snake bite. He counted the money he'd made from the run and considered sending it to Katrina, but after paying his room and board, the dribs would hardly cover the cost to wire the funds. Besides, there was shopping money at the house, and he'd need some petty cash to execute a plan. He stowed it with his Chicago clothes, then crawled into bed. It was only mid-afternoon, but there was no other way to stay warm.

Staring out his window at the stark fields beyond, Frank circled back to the insurance money. His family could only collect it if he were dead—an idea he hadn't discarded yet. There was also the other policy, the one his firm had taken out when he became head trader. "Key Man Insurance," the broker had called it. He hadn't thought about it in years. In this market, the policy made him worth more dead than alive—a hundred thousand dollars more, to be precise. Mr. D would stop at nothing to get his hands on a sum like that. Beneath his folksy charm, James Dutton III was a shrewd son of a bitch; the man hadn't risen to the top of the Chicago brokerage heap on cheesy cornpone alone.

Even under the comforter, he was too cold to think. November promised an endless supply of glacial nights, and he was hoarding the few lumps of coal for just such a night. He headed for the Howard farmhouse. With Will driving cab most afternoons, the house was quiet and warm. Laura-Jean was peeling potatoes, the girls were napping, and Willard was playing in the yard. In a cupboard above the broom, he found a scribbler and pencil. Willard would never miss them. He carved out a spot among the newspapers scattered with Laura-Jean's vegetable debris and went to work on his plan. He wasn't very adept with a schoolboy's pencil and missed the robust weight of his Montblanc pen.

Laura-Jean asked what he was working on, and he lied: "My book."

He immediately regretted it. Soon, she'd be probing for details and insisting that he read excerpts aloud. He flipped to the back of his scribbler and wrote out his title: "The Kingdom of Céyh." He admired it for a moment, then added his name.

The Kingdom of Céyh, By Francis Cork.

As he wrote it, the details of his father's tale came flooding back. That was fortuitous: typically, his childhood memories only appeared during sweat-filled moments of terror in the night. He had a title, but needed a hero, a setting, and a plot. He decided on Fib, the protagonist from his father's dark tale. However, instead of setting his story on a ravaged plain, Frank's Fib would undertake a journey full of optimism and hope, such as the search for the perfect prairie. It would be an allegory—or a parable, perhaps—although he didn't know which was what.

Funny how his writer alibi was creating the impetus to tackle the children's story he had always hoped to craft for Franny and Robbie. At last, he would get out from under the cloud that had cast its long shadow over his efforts in the past.

He'd made a good start: he had his setting, his hero, and his hero's quest. He tucked his scribbler into the large patch pocket on the front of his jacket and marveled at the perfect fit. Now, his parable and his plan would always be close at hand.

THAT EVENING, THE HOWARDS ATE apple wedges for dessert, and Laura-Jean asked him to read from his book. He opened his scribbler and took a deep breath.

"Chapter One."

A hush fell over the room.

"Long ago in a Pictish land lay a barren plain where time began. Mountains loomed to the east and west, and that icy domain was dark and bereft. By and by, the sun awoke, and great sheets of ice shattered and broke. The earth grew warm, and fast-flowing waters flooded the plain. When the deluge subsided into rivers and lakes, unto this land came Cruithne and his seven sons."

"What's Pictish?" Olive asked.

"My father said it was Irish, but I'm sure he was wrong."

Frank smiled and read on. "Cruithne divided his land in seven ways, declaring his realm the Kingdom of Céyh. The seven sons sowed their fields in wheat, casting their seeds far and wide in the welcoming wind. Flanked by the mountains to the west and east, the Kingdom flourished—for a thousand years. Then unto their lands came a withering drought, and the suffering spread all around."

"And the suffering spread all around, all around, the suffering spread all around," Willard chimed in.

Frank nodded encouragingly and read on. "At the dawn of the twentieth century, King Cruithne was sad and full of despair, for he'd seen more suffering than he could bear. With a heart that was heavy, he turned to Fib for help.

'Fib,' said Cruithne to his eldest son, 'we've lost our Kingdom! We've lost our way!'

'Fear not,' said Fib to his father the king. 'We'll search the realm and prosper again. We'll build a new Kingdom of Céyh.'"

FRANK CLOSED HIS SCRIBBLER AND looked around. Laura-Jean was the opinion leader on the Howard farm. To his relief, she had some nice things to say about Chapter One. She relished his prairie theme and was flattered that he had styled his lead character after her: not only was Fib the eldest of seven children as she was, but he also bore her name. Frank nodded as if to say, "Of course."

But with Laura-Jean's praise came criticism, too. "You can't be writing about prairies and plains as if they're the same.

They're not," she said. "They're as different as mountains and hills."

He thought she'd overstated things, although understanding the difference between a prairie and a plain would be helpful when Fib combed the earth looking for the perfect flatland for his people.

Meanwhile, Laura-Jean retrieved *Prairie Song*, the only book on the Howard farm, and read aloud: "The prairies are not the plains. The vegetation differs wildly. The plains are mainly clothed in a short, hair-like grass, russet in color during most of the year. The prairies are rich in blue-joint, crows-foot and wild oats...sunflowers and innumerable and brilliant flowers...with long swells like a quiet sea."

Long swells like a quiet sea—the words were beautiful, but everything Frank had seen was dead flat.

FRANK HELPED WITH THE CLEAN-UP, then joined Will in the yard. They sauntered alongside each other, and Will smoked. The moonlight illuminated a few late-autumn survivors in the garden—coneflowers, poppies, pumpkins, Brussels sprouts, cabbages, parsnips, and butternut squash.

"So, what did you think?" Frank asked.

"About what?" Will replied.

"My book," he exclaimed.

"Oh," Will said as if he'd forgotten about it already. "Well, it's a grand vision with your mythical king and made-up son. I like telling a story as much as the next man. Laura-Jean has heard them all a hundred times. But I stick to the things I know and can see."

"So, you didn't like it."

"When I was a boy, as I told you, I had a few imaginary

friends—Huck, Tom, Aunt Polly, and Pap Finn. I used to conjure them up when I felt lonely or afraid."

Where was Will going with this?

"So, I got to thinking while I listened to your fanciful story that maybe my new friend was feeling that way himself. Next thing you know, I was asking myself, Who is this Frank Cork, and why is he so afraid?

17
PINZOLO

Lewis plopped down on Frank's couch. He was exhausted and in over his head. He was hardly going to take on the mob, let alone waltz into city hall and ask whether the mayor had taken out a hit on Chicago's top trader. No, it was time to bring in the police. He pulled himself up, moved to the desk, and made the call.

"Chicago Police Department," a woman answered.

"I'm calling to report a missing person." After such a confident opening, Lewis waited an eternity for an officer to come on the line.

"Thompson here." It was uncanny: the officer had the same last name as the mayor. After walking him through the facts, Thompson parroted them back: "Mr. Cork's been gone more than a month and not a word."

"Nothing, officer."

"Well, it ain't suicide," Thompson said. "That lot wants to be found. We walk in, and there they are. Usually in the bedroom. Even if they jump off a bridge, their bloated bodies pop up within a few days."

Lewis felt nauseated. He should have handed this off to the police a week ago when Katrina had begged him to. But he kept expecting Frank to show up any day. "So, it's murder."

It was unsettling to say the word out loud.

"He's a missing person right now," Thomson clarified. "But when a rich uptown guy like that disappears, we'll be looking at the big three."

"The big three what?"

"Babes, business associates, and jealous wives."

"What about the mayor—"

"The mayor?"

He almost felt Thompson's spit fly from CPD headquarters on Michigan Avenue.

"Listen, kid," Thompson's voice dropped to a whisper, "if you decide to pursue this—and you'll wanna think carefully about that—there's not a CPD officer in his right mind who will investigate this mayor for murder. Besides, if you think there's a mob angle, you gotta talk to the Bureau."

"But officer—"

"Good luck, son. By the way, we didn't have this call."

He heard the click as the line went dead.

Lewis decided to do some digging on the "Bureau"—the Federal Bureau of Investigation, also known as the BOI. He took the stairs to the firm's library on the eighth. There was a file on almost everything; wagering on the future requires a curious mind and a lot of facts. There was truth to the industry proverb that forecasting is the art of explaining tomorrow why the things you predicted yesterday didn't happen today.

After half an hour of fruitless searching for a file on the Bureau, he was ready to give up. Talk about a culture of secrecy: you needed to be a detective yourself to find anything on the country's top sleuths. But at the back of the bottom drawer of a filing cabinet, he found a slim file marked BOI.

The Bureau, he read, had been around for two decades, but was only now gaining its stride. Its director, one John Edgar

Hoover, had been given the task of quashing the mobster-related crime spreading across America like the plague. The mandate came with a raft of shiny new toys: a fingerprint registry, a cadre of well-dressed young men, and access to a crime detection laboratory up the street.

Lewis completed a round of backslaps with his colleagues—he'd be on the eighth floor again soon enough—then mounted the stairs to make the call. There were no layers of clerical staff at the BOI, and someone picked up on the first ring.

"Pinzolo."

The man sounded like he'd never left the Bronx.

"Detective?"

"Special Agent."

"I'm calling from Duttons, the commodities brokerage firm."

"You're a trader?" It sounded more like "traitor," the way Pinzolo said it.

"No, my boss was a trader...*is* a trader. I'm a trainee." He fiddled with his Parker, examining it for chips.

"That's a pleasant change from our public enemies list. Communists, homosexuals, movie stars—not necessarily in that order."

He liked Pinzolo already. The special agent was a sarcastic son of a bitch. He'd hardly had time to hang up, jot down the man's name, and use the can when Dorothea buzzed: "There's someone here to see you. A client, he claims."

A client? These days, that was a rare event. Without so much as a knock, the door swung open, and someone who could only be Special Agent Pinzolo shambled in. It was easier to imagine this man as a criminal than a cop. Pinzolo was maybe forty-two, more squat than tall, and a colony of ants could live comfortably in the pores of his nose. The agent's wet overcoat hung askew, and his punched-up fedora looked like it had been glued to the tangle of undergrowth below the brim.

Dorothea would have insisted that the visitor leave his soggy stuff in the cloakroom. But no, this was a man who made his own rules. Coat and hat on, Pinzolo flopped onto Frank's pricey couch. A long ash hung menacingly from the end of his cheap cigar. Lewis cast his eyes around for an ashtray. No luck—Frank's office didn't include an ounce of clutter. He mounted the spiral staircase two steps at a time and grabbed a whisky glass from the wet bar. Pinzolo beamed, and Lewis blanched as the hard-boiled agent ground his black ash into Frank's leaded crystal.

Lewis chose the armchair, and Rosie posted herself at his feet, ears forward, eyeing her prey. *So, this is who the BOI has tasked with solving the murder of a prominent citizen by the mayor*, he thought. *There must be more than meets the eye.* He gave Rosie a firm pat, trying to convince them both that this intruder was their friend.

Pinzolo looked around slowly, taking in the lavish furnishings and ruby-red curtains like a hard-boiled detective inspecting the scene of a crime. Lewis followed suit, which launched his imagination into overdrive. He pictured burly assassins shooting Frank while stretched out on his couch, dragging the blood-soaked corpse along the partners hall, and tossing it into the basement incinerator with the day-old trading bids.

Lewis shook off the vision and forced himself to examine the office the way Pinzolo might. It was the well-ordered space of an orderly mind: even the books on Frank's side tables were stacked by color and size. He'd often felt lonely and overwhelmed searching for Frank on his own and welcomed the help of a professional—until the detective's glare landed squarely on him. Why did even good men cringe when confronted by a cop? He felt like he'd been caught sipping the Scotch before the corpse was even cold. It was a mistake bringing in the BOI. An hour ago, he was a caring colleague. Now, he was a suspect in a murder case, with no one to blame but himself.

Pinzolo reached inside his coat and rearranged the contents of his pants. Lewis looked away. The agent finally spoke. "Some might call it brave, others stupid. But telling a roomful of VIPs to ditch the mayor was all mouth and no brain."

Lewis could scarcely contain his relief: the agent's top suspect was the mayor. He wouldn't be handcuffed and marched past Dorothea and out the door, the shortest internship in the history of the firm. He felt the color returning to his cheeks. He made a sweeping gesture toward Frank's bookshelf: "Ask me anything you want about wheat futures, but I know nothing about municipal politics, let alone the mayor."

Pinzolo stood to go, revealing a butt-shaped water stain he'd deposited on Frank's couch. "The Bureau takes on powerful people," the agent said, looking at him stone-cold in the eye. "Men like your Mr. D are not always what they seem."

Mr. D? One minute, Pinzolo was accusing the mayor of whacking Frank, and the next, he's pointing fingers at Mr. D and using the managing partner's nickname, no less.

"Our people do their best work undercover," Pinzolo forged ahead. "Secrecy will be essential if you want us to find your boss. Got it?"

The agent held his glare until Lewis nodded yes. Lumbering out of Frank's office, Pinzolo paused to read the nameplate on the door. Frank Cork, Head Trader, it said.

"Nice office you got here, kiddo. Not bad for a trainee."

18
THE TUNNEL

Frank's second run to the border was easier than his first. He knew both the warehouse workers and his clients by name, and there were even laughs over cigarettes. The humor was not the typical fare served up at the Board of Trade: Shorty acted out the sounds men make when you cut off their roosters, and Wally showed them just how far blood spurts from a gouged-out eye. It was an effort to guffaw.

Yet all this risk was barely netting pocket change. He had to take their bootlegging business to the next level. "How about a visit to Moose Jaw?" he asked Will on the drive back to the farm. "And this time, I'd like to meet your Wapellan."

Will was noncommittal about his supplier but keen on the drive to Moose Jaw. It would be a half-day's drive each way, Will said. They'd leave in the morning, visit the still after lunch, and be back by end of day. Will said he'd get word to Shorty and Whacker that they were going to miss tomorrow's drop, but they'd double up the shipment the next day. Frank couldn't help wondering how one got word to these guys. Was it the elusive Wapellan who did that?

THE NEXT MORNING, FRANK AROSE with the barnyard fowl. He thanked Laura-Jean for the thermos of relief coffee she'd made for the road, then he and Will piled into the Buick. They drove west along the 18, then cut northwest—parallel to the Dominion-Soo railway line, Will said. After the turnoff, the flatlands made way for lakes and trees and, eventually, gentle rolling hills—long swells in a quiet sea, just as Laura-Jean had promised. Even the names of towns became lyrical and French—Belle Plaine, Pense, Rouleau.

By noon, they were in Moose Jaw. Will said the locals were called Moose Javians. Better than Wapellans, he supposed. They wandered into The Brunswick Hotel, and the proprietor introduced himself. "John B. Goodman at your service. Call me Goodie," the man said.

Frank ordered up a jug of beer and three glasses.

"Yep," Goodie said, "there's a still under the town. Down in the tunnels, but it's not for the likes of you."

Frank and Will exchanged looks as if to say they didn't quite catch his drift.

"You're too tall for one thing," Goodie said, sizing up Will. "And you're too nice," he said to Frank.

Frank continued, undeterred: "Who built the tunnels and when?"

"Chinamen. They arrived by the shipload fifty years ago to lay the track." Goodie took a long pull on his beer. "They worked by day and dug by night, hiding out from tax collectors and townspeople, who were always picking on them."

"Where are they?"

"Who? The Chinamen?"

"No, the tunnels."

"Right beneath us." Goodie stomped his foot a few times on the floor. "They run under River Street to Manitoba Street and all the way over to the Soo Line. They use tunnel crawlers to cart the whisky from the still to the train."

"Who?"

"Some hard-luck, local kids."

"No, who runs the whisky?"

"The mob," Goodie said. "Why do you think there's a direct line from Moose Jaw to Chicago?"

Frank was reeling. Was this Capone's operation one floor below? It all made sense: he was standing at the headwater of a mighty river of bootleg whisky. And everything you needed was right here. What had Will said? Water, yeast, and grain was all it took. The Moose Jaw River ran right through town; yeast was clearly plentiful given all the beer and bread; and grain elevators were visible from every window. Check, check, and check. But Goodie was right. What really set Moose Jaw apart was the direct train service linking this northern hick town to the biggest moonshine market in the world. No wonder Goodie called Moose Jaw "Little Chicago."

Frank decided he wasn't leaving town without seeing the tunnels. "How do I get down there?"

Will intervened with a sideways shake of the head that means "No" to every child over two. But Will's family had money coming in, and Frank's did not.

Goodie lowered his voice: "Go to 51 River Street. Walk through the diner like you own the place and head down the back stairs. You'll find a locked door. Knock twice. Today's password is 'Storm Tonight.'"

Frank stood to leave. Goodie yanked his arm and gave him a warning look: "It's full of ethanol alcohol down there, and there's not much light or air. One fart and the whole place could go up in smoke. And that's the least of your concerns."

SURE ENOUGH, THERE WAS A staircase at the back of the River Street diner; Will followed reluctantly behind. Frank called out the password, and when the door opened, he half expected a genie to come billowing out. But no, he was staring into a black abyss. The long, low roof of the tunnel was propped up with railway ties, and there was a single murky ray of light from what looked like a manhole cover ahead. It certainly wasn't the skylight over the trading pit at the Chicago Board of Trade. The whole place reeked of solvent, danger, corruption, frightened boys, and bad men. He'd come to the right place.

In the gloom, he made out a man's face: his pock-marked skin, a scar above the left eye. Jesus, Mary, and Joseph, it was the shooter from North Clark Street—here in the Moose Jaw tunnels. But the look of recognition went both ways. "It's the witness in the green car," the shooter's expression seemed to say.

Frank's heart raced, and his sweat glands went into overdrive. The smell of fear was oozing from his pores, and the shooter savored it like a man who'd caught the scent of a steak on the grill.

"Jimmie Gawdini," he said, thrusting out his hand.

"Tony Bonanno," the shooter replied, sticking out a pistol instead of a hand. At least it wasn't Al Capone.

The door banged shut, locking Will out and Frank in. With one look, he could see his only hope of appeasing this man was with money.

"I sell wheat futures, Mr. Bonanno," Frank said.

"Yeh, I know."

What did Tony Bonanno know? Did he know about his shed in the wheatfields on the Howard farm? Did he know where his family lived in the village of Glencoe?

"The boss tells me you're workin' with Shawty."

Tony Bonanno's accent made Shorty sound like he'd been to finishing school.

"How's your dawg?"

The man must have seen Rosie on North Clark Street, barking hysterically in the Hudson's front seat before diving for cover. Frank had read in the press that the only creature to survive the St. Valentine's Day Massacre was Highball, the dog. Maybe Rosie was the reason he'd been spared.

He brought the focus back to money. "I can offer you a thirty-day turnaround and a 33 percent return, less my 20 percent commission." The terms were pouring out of him like moonshine from a pot still.

"Wheat? That'd be a new one for the boss. The world's gotta eat, I s'pose."

There they were—his favorite words. He tried not to flinch.

"Lemme talk to the boss," Tony Bonanno said. "He's always looking for new ways to put our money to work, if y'know what I mean. Besides, we like the tawl guy, the one with the good sense to stay on the other side of this door. Talk to Shawty. He'll let you know. Now scram."

He was sweating bullets, but Frank had one more thing he had to make clear. After this gambit, they'd be square: there would be no more wheat futures and no more witness in the green car.

"These are highly unusual market conditions, Mr. Bonanno," Frank began. "This is the first time in a decade that prices have dropped this low and stuck. I cannot possibly invest your money in wheat futures after this. So, here's the deal. We do this once, then we're done."

In the darkness of the tunnels, it was difficult to tell whether Tony Bonanno had agreed. Frank knew that if this contract didn't close, it would not be for want of money. These men were chomping at the bit to find places to park their ill-gotten cash. No, the risk was that he was a loose end, a threat. If he wanted to close, he'd have to reassure them he wasn't one to squeal.

"My clients are wealthy men, Mr. Bonanno," he said. "Many have made their money through means that do not bear scrutiny in the light of day." He thrust out his arms as if to say his natural habitat was a pitch-black tunnel.

"Your secrets, whatever they may be, are safe with me. You have my word." Maybe he was nervous or simply couldn't help himself, but he should have shut up then. "I'm no mobster," Frank said. "One deal, then we're done."

He might have safely called the man a mothafucka, but "mobster" had struck a raw nerve. His mouth had brought him to the brink again. Some men speak their minds, but Tony Bonanno shared his feelings by tightening his finger on the trigger. Frank forced a bootlicking smile and corrected himself. "What I meant to say, sir, is I'm not cut out for your line of work."

Tony Bonanno shoved open the door and scuttled away like a rat in a sewer.

FRANK WAITED A MINUTE OR two, then ventured into the stairwell. Will emerged from the shadows, looking relieved, and they mounted the stairs to the River Street diner.

"How'd it go?" Will asked.

"Let's just say that Stets has nothing to worry about. We won't be switching to Moose Jaw during my lifetime," Frank said.

Will nodded his assent. Their partners' decision was done.

During the long drive home, Frank said nothing about his proposal to do a wheat futures deal with their clients. It was outside the scope of his partnership with Will; besides, he'd promised Tony Bonanno he could keep a secret. There was that story on the news last year during the St. Valentine's Day Massacre about one of the gangsters taking fourteen bullets to the head. When the police arrived, the gangster, bloody and dying, swore he hadn't been shot. There was a man who knew how to keep his mouth shut. Tony Bonanno was cut from the same cloth. Frank was saying nothing to anyone.

He'd found his investors. There was only one nagging question.

Would he ever be free of these men?

19
SUSPECTS

"I have Mrs. Cork on the phone for you," Dorothea announced. And when Lewis picked up, it was a furious Katrina on the line. She fumed that she'd had no visitors since her husband disappeared more than a month ago.

What about her parents?

No, she couldn't face them.

And the children?

They were fed up with the constant fibs. She'd had to move them to the public school, and they'd stopped bringing home friends. "And to top it off," Katrina seethed, "the federal police were parked outside my door half the night."

An ugly mix of outrage, jealousy, and guilt washed over him at the thought of Pinzolo lurking outside Katrina's door. "I promised you I'd find Frank. Believe me, I've looked. But I need help. The Bureau is our best chance."

"You might have warned me, Lewis."

She had a point. "They work discreetly. I wasn't sure they'd come by. At least you're not a suspect."

"Really? The creep sure treated me like one."

"You have nothing to fear. You didn't murder anyone."

"Murder? Are you back on that again?"

He was always on a tightrope talking to Katrina. She was so

clever, so vulnerable, so—

The cursed intercom buzzed.

"Special Agent Pinzolo is heading down the hall," Dorothea warned.

He bid a hasty goodbye to Katrina and felt a foul mood coming on.

Pinzolo flung his hat and coat on Frank's chair as if it were fresh territory to soil. Seeing the agent stripped down to his suit for the first time, Lewis was surprised to discover a menacing build and a head full of black hair.

"Quite the peaches 'n' cream that Mrs. Cork," Pinzolo said. "And not fond of curtains. It's enough to make you wanna work at the BOI."

The heat rose from Lewis's collar to his face. "Is there anything I can help you with?"

"Not much of a marriage, those two. Wouldn't be surprised if it was the wife who popped him."

"You're the expert, sir. I deal in agricultural commodities," he said, tight-lipped.

"Or one of her male visitors," Pinzolo added.

Was the agent talking about him? He'd seen her twice—once to drop off the car, and the other time to borrow it. It couldn't be him, yet Katrina had just told him she hadn't seen a soul all month.

"And if this is a domestic," Pinzolo ragged on, "it's a matter for the local police, not the BOI."

God forbid the file went back to Officer Thompson. "What about Frank's family. Any leads there?"

"The mother is in Chicago State—the asylum, that is, not the jail. And the old man is NFA."

"NFA?"

"No fixed address. Like me," Pinzolo said.

Lewis gave him a blank look.

"When the Bureau came calling, I packed up my place in the Bronx and was here the next day."

"No wife or kids?"

"Just me."

The agent could spend days sifting through other people's dirty laundry but didn't have a thing to say about himself. "How did it go with Bobby?" Lewis asked.

"Dynamite. Seems that your Mr. Frank P-for-Perfect Cork was under investigation by the Board of Trade. I'm not talking unpaid parking tickets here. I mean career-ending, sensational stuff." Pinzolo flipped through his notes and read aloud: "A cross-border, quasi-criminal investigation. Churning the price of wheat—driving prices up and down, collecting fees with every churn." Pinzolo closed his notebook for effect and stared him in the eye. "You shoulda told me, kid."

He couldn't remember much about the investigation besides that scrap of paper Frank had handed him and the memo he'd prepared on whatshisname from the Wheat Pool.

"Our work is pretty simple here," Lewis said. "We don't set prices, and we sure as heck don't drive them up, down, or anywhere else. We look in our crystal balls, we fiddle with our cufflinks and pens, and then we wager. Sometimes, we even get it right." The name came back to him. Yuri Dyachenko.

Pinzolo retorted, "The Board of Trade has a different view."

"Ha. If only we were as powerful as others think," Lewis laughed, something between a whoop and a sneer. "If a bookie's clients all bet on the same horse, does the horse run any faster? You tell me."

Lewis wasn't the type to sit for long. He walked from his desk to the window. The city looked bleak; Thanksgiving was next week. "I haven't seen the Board's file," he said. "If there is one. No such paperwork has crossed my desk. But in my limited experience, I see no merit to such a claim. Men don't make markets; markets make or break men."

Pinzolo lifted his head from his notes, and Lewis saw the light go on in the agent's eyes. It always took people a bit of time to make sense of markets. Some spoke of them as tangible things, like roulette wheels or Bingo. Others thought of them in abstract terms, like God or the weather. After a year in the pit, he'd come to see markets as all of that and more. As everything and nothing. And while he was down a rabbit hole thinking about markets, Pinzolo said, "Kind of a jealous guy, that Bobby."

Was there no one beyond Pinzolo's cynical reach?

"A rich kid with his daddy's big shoes to fill," the agent persisted. "Then along comes this boy wonder—Frank." Pinzolo was up from his chair, picking up photographs and ogling the family's movie star looks. "The brash kid from the South Side beats Bobby at everything that ever mattered to Bobby's old man. Better looks, better athlete, better grades. A few years later, better job, better house...perfect wife."

Pinzolo licked his lips like a tomcat, and Lewis almost erupted. But the agent was oblivious, building his story. "Finally, Bobby gets his break. An international investigation, no less. It's gonna bring the famous trader down. But Frank disappears, and Bobby's been one-upped again."

If Pinzolo hadn't become a special agent, he could have made a living writing for the *Tribune*. But maybe the man was right about Bobby. "I thought you were looking into the mayor. Now it's Bobby?"

"Police investigations are like markets, Lewis. Things are never quite what they seem."

20
THE PLAN

Frank was walking alone in the wheatfields, choreographing his plan. November had become December, and his one-month partnership with Will had morphed into two. As for his futures deal, Bonanno had said Shorty would let him know. He'd heard nothing at this morning's drop. But what if Shorty said yes tomorrow?

These were men who were not likely to dither. They had no boardroom politics, were unconstrained by the law, and had more money under their floorboards than some banks had in their vaults. No, these were impulsive men, weaned on adrenalin and addicted to risk. They were precisely the kind of investors he required.

And what if Shorty said no? He would give his life to do this deal. His book was progressing, yet his plan hadn't moved beyond his one-word start. What he really needed was a little luck; he looked around for a sign. Yet all he could see was rows of stubble under a shroud of snow. Frank closed his eyes, and an image of something else emerged. He was a boy again, peering over the pews at St. Stanislaus church at rows of lacy white headscarves bowed in prayer. And there was Katrina, the little Polish girl, beckoning him with her sweet smile. It was a sign—and exactly what he needed to inspire a plan.

Frank retrieved his scribbler and pencil from his shirt pocket and went inside. The *Leader-Post* was on the kitchen table, and the headline couldn't have been bolder: "'A Billion Bushels:' global wheat surplus reaches new high." The over-supply of wheat had reached almost one billion bushels, declared the fine print below the fold, and efforts to reduce it were underway. Desperate farmers in the American Midwest were burning their fields and flushing their crops into creeks. It was wrenching to even consider the waste. Yet these were mere nods at the problems. He read on. Groups in Canada and the US were making large-scale donations to organizations like the International Red Cross. Generous gifts, indeed, but Frank knew dumping grain into third-world markets had more to do with propping up North American agricultural markets than charity.

CJGX was reporting the latest price; it had barely budged. Such drastic measures, yet all to no effect; the surplus was just too big. There was no getting around it: the world was awash with wheat like never before. It would have to be the defining feature of his plan. Yet a successful futures contract required a change in price that others did not foresee: *his* date and price had to be right, and others wrong. No one was predicting a price increase with so much excess supply. The only scenario that could possibly drive a bump in the price in this market was an intervention by the US government. Herbert Hoover was hardly the man for that: the arch-conservative was too steeped in free-market values. However, wheat was the beating heart of financial markets and accounted for more of the world's diet than any other crop. Would the president stand idly by as the American people went hungry and its economy went belly up?

The radio station moved seamlessly from grain news to

opera, and Laura-Jean threw a handful of chopped vegetables into the cast-iron pot. Its contents rose and fell on a continuous loop: up with leftovers, down with meals. The woodstove, too, had an insatiable hunger cycle of its own—feeding, stoking, burning, and feeding again. Her family depended on it for food and warmth, yet the thing had seen better days. Its white enamel had yellowed, the turquoise trim around its warming drawer was chipped, the temperature gauge was broken, and there was no window in the oven door. In the Howards' kitchen, Laura-Jean had come to know when the apples in her cobbler had turned from blush to brown without a window or a gauge.

Would Herbert Hoover intervene? Might his government buy up enough wheat to cause wheat prices to rise? Frank was willing to bet yes to both. It was the kind of forecast few others would make—the kind that could deliver a winning wheat futures contract.

Antonio Scotti was belting out the character of Scarpia, the baritone chief of police in Puccini's *La Tosca*. Frank knew the opera well, with its momentous depictions of suicide, torture, and murder. Somehow, it provided a propitious backdrop as Frank created his plan.

It all depended on the weather. By mid-March, the winter wheat, long dormant under its blanket of snow, should throw off the covers and light up the Prairies like a Broadway show. Year after year, like an annual revue, the springtime ritual promised bounty and renewal; this season, it carried the dark message of excess supply. The *Old Farmer's Almanac* warned of drought, which would inhibit production, yet any new wheat would cause prices to drop. Frank was willing to bet that even the free-market Hoover government would not stand by and let the economy suffer a further decline. No, the feds would intervene in an effort to stabilize the economy and drive the price up.

His forecast made sense, and he'd had a sign. Besides, there was no backing out on Bonanno. If Shorty came back with a yes tomorrow, he'd confirm they had a deal. Still, his plan was a long way from done—it was a skeleton with no guts. He'd promised Bonanno a 33 percent return in thirty days, less his commission. My God, he could never deliver that. But he was stuck with those terms. It was time to do the math.

According to CJGX, wheat was sitting at 45¢ a bushel. If it hit 60¢ in mid-March—a 33 percent increase—it would yield the stated returns. Perfect. He had his price. Next came the dates. Counting back thirty days from mid-March took him to...St. Valentine's Day. Ha! St. Valentine's to St. Patrick's Day—February 14 to March 17. Thirty-two days. Close enough.

Laura-Jean was suddenly yelping and scooping up baby June, who had toddled too close to the stove. He leaped from his chair to help. Brushes with the woodstove were rites of passage, but happily, there would be no carmine tattoo this time.

Frank returned to his plan. There were still gaping holes. For one thing, selling wheat futures was illegal in Saskatchewan. For another, thirty days was a helluva long time. Will had said turnover among these men was as fast as a round of Chicago lightning. What if Shorty was arrested or Bonanno shot before they could complete his deal? Still, he was excited. Now, all he needed was for Shorty to say yes.

In December on the Prairies, the sun rose at an ungodly hour and set just as you were swinging into your day. Frank accompanied Laura-Jean into the yard; it was the outer limits of her world. She sprinkled a handful of dried corn for the birds, and he hung wet nappies on the line. They chatted and shared stories while they worked. "Politicians are like diapers," he told her. "They need to be changed often and for the same reason." It was the only diaper joke he knew.

They moved to the barn. He milked the cow, and Laura-Jean tucked a wren's egg under the broody hen. He wasn't sure where he stood in her pecking order between the wren and the hen, but he knew they'd become friends. During the past month, he'd put in more time chopping vegetables with Laura-Jean than helping Katrina in the kitchen in the previous ten years. Candidly, he'd enjoyed it immensely—the persistent presence of food, of news, even the chores. Why hadn't he shared those pleasures with his own wife? He'd told her once, "I can be a family man or a businessman, but I can't be both at the same time." Katrina had countered that she could host his clients, but not on a sailboat with the wind whipping her hair in her face and her husband shouting, "Coming about!" The line distinguishing their roles had sharpened after that. He had his study, his closet, the car, the boat, the garage, and his golf course; she had everything else.

Back from the barn, he competed with Laura-Jean in the daily CJGX spelling bee, and they got caught up on recent events. Britain was renewing diplomatic ties with the Soviet Union, the Museum of Modern Art had opened in New York, and Leo Diegel was the new PGA golf champion. As their hours in the kitchen multiplied, so too did the subjects they discussed. She was drawn to conversation like a moth to a kerosene flame: entire seasons had passed when she hadn't ventured off the farm.

Seated at the kitchen table, he took in the view from the farmhouse's only window. It reminded him of a picture he'd seen in an arthouse book that Katrina had brought home. It had been painted immediately before the artist killed himself, Katrina said. Was it *Wheatfield with Crows*? By Van Gogh? He'd never forget its vivid display of rapture and torture, heaven and earth, two sides of a horizon's fine line. Then, with his face still turned toward the fields, he told Laura-Jean about his mother.

"She started life as Magda Kowalski," Frank said. "When she married my father, she became Magda Cork. Then, she took to calling herself Mary. She lost herself somewhere between Magda Kowalski and Mary Cork, one name at a time."

Laura-Jean removed the round of bread dough rising in the warming drawer. She lifted the damp tea towel covering the stoneware bowl and took a peek. It was as swollen as her belly. He sprinkled flour on the table, she handed him the round, and he punched it down more vigorously than required. "Our life was consumed by poverty," he said, eyes down, kneading, almost frantic now. "And violence. The only memory I have of our kitchen is the broom closet. I'd hide in there, helpless, crouched down with my hands over my ears, trying to block out my mother's pleas as my father clobbered her again and again. Sometimes, I think her mind was her only means of escape, and she took it."

"Where did she go?" Laura-Jean asked. She laid her fingers on the back of his hand to direct a gentler touch with the loaf.

"To a place of her own making. To a mythical place, far from our home."

"Like the Kingdom of Céyh," Laura-Jean said.

Yes, he nodded.

And for the first time in his life, he felt fully understood.

21
CHRISTMAS

Lewis stopped at a vendor on LaSalle Street to buy a small evergreen tree. He was probably the only person in the history of the Board of Trade building to ride its posh elevator with a tree, a dog, and bags of ribbons and bows. When he arrived in the Duttons foyer, Dorothea nearly squealed with delight. She flicked on the radio, and Louis Armstrong horned "Ain't Misbehavin'" while they transformed the simple spruce into a tribute to Christmas. Fanny Brice was next, crooning "My Man," and Lewis moved closer. The tree smelled as clean and fresh as mountain air, but it was Dorothea's perfume that was—what was the word? Unforgettable. He slipped a candy cane over a bough, and they touched, her red lacquered nails brushing the back of his hand. His breathing quickened, his heart pounded, and his blood pulsed upward from his toes to his head.

Wait, what was he doing? Could he have them both? Dorothea was all tinsel and Christmas carols, her finger on his hand; Katrina was virtuous and sublime, even illusory, perhaps. It was an easy choice. Besides, the promised deadline had arrived. He made an excuse, then hurried down the hall to call Katrina.

"It started with a single car parked outside my door. Now I have a string of men parading past my house," she said. "Not only Bobby and Pinzolo but an around-the-clock team from the BOI."

It was a far cry from the Santa Claus parade, he thought.

"What did my husband do to merit all this attention? He's been gone two months without a word. I'm hardly expecting him to waltz in the front door with a tree."

Damn. He should have bought two trees. "What about Frank's mother? Have you been in touch with her?"

"No, she's ill. She was committed to the State Hospital when Frank's father walked out—it's becoming a habit among the Cork men, it seems—his mother was incapacitated by poverty and despair. Even as a boy, Frank has been the one trying to provide for her."

"In an asylum?" he pressed.

"She has depression."

"He's never mentioned that."

"He doesn't like the word. He says it's an economic term and he's not willing to apply it to his mother's health."

Lewis tried not to snicker. He missed Frank and his smart-aleck mouth.

"When she was admitted," Katrina continued, "I bought him a book by the renowned neurologist Sigmund Freud. I had hoped Frank and I...that *we* could read it together. Since he'd vetoed the word the doctors use, we needed a vocabulary to discuss her condition and her care. But he stuck my gift on his bookshelf and never so much as cracked the cover."

Lewis had to admit he wasn't very likely to read it, either. Neurology, the science of the soul, he'd heard some quack call it. It sounded like an oxymoron to him.

"Do you think they're connected—his mother being committed and Frank's disappearance?"

"No, not at all," she said firmly, dismissing the notion that Frank would put his mother before she and the children. Then she paused and reflected. "His visits to the Chicago State left him very upset."

"Well, then, why *did* Frank disappear?"

"He left because . . ."

Her voice trailed off. What was it she was about to say? Even he felt wickedly wronged by Frank, he could hardly imagine Katrina's sense of betrayal and loss. Now, the deadline for finding Frank was upon them, with no sign of the man. Did he have a chance with her? Sure, he was a decade younger, but he couldn't care less. He'd never longed for anyone the way he longed for Katrina. Was it her beauty? Her vulnerability? Or because she was Frank Cork's wife?

There was so much to say...and yet so little.

"Merry Christmas," he said.

LEWIS WAS THE LAST TO leave Duttons that Christmas Eve. He turned out the lights and trudged with Rosie to the 'L.' They rode the train to South Side for a late dinner with his mom. It was good to be home. She'd baked a ham. He'd considered perfume, but it was well beyond his budget. Instead, he brought her a beautiful brandy fruit cake he'd found in the pantry at the firm. She gave him a tie that wasn't really his style.

Making his way around the old neighborhood after the meal, he stopped in to see a girl from his high school days. Hours later, kissing her goodnight on her porch, she said, "Come by any time."

When he finally made it home that night, he thought about all the women who'd made his Christmas special: Dorothea, his mother, the girl from the hood, and even Rosie, who was asleep beside his bed.

But when he turned out the light, he dreamed of Katrina.

22
PLONK

It was hard to say which came first—the smell or the announcement by Laura-Jean that the coffee was gone. Either way, there was relief coffee instead. When Frank gave her a puzzled look, she explained how she'd toasted a pan of wheat in the oven, ground it in the coffee mill, and boiled it with blackstrap molasses and water until it was as thick as stew. The pantry shelves had no doors, and he could see with a glance they were growing bare. At least he was paying room and board and contributing to the Howards' household, if not to his own. Laura-Jean handed Will their thermos, and they were off to the drop.

Today, he hoped, would be the day Shorty said yes. At the border, he filled their mugs and stealthily emptied his share onto the ground. Whether it was that simple act of deception or the waste, he was left with a sense of foreboding about what was to come.

Shorty and Wally Whacker arrived late. Everyone gathered around the Buick, lit smokes, and passed the bottle. As the client, Shorty always took the first slug. Before anyone else could sample the wares, Shorty was doubled over, gagging and gasping for air. When he spat out a yellow splay of sour mash, Wally Whacker drew his gun. In an instant, the pleasure of the daily nip had turned to peril.

Everyone waited for Shorty to recover enough to talk. "You picked the wrong men to mess with," Shorty said. It was the longest sentence he'd heard the man utter.

Will intervened, as calm as a convent. "Very sorry, gentlemen, I—"

"I'm sure we can sort this out," Frank said, backing up his partner and managing a pounding heart.

Whacker snatched a bottle from the case, tossed it high in the air like a skeet, and blasted a hole clean through the middle. Toxic liquid and shards of glass rained down from the sky. He wasn't sure whether to stand his ground or run. Then Whacker turned his gun on Frank.

The best he could do was appeal to Shorty: "We'll bring you a new batch." He barely recognized the sound of his voice; it sounded like it was stuck below the lump in his throat. He tried again. "We'll be back in one hour, mark my word. And there will be no cost for today's run."

The promise of a free batch seemed to work: the pint-sized gangster signaled at Whacker to lower his gun. Frank backed up slowly, Will followed, and then they both turned and made a mad dash for the car.

"The great thing about stupid people," Frank said as they peeled up the 256 North, "is they make the rest of us look smart."

But Will wasn't easily consoled. They drove to the warehouse in silence. Frank suggested they take up the matter with their elusive supplier, but Will nabbed a sample from the stockpile to taste-test. It took every ounce of Frank's willpower not to drink the entire bottle.

FRANK AND WILL WERE BACK at the border within the hour. It was clear from Shorty and Whacker's behavior that the rotgut had been eminently drinkable after all. There were shattered bottles and sticky liquids everywhere, and the international border was demarked with the debris from multiple rounds of ammunition. Clever Wally Whacker. For the first time in history, the two Antlers were separated by a line.

Frank was hankering to restore the camaraderie and get his futures contract back on track. Was his plan already an idea whose time had come and gone? "I assure you, gentlemen," he said, "our whisky is made from the finest products, home-grown in Saskatchewan." On reflection, he should have stopped there. "Grain storage is challenging at this time of year," Frank added. "Too damp and the weevils spread like the Spanish Flu; too dry, and the whole supply can go up in a blaze of smoke."

"That's your problem," Shorty said. The mention of weevils in his alcohol had made Shorty angrier than a cross-eyed mule.

Will saved the day. "We've added a new taste test at the warehouse before we load the car. We will not have this problem again."

"Better not," Shorty said, staggering the way men do when kicked out of a speakeasy after closing.

Everyone tasted the new batch, and Shorty made best efforts to nod his consent. With crates and envelopes exchanged, Frank crumpled into his seat for the drive home. He'd never get a chance to pitch his plan; there wasn't a single damn thing to show for his time on the Prairies. Worse, even if Shorty did say yes, the risks were now clear. A case of spoiled whisky had merited a gun to his head—imagine the consequences if he lost the mob's money.

IN THE AFTERNOON, FRANK FOLDED the clean sheets with Laura-Jean. They grasped the corners and stepped forward until they bumped, then grasped, stepped, and bumped again in a kind of sheet-folding waltz that was new to him. Under her apron, pockets laden with wooden spoons, she wore a simple frock with a long hemline and a neckline that could barely contain her ample bust. His mind and his body remembered the first time he'd reached up under Katrina's blouse. There were soft handkerchiefs folded into triangles and stitched to a silky ribbon winding around her slim frame. Women were making do, she'd explained. Every scrap of metal, even the wire supports in brassieres, had been salvaged for the military supply. Oh, how he'd loved those delicate cotton corners and the glimpses of lace through her blouse. Laura-Jean handed him a stack of nappies to fold. The sheets and his reveries were done.

Willard came in from the yard and laughed at the spectacle of a man folding the baby's things. Frank took the heckling with grace, flung a few muslin squares at the boy, and demanded his help. But Willard scoffed, plunged the ladle into the pail of Queenie's milk, let out a loud slurp, then dashed back out to the yard. It was at that moment Frank knew he'd become a fixture on the Howard farm.

AND THEN IT WAS CHRISTMAS. He longed to call Katrina and the children, but the house phone would be disconnected. He'd been away two months. Is there a point, he wondered, when away becomes home, and home becomes away? He traipsed outside and down to the root cellar to search for vegetables for the festive meal. The bounty from the Howards' garden was diminishing day by day. He selected an onion and a couple of turnips and brushed off the rich black loam. It smelled of a million years of mountain run-off. He rubbed it between his thumb and fingers until it resembled rosary beads and prayed that Shorty would say yes.

In the yard, Willard plucked the feathers from a chicken; in the kitchen, Laura-Jean placed sprigs of holly on the plates. After the Christmas meal, she asked him to read from Chapter Two, and he did.

"Fib's mission was clear: he must find a new homeland for his people. If he succeeded, he'd become king...but if he failed? Fib and his people would perish."

The Howard children stirred in their seats, and Willard chanted, "And the suffering spread all around, all around, the suffering spread all around."

Frank rustled the youngster's hair and continued his tale: "Poor Fib grew wary. How would he find the perfect prairie? The lava fields were too hot, and the ice fields too cold. The rainforests were too wet, and the deserts too dry. But lo, a gentle wind blew from the east to the west and whispered to Fib like an angel's breath: *Kisiskâciwan*.

"Fib gazed beyond the mountains and across the sea. 'Father,' said he, 'I have found a new Kingdom of Céyh.'

"'What is it called, this faraway realm?'

"The wind stopped blowing, and Fib tried his best.

"'Go now,' said Cruithne. 'To Saskatchewan.'"

FRANK PUT DOWN HIS SCRIBBLER and waited in silence.

"We're honored to host you on the Howard farm," Laura-Jean said, seemingly enchanted.

He let out a quiet sigh of relief. Now, if he could only advance his plan as smoothly as his tale.

In his shed that night, Frank found the Hudson Bay blanket spread across his bed. Other than his cufflinks, it was the most thoughtful gift he'd ever received. He couldn't possibly keep it; Laura-Jean's blanket belonged on the Howard farm. But for now, he welcomed its warmth and alluring smell. Nestling under the new layer, all he could smell was warm cobbler and woodsmoke.

Hours later, in the cold, dark stillness of his small space, he awoke in a petrified sweat. Men were breaking into his shed, suffocating him with his pillow, clubbing him over the head—Bonanno, Whacker, his father, even Cruithne, his mythical king. Where was he? In the broom closet in his childhood kitchen, immobilized with dread? No, he was thrashing under the blanket in his shed.

Would he ever make it home?

23
LUST

With January came the beginning of a new decade and the chance for a fresh start. Yet Lewis felt stuck. He didn't even know whether Frank was dead or alive. If he believed Pinzolo, Frank was dead, and everyone in the world was a suspect. Yet Bobby seemed certain Frank was alive, hiding to protect Katrina after his encounter with the mob. The Chicago police ruled out suicide and favored foul play by a wife, lover, or friend. He liked CPD's list of three and decided to work through it, starting with the wife.

By the time he'd completed a single lap around Frank's office, the idea of Katrina killing him was beyond the pale. True, Pinzolo had pointed a finger at her, but it was more of a measure of the agent's cynicism than anything else. So, Lewis struck wife off his list and set out on his second lap: lovers. Eek, this was uncharted ground. Did Frank have a mistress? Women were undeniably drawn to the man. Lewis had hauled a tree for Dorothea at Christmas and hand-carved a pumpkin for her at Halloween, yet the firm's receptionist only had eyes for Frank.

But why would Frank throw away his diamond for a rock? No, it was easier to picture Katrina fishing for trout upstream. He called Bobby. "Was Frank having an affair?"

"Frank? God no," Bobby said. "Would you, if you had Katrina to go home to every night?"

Just as he thought. Even so, he decided to pop by the Drake. It should have been at the top of his list, but asking strangers at the morgue whether his boss was dead or alive had been easier than asking the man's friends if he was having an affair.

In the lobby bar, the bartender sized up his ability to tip. He pulled out a dollar bill to settle the question and ordered a fizz. Then, lowering his voice, he asked for a shot. If he could secure an illegal drink from this man, skanky information should follow at the right price.

"Yes," the bartender admitted, topping up his drink, "Frank's a regular, but always with clients or colleagues. He never showed up with a broad at my bar."

Lewis dug deeper into his pocket, and the bartender agreed to ask around. The man was back in a flash. "The high-rollers go to Hollywood these days, so I'm told. Apparently, Joan Crawford and Lillian Gish look-alikes are all the rage. But not Mr. Cork. Have you seen his wife?" The bartender let out a whistle.

Lewis savored his drink. Did gin taste better when served from an unmarked bottle on the sly? The lobby bar, he'd discovered, was a delightful place to pass the time. The fact that it was the middle of a business day added to its allure. There must be a trick to deciding you'd had enough; if so, someone should probably share it with the partners. Yet, for all this enjoyment, he wasn't any further ahead. Was there a lover to be found? Having queried Frank's friend and checked out Frank's bar, he had no choice but to ask Katrina. There would be no easy way to do that over the phone. He called from the concierge desk: "I was wondering if it might be a good time for a visit; the children might welcome some time with their dog."

To his utter surprise, Katrina said yes.

Lewis swung by the office to pick up Rosie, then hailed a cab to Glencoe, stopping by the local hospital to make his usual inquiries. "Oh, Mr. Cork," a nurse who was reason enough to move to Glencoe said. "He's one of our biggest donors. But no, he's definitely not here. Is he okay?"

The cab carried on to the Cork residence, and Lewis ponied up the fare. Having heard about Katrina's allergy, he settled Rosie in the garage, then tapped at Katrina's impressive front door. She greeted him in slacks and a sweater set, as soft and curvaceous as her hair. The last time he'd appeared at this door, he was delivering documents to her husband. She'd been Mrs. Cork, Frank's wife, then. But there was a new ambivalence about her: Mary Magdalene, he thought, not quite a widow and not quite a wife. He found it exciting, even intoxicating, although it may have been the gin.

The house mirrored her beauty; everything was luxurious and soft. The curtains landed in creamy puddles on the floor, and the chairs were as welcoming as feathered nests. He watched as she laid out a light lunch, transforming food and household effects into small works of art. The sandwiches were arranged in contrasting colors and shapes, some round, some square, some brown, some white, and the big-handled coffee mugs towered over delicate cups for tea. She handed him a bottle of something sparkling, and he popped the cork.

The only thing missing was any hint of Katrina's past. There wasn't a trace of her Polish roots: no pictures of the motherland, no Pope on the wall, no Jesus on the cross. The record of her journey from South Side to the tony northern suburbs had been expunged. He thought of his own upward climb, replete with the markers of his past like stamps on a well-traveled envelope: his crew-cut hair, military-style workouts beside his bed, Sunday dinners with his mom, and touch-football games on weekends with his same old friends. How far can one travel from one's past without getting lost? Maybe that's where Frank was—lost.

They spoke of practical things. For Katrina, money was top of mind. Every last cent that she'd squirreled away for groceries and the children's tennis was gone. She'd received threatening letters from the bank about the mortgage not being paid, and her philosophy degree hadn't opened the door to a single job. Art was her only skill, she said. She'd submitted some illustrations to publishers of children's books and reached out to friends at the Chicago Art Institute, but neither was a path to money. Tears were welling at the corners of her eyes. She dabbed at them and gasped, "What will we do?"

Her composure diminished in lockstep with their lunch: cookies lay half-eaten, and the coffee had grown cold. The napkins were soiled, and the bubbles gone from the sparkling wine.

Lewis had never even said sex out loud; how was he going to ask Katrina about her husband's affairs?

"The Bureau advises that the usual situation with missing men is they've run off with another woman. I've assured the agent this is not the case here. But they can't handle the file if it's about matters of the heart, shall we say."

"Frank? An affair? Over my dead body. Frank adores Dorothy Parker—absolutely loves her columns in *Vanity Fair*, but he's not holed up with her. My husband is many things: orderly, disciplined, and kind. But he's no philanderer. Women throw themselves at him—believe me, I know—but Frank's mind is on his family and work."

"Was he home most nights?"

"Every night. Like clockwork." She was confident and unequivocal in her replies. The tears were gone.

Lewis was out of his depth. What did he know about marriage? He was just past being a kid. "Did Frank take a suitcase when he left?"

"No, nothing. Not even Rosie, as you know. It was business as usual. I slipped in his cufflinks—it's our morning ritual—and we kissed goodbye." Lewis could almost feel Katrina pushing those golden sheaves through his own showy cuffs.

"He left in the Hudson at his regular time, and I haven't seen him since," she said.

The tears were back. He couldn't say for sure whether it was grief or red-hot fury, but his own sentiments were clear: he was smitten.

"The children are distraught," she said. "At night, I hear them crying in their beds. I take turns lying with them until they fall asleep." Her voice rose in an upsurge of anger and betrayal, then plunged into sadness and loss. It was operatic, he thought, although he'd never been to an opera in his life. She lifted a window, and the room filled with the smell of frosty January air. He longed to kiss her, to bury his face in the softness of her sweater, her skin, her hair.

Franny and Robbie bounded in from school. He dodged their questions: your father is busy with work; we all miss him; yes, he'll be home soon. But he could see these lies had grown stale. She invited him for dinner—to give the children more time to play with their dog, she said. An hour later, they were begging their mother to let Rosie spend the night, and for one excruciating minute, Katrina let that laden question dangle in the breeze. What was she really thinking behind those emerald eyes?

"Help yourself to anything in Frank's closet," she said.

Frank's closet? Was it inevitable that he would end up here, in Frank's home, with Frank's wife, changing into Frank's polo shirt or pajamas?

The children went to bed, she poured them drinks, and he walked to the window. There were cars on the street. Was it Bobby? Pinzolo? Frank? Lewis shut the curtains.

No one was going to watch whatever happened next.

24
STILLBORN

As 1930 got underway, the chilly winds of winter carried almost no snow. With Christmas over and the decade, too, the Prairies dried up like the Kingdom of Céyh. An unforgiving drought descended over the wheatfields, and the rich, dark loam turned to cracked cement. If it continued into summer there would be hailstones instead of rain. Mother Nature had grown mean-spirited and cruel, sucking every drop of moisture out of people's lives and their land.

For Frank, making his way to the outhouse from his shed was an ordeal. Russian thistle and tumbleweed pummeled his face as if he were crossing a desert in a sandstorm. Then, in the third month after the Crash, the land aggregators came. A few were deep-pocketed investors, although there weren't many of those in sight. Most were conglomerates—banks and mortgage-holders foreclosing on farmers who couldn't make their payments for the third month in a row. Many were backed by corporate agricultural giants, grabbing up lots at rock-bottom prices and consolidating them. They stitched together quarter sections like cheap squares of cotton in a patchwork quilt.

At the Dominion and in the shops in town, Frank could hear the political mood change. The Prairies had beckoned with the promise of free land and self-sufficiency. Millions had come to escape the tyranny of oppressive governments, searching for freedom from heavy-handed churches and states. Many were despondent and in dire need of help. The papers were full of talk of new political parties, and there were rumblings in America of a new Roosevelt and a New Deal.

All of this was good for his plan—if only Shorty would say yes. It seemed ever more likely that some administration might intervene to put the economy back on its feet. But which government, and when? Was there a politician anywhere willing to make a large-scale purchase of wheat at an inflated price? The Saskatchewan Wheat Pool could barely keep its lights on. No, it would require American money, but would the tough-talking Herbert Hoover really eat crow?

Frank felt frightened and alone. Other than Bobby, no one even knew where he was. Thank heavens for Bobby. His friend had put his integrity and career on the line for him and would care for his family if it ever came to that. Knowing Bobby, he'd be driving by the house now, looking for signs the heat was on, checking on his kids, ready to step in.

That night, the temperature dropped to forty below. He didn't remember lighting the potbelly stove, but he awoke gagging, his lungs filling with thick, black smoke. He leaped from his bed, the flames licking at his bare feet. He seized his wash basin to douse the fire, but the red-hot metal singed his fingers, and he screamed at the searing pain. There was no putting it out; all he could do was escape. He pulled his bedding around him and snatched what he could—the mattress and Hudson Bay blanket, his scribbler, and his Chicago things. He smashed open the door and hurled himself into the yard. There was Queenie, too dazed or stubborn to move. He grabbed her cowbell and guided her out into the cold.

In the light of the fire, he saw Will running from the house with a bucket in each hand. It was the only time he'd seen the man pick up his pace. Will hurled the water on the blaze then rushed to the pump for refills. The douses of water were about as effective as a light snowfall during a drought. The flames grew larger. Frank tried suffocating the inferno with the chicken-feather quilt to no avail. They huddled under the Hudson Bay blanket and watched from the sidelines as the Howards' shed went up in smoke.

The fire was done as quickly as it had started up. On a base of frozen soil, with no trees in sight, it simply burned itself out. They plodded toward the house—dirty, downtrodden, and exhausted. Will went back to bed with Laura-Jean. Frank hauled the grimy tick mattress onto the floor beside the children's bed, lay down, and pulled the smoke-filled blanket on top.

THE SUN HADN'T RISEN WHEN Laura-Jean's labor began. Will drove to town to retrieve Dr. Fyfe, and Frank and the children prepared for the birth. He gathered up the linens and threw a log on the woodstove to bring the water to a boil. The children tried to comfort their mother through each contraction, but the house had gone quiet by the time the men arrived. The doctor stooped to deliver his grandchild, but the mewling cry that signals new life never came.

"Stillborn," the doctor said. A single word was all he could manage.

Laura-Jean's father wrapped his grandson's tiny corpse in the wee blanket she'd knit for him and walked toward Laura-Jean. She closed her eyes and turned away.

Frank was silent. Had the fire brought on the labor and triggered the stillbirth? As if reading his mind, Will provided some relief.

"The stove was old, and the shed was not really for sleeping. You seemed to be a man who needed some help. The baby—"

Will cut himself short as his eyes filled with tears.

After a long pause, Will put his hand on Frank's arm and said, "It's not your fault."

The next day, the Howards buried their lost boy at the Gainsborough cemetery in a communal grave for infants who didn't survive childbirth. The ground was as flat and treeless as the surrounding terrain.

Back at the Howard farmhouse, Will took Frank aside.

"We've hit a difficult patch. With the shed gone, there's no place for you. It's time to move on."

Laura-Jean sat in her rocker, as tender as a bruised peach. He brushed his hand gently on her shoulder, but she continued to stare out the frost-covered kitchen window. He followed her gaze to a grouse wintering in the yard. On the radio, Laura-Jean's favorite soprano, Florence Easton, sang, "*O mio babbino caro,*" and her transcendent voice filled the small room.

"Where will you go?" little Olive asked.

"Down the road," he replied.

"That's too far," Willard said.

"Yes," he agreed, understanding that in a wheatfield, down the road is a very long way.

Frank closed the door, and Willard called after him: "Say hello to Fib and the King."

25
KEY MAN

Lewis was pacing, practicing his lines. His meeting with Mr. D was in an hour. Ricco had called to say the boss wanted an update on Lewis's search for the firm's head trader. His hands were getting clammier with every lap around the room. The man was as trusty as a crooked politician.

Lewis had adopted Frank's habit of sticking to three points at any meeting: two points left your listeners wanting, but four ensured everyone was confused. First, he'd announce Frank was dead. Second, he'd insist it was time for a funeral and financial relief for Katrina and the kids. Wait, his pitch would be easier if there were insurance to cover it. Had the firm taken out a policy on Frank's life? He called Ricco. It was a long shot. He'd never met anyone with life insurance; in South Side, you were lucky if your family could afford to bury you in a pine box.

Ricco seized the opportunity to remind Lewis he had better things to do than fetch documents for the firm's underemployed intern.

"I'll pick it up," Lewis conceded.

Five minutes later, a brick of paper sat on Ricco's desk. Lewis pretended it was just what he had expected. But under his breath, he cursed the fact that even Ricco knew about this policy, yet no one had told him.

Back at his desk, Lewis flipped open the file. Titles matter, and this one said it all: Key Man Insurance. The next line was even better: "One hundred thousand dollars." He let out a long whistle. On slow afternoons, he dreamed of owning a house, but the sticker price of five thousand dollars was an impossible sum. The insurance was enough to buy twenty homes. Yet there was something crass about the bold, black-and-white sum and the way it reduced Frank Cork to a dollar sign. Granted, it came with an impressive string of zeros after his name. For the first time, Lewis understood the relentless pressure the head trader must have faced to earn his keep. And how futile Frank must have felt in those final days. He flashed back to the morning he'd rushed to the eighth floor to add Wally Caldwell's check to the Pool. Surely, Frank had still been clinging to the hope of a correction when he put that money at risk. The school board loss alone would have been enough to break a man.

He scanned the reams of paper for any mention of Katrina or the kids. But no such words adorned that tedious tome. The whole kit and kaboodle was payable one-third to Mr. D and two-thirds to the firm. Mr. D got thirty cents on every dollar generated by every trader in the firm, whether they were dead or alive. Being the managing partner was quite the gig.

Lewis revisited each page to ensure he'd understood the terms. His finger stopped on a section called "Exclusions." There were two: the first was suicide—if Frank killed himself, the insurer wouldn't pay a dime. That seemed fair. The second was murder. If Mr. D or any other beneficiary killed Frank, the policy was null and void. Fair again. But if Frank was killed by any other person (such as the mafia or the mayor), Mr. D and the firm collected the entire sum. This was a new angle from which to assess his suspects.

The second section of interest, "Purpose," had seemed self-evident his first time through. But no, there were some surprising details there. The purpose of the policy was to cover five years of revenue generated by Frank: $20,000 a year—$100,000 over five years. It was a staggering sum. In this market, there wasn't a trader anywhere who could pull that rabbit out of any hat. However, if Frank were dead, the firm would receive the entire amount in a lump sum. The penny dropped. Frank was worth more to his firm dead than alive.

It was time to go. What was he going to say about all or any of this to Mr. D? Sure, Frank had a few enemies, but the only person with a motive to kill him—a $100,000 motive, to be precise—was Mr. D. He donned his suit jacket from the back of the chair and scooped up his daybook and pen. While he was striding from one corner office to the other, the idea struck him as hard and fast as a line drive to the mound. He was being used.

WAITING FOR RICCO TO SHOW him in, Lewis had seconds to come up with a new script. The managing partner yelled from behind his shut door for Lewis to come in.

"Where's Frank?"

"I haven't found him, sir."

"It's a lot easier to be lost than found," Mr. D said.

"Yes, sir."

"Any theories?"

Lewis pulled himself up to his full height, dwarfing Mr. D. If he'd learned anything at West Point, it was how to look big and stay composed. He slid his Parker into his pants pocket and gripped the pen for dear life.

"In this city, we're more likely to find him at the bottom of Lake Michigan than vacationing on a beach."

Mr. D laughed, almost a snort. "Who's the egg-suckin' dawg that's stolen our head trader?"

"It's time to make an announcement, sir. We need to host a funeral and provide some money for Katrina and the kids. Shall I develop a plan?"

"As fast as a prairie fire with a tailwind." Mr. D concurred, then quickly threw himself into reverse. "Of course, we'll need a body. An empty casket at a funeral is as useless as a trapdoor in a canoe."

Lewis clutched hard on his pen. "I assume there's insurance to cover it?"

"Insurance? No, not that I know of, Son." Mr. D made tracks to Lewis's side of the desk. "You've been busier than a moth in a mitten. That'll be all," Mr. D said, nearly pushing him out the door.

26
NEW DIGS

Frank followed Will to the Buick. "I've arranged for you to stay with Elzier Duret." El-zeer Doo-ray, Will said. In the midst of the most profound trauma of Will's life, the gentle giant had managed to find housing for him. He was humbled and ashamed. "That's not a name you hear every day."

"He's French Canadian. He's also my best friend," Will said. "Most importantly, he has that rarest of gifts on the Prairies these days—a job."

Pulling up to the Durets' home, it was immediately clear his new digs were a step up. Will Howard ran rum, but Elzier Duret ran the lumber store on the edge of town. Beaver Lumber was the biggest enterprise around. The Duret's well-built, two-story house was behind the lumber yard on a small acreage with a shed, a barn, and a large frozen pond. Elzier was either in the shop or the mill, so Will gave Frank the tour. They began at the barn, passing an impressive red tractor, two horses, a pig, and a cow, and finished up at Elzier's workshop—Frank's new home.

He was relieved to find a thermometer beside the front door; he'd grown accustomed to checking the temperature multiple times a day. Inside was a desk, a couple of chairs, a bed, a large window, and a modern new woodstove. A pair of towels hung from the hooks beside the washstand, embroidered with the letter "D"—for Duret, he supposed. Curiously, it bore a striking resemblance to the monogram on the Duttons masthead and business cards. A prairie sampler hung above the bed; the timeless lament of Thomas Paine's cross-stitched into the burlap: "These are the times that try men's souls."

Will brought the Hudson Bay blanket and a mickey of whisky from the car. They beat the blanket with a broom and hung it over a rail to soak up the winter air, then inside, they threw back a couple of shots. The thick, cedar-plank walls provided a meaningful barrier against the cold. He inhaled deeply; it smelled like whisky and cedar. It was going to be a great place to work.

FRANK'S TOUR OF HIS NEW digs included a briefing by Will on Frank's new host. "Elzier and I couldn't be more different," Will said.

"What are you talking about?"

"Well, I'm tall, for one thing, and Elzier's about the size of Laura-Jean. Also, Elzier grew up in a monastery, and I did not. When I was hiding in the corners of saloons reading *Huckleberry Finn*, Elzier was being weaned on the Apostles. To sum it up, I'm the sinner, and he's the saint."

"Got it," Frank said with a tentative smile. "And what else?"

"Elzier's the jealous type."

"Meaning?"

"He probably put this desk here just so you're not loitering in his kitchen with his pretty wife." Will winked, and Frank blushed.

"And?"

"I told him that helping Frank Cork would work out well for everyone in the end."

More pressure. Not only did he have to save himself and his family, but his plan now seemed as fanciful as his book. He'd delivered a case of rotgut to his only client, which was not a great segue for pitching him on a securities deal. If he didn't get the nod soon, he'd have to revisit some long-discarded options like riding the rails or stealing a car. His scant savings still wouldn't cover a one-way ticket home.

Then Will left, and Frank was alone in Elzier Duret's workshop.

AFTER AN ENTIRE AFTERNOON FLIPPING aimlessly between his book and his plan, there was a rap on Frank's door. From the outset, things did not go well with Elzier Duret. The man, who was about his age, seemed agitated to discover a stranger who'd been working at his desk, lying on his bed, and using his towels. Frank's hopes of pitching the lumber manager on a futures contract evaporated.

Frank stood to greet him—compared to Will, Elzier was a man who could make you feel tall. He poured them drinks and asked Elzier if he'd grown up on the Prairies, which seemed to settle him down a bit.

"I'm from Rimouski, Québec." KEH-bek, Elzier said.

Frank looked puzzled.

"Downriver from Montréal."

It wasn't the geography that was stumping him; it was Elzier's accent. It didn't sound anything like the English—or the French—he'd heard in Chicago. But Frank got the hang of it. Consonants were soft, THs sounded like Ds, and Hs simply disappeared. *'Dare ouse'* meant their house, and *'da turd ting'* was the third thing.

Elzier said that his mother had died giving birth to him, her only child, and his father, who was a lumberjack, had deposited him at the Ursuline Monastery in Rimouski and returned to camp. The story made Frank wonder which was the more difficult path to manhood: having a brute for a father or no father at all.

"Sounds like a cruel start. Yet things have gone well for you," Frank said, gesturing widely to take in the man's house, barn, and land.

"People come to the Prairies for one of two reasons," Elzier said. "They're leaving something behind or searching for something new."

Or both, Frank thought.

ELZIER INVITED HIM UP TO the house for dinner. He could hardly believe there was a bathroom of sorts, with a toilet, wash tub, and mirror above the sink. He caught sight of himself for the first time in months. He was startled to see this version of himself—his long hair, bristled chin, and burlap shirt. Chicago trader Frank Cork had disappeared.

In the living room, he met the three Duret children—Maurice, Eugene, and Victor, seven, six, and four. They were fighting for control of a comic strip featuring Popeye the Sailor and Olive Oyl. Franny and Robbie had also loved the characters when they showed up in the newspapers last year.

Elzier's wife was making doughnuts in the kitchen, looking lithe and winsome in her calico frock. He watched from across the room as she pinched the warm, deep-fried dough between her fingers, then dipped it into a shallow dish that smelled of cinnamon and brown sugar. She peeked up from under a dense mound of chocolate-colored hair, licked the sweet red dust from her fingers, and held out a warm sample for him to taste. He blushed, as hot as July.

"Welcome to our home, Francis Cork." She had plump lips,

English skin as fine as baking flour, and an accent to match. "I'm Gabriella," she said.

FALLING ASLEEP THAT FIRST NIGHT in Elzier's shed, Frank missed Queenie the cow. She'd slept on the other side of his wall for the past two months. Some of his partners' affairs didn't last that long. Eek, it was the type of snide remark Mr. D might have made at some poor animal's expense. There was a time when he'd respected the man: James Dutton III had picked him out of a crop of graduating students and mentored him from intern to head trader. During those first five years, Mr. D was the closest thing he'd had to a father. Maybe Katrina was right; he'd outgrown the man. On the other hand, he was the one living in a shed.

In the morning, there was real coffee and indoor plumbing. Gabriella shone so brightly she could shame a star. Over breakfast, she told him she was born in London, her father was British, and her mother French. She had lived in Paris with her aunt for a few years; he almost melted when she said, "*Ma tante Isabelle.*" During the war, she'd worked in ladies' fashion at Liberty's, the famous West London department store. Even now, she managed to look shapely and elegant in a baker's apron with flour in her hair. Her sister, she said, took her life at the end of the Great War, and Gabriella had found her in their back garden, the poor girl's toes grazing the tops of the Cox's Pippins that had fallen from the tree. Her parents had sent her to the colonies to escape her gruesome loss, with two preachy spinsters as chaperones. Their "Tin Lizzie Tour" had taken them through prairie towns with funny names, like Entrance and Eyebrow, Fertile and Forget, and Moose Jaw and Mozart. There was even a town called Climax, Gabriella said with a playful wink, and Frank blushed again.

Will pulled into the yard, and none too soon. Frank dashed out the door before Elzier could catch him in the kitchen, looking flushed. At the border, they unloaded their crates and collected the cash. Shorty signaled to him to step behind the Hup. What was this? Had the moment of truth arrived? Was Shorty buying securities from him, or was Whacker about to execute the witness in the green car?

"We're gonna do this t'ing with youse," Shorty said, then elaborated a bit. The boss had been impressed by the numbers—the quick turnaround and handsome returns—and thought Frank's dibs were fair. Sure, it would be their first investment in wheat, but the price could only rise. "The world's gotta eat," Shorty said.

Frank feigned middling interest; there were matters to clarify first. "One deal," he said, "and then we're square." Neither man budged for what seemed like an eternity. When Shorty finally nodded yes, they shook hands, and Frank emerged from the shadow of the Hup. Will fired up the car. Neither said a word as they drove back to town.

The mob was in.

27
DUPED

When Pinzolo called to say it was time for an update, Lewis was anything but pleased. He was disgruntled by the special agent and his ever-changing reports. Lewis knew in his bones that Frank was alive, yet the agent kept insisting his boss was dead. One day, the culprit was Mr. D, and the next, it was the mayor, or Bobby, or the mob. He was sick of the agent's constant inferences and disparaging remarks, especially when they were aimed at Katrina, let alone him.

"Come for a tour of the new crime lab," Pinzolo said. "It's on the downtown campus at Northwestern University in the Law faculty. Meet me there."

His work was less than demanding—he had no boss, no clients, and nothing to trade. A field trip to the city's new Scientific Crime Detection Laboratory would be interesting, maybe even fun. He managed to flag down a cab; it always took time with a dog. He was at the Crime Lab twenty minutes later.

Pinzolo snarled at Rosie, and Rosie snarled back. With that out of the way, the grubby cop showed him around.

Lewis was impressed. "Got an opening for a West Point drop-out at the Bureau these days? If the market doesn't pick up soon, I'll be needing a new line of work."

"We hire all types," Pinzolo said. "Even women—Betty Bureaus. There'd been a Black guy once, too—a former bodyguard to Teddy Roosevelt."

"That figures. If you're Black, you need the president of the United States on your résumé to get a job with the BOI. How's the pay?"

"Lousy," Pinzolo said. "Six bucks a day."

Lewis decided to stick with trading.

PINZOLO GAVE HIM THE GRAND tour. The man was as puffed up as a blowfish; he was proud to be a member of the nation's most elite force with its dazzling crime detection facilities. Lewis remembered a similar rush of pride when he'd moved from the eighth floor to the ninth, although the feeling hadn't lasted long. Pinzolo acknowledged that the lab was really for academics and researchers, but they seemed to like him on site.

Lewis nodded. Every lab needs a live rat.

As they wended their way among dozens of scientists stooped over their work, Pinzolo handed out back slaps like a beat cop issuing parking tickets. And when he wasn't smacking the scholars, he was manhandling the gadgets and guns.

"It's all very interesting, sir. But why am I here?" Lewis asked.

Pinzolo went back to being a sonofabitch. "That's quite a price on your guy's head."

Did Pinzolo know about the life insurance? Was everyone aware of it except him? "Frank was our top earner," he said, keeping his answer vague.

Pinzolo took another jab. "The insurers tell me Duttons reported your guy dead months ago."

"I'm not sure I follow." Lewis was reeling.

"I'm no expert, but our people tell me you gotta call in a

death at the earliest moment if you're hoping for a check."

"Can you be a little clearer, please?"

"The trail goes cold pretty fast. If a death doesn't get called in right away, the insurer can't do its job," Pinzolo said.

When God handed out voices, the agent got one with no volume control. The scientists glared, pleading for quiet. Pinzolo and academe were as incompatible as John Adams and Thomas Jefferson.

"So?"

"So, your firm called in Frank's death back at Halloween."

Lewis made every effort to keep the sinking feeling in his stomach to himself.

"Here's how things went down," Pinzolo said. "The insurer hears about the death at Halloween. It calls CPD, who's supposed to find the body and declare it dead. The police issue a death certificate within sixty days, or the insurer declares the case closed. In Frank's case, CPD never found him—probably never even looked—and the sixty days were up around Christmas." Pinzolo gave a loud smirk. "Frank was the only man in town willing to stand up to Big Bill, and now he's dead."

"What happens next?"

"Your guy is what we call 'deemed dead.' No one could find him, so the insurer deems him dead. The check is already in the mail. Dorothea will be sticking it on Mr. D's desk any day."

Pinzolo's upper lip curled when he said "Dorothea" and "sticking it" in the same breath. Lewis was repulsed.

Then Pinzolo stepped down from his soapbox and gave Lewis a hard-boiled look: "Did you ever ask yourself why half the people in this city know about this insurance claim but not you?"

For a slow-moving guy, Pinzolo had a way of squashing people with the fewest of words. And the agent wasn't done.

"Did Mr. D set you up in Frank's pretty office and keep you busy while he collected the cash?"

Pinzolo signaled that the meeting was at an end. "Next time, leave the dog behind, will ya?"

Lewis decided to walk back to Duttons with Rosie. God knows he needed the air. It would be two miles, tops—time enough to clear his brain.

Turning south onto Michigan Avenue, Lewis was assaulted by a powerful gust. The new skyscrapers had created a blistering wind tunnel right up Chicago's main drag. Just what the Windy City needed—more wind. He and Rosie battled their way to Wacker Drive, where, miraculously, the sun came out, the winds quieted, and Lewis poked his head above the turned-up collar of his overcoat. He was dazzled by two glorious new feats of architecture—the Wrigley Building and the Tribune Tower. He felt like Dorothy with her Toto, carried away by a twister only to find themselves in the land of Oz.

From Wacker Drive, Lewis walked along the river toward LaSalle Street. A thick mist had settled over the water, and his brain was as foggy as the air. When he'd asked Mr. D if there was insurance, the old codger had said no. Yet, Lewis now understood that Mr. D had filed forms with the insurer declaring Frank dead months ago. Apart from wasting Lewis's time searching for Frank, what else was Mr. D up to?

AT DUTTONS, LEWIS HAD BARELY removed his overcoat when Dorothea put Pinzolo through. "Figured it out yet?"

"Listen," Lewis said, "you're a trained professional with a lab full of tricks. I don't believe for a minute that Frank is dead. Or that this firm will collect one cent from staking a claim on it. Drop your fancy gadgets, get in your goddam car, and go find Frank."

28
THE WIZARD

No sooner had Frank returned to the Durets' shed than he was beset by doubts. What were the chances of guessing the right price of wheat on a distant date, especially with no briefing binders or interns and only the scantest news? Weeks of torturous uncertainty lay ahead. Seated at Elzier's desk, he mulled over the date he'd picked for the contract to come due—March 17th, the Feast of St. Patrick. It was an obvious choice for any Irishman, but was it the best date? By mid-March, the snow would be melting, and a new season of wheat would be contributing to the global over-supply. Yes, he'd got it right. If the federal government were to intervene, there couldn't be a more prudent date. But what about his price?

Frank poured himself a whisky and swirled it in his cup, swilled it in his mouth, then coaxed it along its course like a father teaching his child to ride a bike. One shot was always a delight, two was just right, and three made him feel like he was on the path to becoming a yeasty, shapeless inebriate, like his father. Thoughts of his father always left him upset, so he distracted himself by working his way through the alphabet, searching for other words to describe him: boozer, barfly, binger, debaucher, dipsomaniac, drinker, guzzler, imbiber, lush, sot, souse, sponge, tippler, toper, tosspot. He suspected his father had stood in a long line of blotto Corks, although he'd never heard a thing about any of them. It was one more example of silence being more powerful than words.

Happily, Frank had never sought comfort from that altered state: most days, it was difficult enough keeping his wits about him. Sure, some days you were tempted by another round, like a second slice of hot apple pie, but he'd never felt the urge to scarf down the entire pie—or bottle. Maybe the need to obliterate oneself only showed up every second generation—or every third, for Robbie's sake.

Getting back to his price—after all, his very future depended on getting it right—it was late January, and wheat was trading at 45¢/bushel. His wager had the price hitting 60¢ on March 17th. If Shorty bought a hundred units, his clients would recover their $20,000 deposit plus a profit of $15,000, for a total of $35,000. At 20 percent, his cut would earn him another $7,000—more than twice what he'd paid for his house. It was also five times the average annual salary in America that year. Not stunning returns, but not bad for a thirty-day contract after the worst market crash in history.

He had one more thought. If he used some of his client's deposit and repaid it when the deal generated winnings, he could also wager on the contract on his own behalf. It would be like borrowing from his margin account, which had worked so well for so many years—until it didn't. The mobsters would never know. Of course, if the contract was off the mark, he'd have dug himself a very deep hole—not including the penalties for unauthorized use of clients' funds. In 1920, Charles Ponzi, a wheeler-dealer in Boston, put the issue to the test, raking in some $15 million in eight months by borrowing from his clients' accounts. The problem was he never paid back the money and was convicted the year Frank joined Duttons, of eighty-six counts of mail fraud. Frank dismissed the idea.

DINNER THAT NIGHT BEGAN WITH a simple prayer, then pandemonium ensued. At home, his children ate first, but here, the Duret boys dominated the meal. They attacked each other under the table and relentlessly drew Frank into their games. Meanwhile, Gabriella and Elzier, seemingly oblivious, told him about how they'd met. They were as clever as a wisecracking comedy team.

"I'd thought I was in love with a young novitiate at the convent. She had the face of an angel and a voice to match. Then I met Gabriella. It was a relief not to have to call her Sister," he said.

"And Elzier. It was his smell that attracted me first—pine sap and maple syrup. What I really wanted was to spread him on my toast."

"We were married on the train platform in Tweed—it's in Ontario, not far from Kingston. Then we boarded and honeymooned all the way to the Prairies," he said.

"We chugged alongside the Mattawa River and choo-chooed through the rocky shield," she said.

"We rounded the Lakehead, between Sudbury and Nipigon," he said.

"We entered Manitoba at full throttle," she said.

"We came to a triumphant halt in Saskatoon, accompanied by bleats of the steam whistle and billows of smoke," he said.

"Maurice was born nine months later," she said.

"You are my sun, my moon, and my northern star," he said.

The sun, the moon, and the stars? By God, his luck was back.

FRANK WOLFED DOWN HIS DESSERT, saskatoon berry pie, and Elzier fed dried cow dung into the fire. Buffalo chips, he called them, a sensible fuel on a treeless plain. They made the Durets' home smell like warm grass. Elzier announced that Uncle Frank would read from his book.

Why had he said he was a writer? He'd never dreamed of being one and couldn't imagine himself as such. He should have said he was a food critic writing a feature on luncheon specials in railway towns—now that was a subject he could write about. Or he might have told the truth, although most people had trouble understanding what a wheat future was. He once overheard his mother telling her neighbor that her son traded futures for a living. "I'm so sorry," the woman had said.

Now, he was trapped in a lie. Having pretended to be a writer, everyone was waiting for proof. At least he was widely read. He had browsed the *Old Farmer's Almanac* almost every day of his adult life and had been reading E. M. Forster's *A Passage to India* when he left. He approached all his reading with a view to what it meant for wheat. How would a soggy season affect the supply of wheat? And if the Brits left India, would the country give up chapati, paratha, and naan?

"Tell us about the king and his seven sons!" Maurice begged.

"Why aren't there any sisters?" little Victor asked.

He could give a speech at the university with barely a moment's thought, yet reading his own tale made him tense. Was Fib's fate too bound up with his own? He muttered an excuse and decided to make up a story, borrowing from well-known books. "Tonight's story is 'The Wizard of Wheat,'" he began, and the children hooted and nestled in.

"Queenie the Cow lived in a wheatfield at the corner of Thirteenth and Fifth. Queenie was a happy cow with many barnyard friends, including Magpie and Gip the Backward Pig. Magpie knew how to fly and brought news of the great beyond, and Gip did everything back to front, even the way he spelled his name.

"One day, Magpie invited Queenie and Gip to see where the wheatfields meet the sky. Magpie flew overhead, Gip followed his clever tail, and Queenie trailed behind in a swarm of flies. They roamed far and wide, but all they could see was grain.

"'When will we see where the wheatfields meet the sky?' Queenie sighed.

"'We must ask the wizard,' Magpie replied.

"'Where is the wizard?' asked Gip.

"'The wizard is in a grand hall in a gilded tower, in a faraway place called Chicago,' Magpie replied.

"'What does the wizard do?' Queenie asked.

"'The wizard predicts the price of wheat. But one day, he had a problem. There was too much wheat. So much wheat that everyone feared the price would go down, so they sold their wheat, and sure enough, the price went down, and everyone lost their money, and the wizard did, too.'

"'What happened to the wizard?' asked Gip.

"'The wizard wandered too far from his gilded tower and got lost where the wheatfields meet the sky. Now, he must find his way back home.

"'And so must we,' Magpie replied, flapping her wings and setting off with Gip to their farm."

FRANK SWALLOWED THE LUMP THAT had grown in his throat and tucked the children into bed.

29
DUTTONS

No one was more surprised than Lewis when he arrived at Duttons that February morning with Rosie in tow. Waiting for him at reception was none other than the president of the Board of Trade. Bobby was seated, sipping a coffee and flipping through the *Tribune*. With Frank gone, he must have decided that industry rules no longer restricted him from venturing upstairs to Duttons. But that wasn't the only change. Over the winter, Bobby had grown out of his suit.

Lewis winked at Dorothea and whispered, "You should pass him the name of Mr. D's tailor."

Then, as Lewis plunged forward to greet Bobby, Pinzolo shambled out of the client washroom. The agent gave his hands a vigorous flick, and Lewis tried to dodge the droplets as they flew in his direction. Two visitors at the same time. A new record. He squired the men along the hushed corridor, past the offices where the deals that moved markets had once been done. A full quarter after the Crash, such successes were a fading memory, which might explain why everyone had time for Lewis today.

Bobby took the couch. Lewis saw a spark of recognition flash across the executive's face: the ceilings of Frank's office and the Great Hall were a matched set like a scepter and a crown. The look on Bobby's face was so telling that Lewis realized Pinzolo was right: Frank had outdone his friend at everything, and the proof was hanging right over Bobby's head. Would the simmering jealousy lead to a betrayal, or was Bobby a proud and protective friend?

Pinzolo also chose the couch, crushing Bobby and putting pressure on the man even as he sat.

Lewis settled into the big armchair, a safe distance from both men: Bobby and Pinzolo, one opaque, the other wily and crude. Still, he'd love a photo of the scene. He'd have it framed and display it on Frank's desk. Here is Lewis Montgomery, he'd say, hosting a pair of the city's leading lights.

Pinzolo took command of the meeting, his hot breath right in Bobby's face. "How's your investigation going?"

"It's not," Bobby said.

"What's the holdup?"

"The subject of our inquiry—one Francis Cork—has disappeared."

"I thought you were pursuing Mr. Cork and his firm," Pinzolo insisted.

"They're one and the same. As its chief trader, Frank Cork is the firm," Bobby pushed back.

"Surely, if your Board has a complaint against this firm, there are other partners to pursue. Why not the managing partner, James Dutton III?" Pinzolo looked from the couch to the chair. "Isn't that right, Lewis?"

"Yes, sir." Where was this going?

The detective turned back to Bobby and, with great fanfare, pulled out his notebook and pen. He swiped his thumb across the tip of his tongue and used the wet digit to literally thumb through his pages, posing his pen over the page and making clear that their answers were on the record.

"And yet, Mr. MacNamara, you've chosen to focus only on Frank. Didn't you consider other avenues, given that your perp was gone?"

Perpetrator, Lewis supposed. It was yet another identity for Frank—head trader, missing person, the insured, the deceased, and now, the perp. Bobby hedged and fiddled, and Pinzolo put down his pen as if to say I'm here for as long as this takes.

"Yes," Bobby replied, "there was some discussion about that with Mr. D."

"When?"

"Halloween. I remember Mr. D making a wisecrack about it being as cold as a witch's tit." The three men sneered; somehow, you couldn't help liking Mr. D.

"Let me guess," Pinzolo jumped in. "Mr. D proposed payment if you dropped any investigation against him or his firm. I suspect Mr. D called it a penalty or a fine—certainly not a bribe."

"No. I mean, yes—"

"Have you received those funds?"

"The penalty? No. Not yet. Mr. D reported that his firm is expecting a large payment. And he...his firm, that is... will pay me...I mean the Board...when the money comes in."

"And this large payment would be the insurance claim on Mr. Cork's life?"

Bobby blanched, and Rosie, seeming to sense the tension in the room, thrust her snout in the air, perked her ears, and pounded her tail rhythmically on the carpet.

"Where this firm gets its funds is not our affair," Bobby retorted.

"I see," Pinzolo said, laying his notebook down. "Let me recap. Mr. D decides Frank is underground pushing worms and claims a hundred thousand buckaroos from the insurer, even though there's no corpse. He promises you a cut of the cash if you let the investigation disappear forever, like Frank." Pinzolo pulled a used handkerchief from his pocket and wiped it across his rheumy nose. "I've been waiting for the right opportunity to try out some of our favorite words at the Bureau. You must know them: embezzlement, conspiracy, fraud."

Silence. You could hear a pin drop.

"By the way," Pinzolo, relentless, said, "my men tell me they see you hanging around the Cork's house after dark. Quite the catch, that Katrina. All alone in her swank house, curled up like a kitten with her kids at night."

"Enough," Lewis jumped in, feeling valiant.

Bobby undid the buttons on the too-tight vest of his three-piece suit. "The Board proposed that the firm pay a fine and the Wheat Pool drop its cross-border complaint. That's what we do at the Board. We steer the industry through troubled times. As for the Cork's home, he—"

"He? Or she?"

There was a new passion in Pinzolo that Lewis hadn't observed in the agent before. It was becoming clearer how these BOI agents worked. They skulked about until they cornered their prey, then pounced.

"But you don't use telephones or knock at the front door," Pinzolo pressed on. "You like to lurk, don't you, Bobby?"

Pinzolo knew how to pick the scabs off a man's skin, even two men at the same time.

"One final question," the special agent said, flipping open his badge on the table and letting the tension rise. "Have you heard from Frank Cork since his disappearance on October 29th?"

Bobby hesitated. It was a simple yes or no. Why the pregnant pause?

"I am not prepared to answer that question at this time," Bobby said.

30
THE DEAL

After their run to the border, Will proposed they swing by Beaver Lumber and let Elzier show them around. Frank couldn't care less about lumber, but it was a good idea to grease the wheels with his new host. Elzier was delighted and brought them coffees made with real java beans. A parade of employees filed in and out, helping themselves to mugs of the good stuff. Elzier seized on the opportunity to share his pride in his staff.

"I've built my team by hiring veterans. They came home from the war with amazing skills—they're disciplined and bring a lot of technical know-how to their jobs. But I've seen first-hand how war can break a man. Verdun, the Somme…I used to wish I'd served overseas, but not anymore."

Frank and Will nodded in assent and, after a quiet moment, followed Elzier to the yard. Their host pointed at stacks of wood and shared minute details that he found fascinating. No, Frank did *not* know that the actual size of a 2x4 was 1.5 x 3.5 after it was dried and planed. By the time they'd reached the planers and the saws, Elzier was telling them about life after the monastery.

To Frank's surprise, this Canadian had crossed the border and enlisted in the US Army. But because he could recite the

Old Testament from cover to cover, Elzier had been assigned to the Morality Squad instead of the European Front.

"I spent two years traveling from state to state preaching the evils of alcohol and assuring state governments that the army would help them enforce the new federal Prohibition laws. Now, here I am, standing in my lumber yard with a pair of bootleggers," Elzier laughed.

Frank forced out a guffaw—he'd worked so hard to keep his livelihood secret. But the rotary saw roared, and Elzier led them to a quieter corner of the yard.

"I didn't stay long in the army," he said. "The sergeants were stricter than the Ursulines." So, he'd quit and headed out west to the lumber camps.

"I came to appreciate the quiet allure of a forest. Over time, I forgave my father for choosing trees over me."

Frank had never considered absolving his father for his sins against his family. He wondered whether he could—or should. But Elzier continued his story.

"When I saw an ad to manage a Beaver lumberyard, I got the job. On the Prairies, everyone knows a lot about wheat. They can talk forever about the difference between Durum and Marquis. When it comes to lumber, they don't know red oak from knotty pine," Elzier said.

WILL DROPPED OFF FRANK AT the Durets. The visit to the yard had gone well, and for a few weeks, things were harmonious between Frank and Elzier. In the mornings, Frank ran rum with Will, and in the afternoons, he choreographed his plan.

There were two weeks to go until February 14th, St. Valentine's Day. Since trading wheat futures was illegal in Canada, everything had to be executed state-side. Frank suggested to Will they try out the diners and bars across the border. For fourteen days, they ate fries instead of mashed potatoes and drank Coca-Cola instead of beer. After lunch, he'd pop into the local post office under the pretense of making a phone call or mailing a letter and execute one more step in his plan.

His first step was setting up a company to carry out his trades. Strictly speaking, a company wasn't required, but it kept his own identity more discreet: everything would be done in the company's name instead of his own. In the securities industry, these one-man companies were called "bucket shops." There was also a special place in hell for traders who ran bucket shops. As small businesses, they had more in common with off-track betting kiosks than professional firms. They were popular among small-time investors because they offered discount pricing and a convenient place to purchase securities, such as the back of a pool hall. However, trading houses like Duttons hated them because they lured away their smaller clients and deals.

In Canada, bucket shops were illegal, and in the US, Congress held varying views on them at various times. Just last year, Congress had threatened to shut down bucket shops under pressure from the head traders of big firms, including Frank. But politicians collect votes from the many, not the few, so Congress had resorted to a tried-and-true political trick—passing legislation to curtail them while ensuring the measures had no teeth.

At the Antler post office, creating his bucket shop was easy enough. Frank filled out an application and came up with a name—James Gordon Enterprise. The postmaster mailed the form to a state official and assured him his company would be operational within a matter of days. He now was the owner of a bucket shop—Jimmie Gawdini Enterprise, as his clients would say.

Frank executed his second step the following day. He registered his deal with a clearinghouse, which allowed him to delegate all the grunt work to someone else. Its key role was to find someone who actually wanted the wheat. Investors almost never wanted the product they bet on—they'd be flabbergasted if the pork bellies or cotton bales ever landed at their front doors. No, all investors wanted was the cash from their wagers. But to ensure there was no misunderstanding with the mob, he added a "No Delivery" clause to their contract.

The clearinghouse also ensured Frank got paid. His winnings would only materialize if his price was in line with market prices on St. Patrick's Day. If things panned out that way, the clearinghouse would collect the funds from the buyer and wire them into his James Gordon Enterprise account. But if his price missed the mark, he wouldn't live to tell the tale.

By the time Frank was ready for step three, he and Will had worked their way through the entire lunchtime menu at the Antler diner; he was also sick of Coca-Cola and fries. It was time to present his contract to Tommy and Chopper. Did the men behind the weapons even know how to read?

Frank kept his contract to the point. At their simplest, contracts were an exchange of promises: I will if you will. So, that's what Frank wrote: "I will invest your money in a wheat futures contract, and you, Shorty, will give me the cash." He added the terms he'd laid out for Bonanno in the tunnel, the no-delivery clause, and a signature line. It may have been the shortest contract in the history of the securities industry.

St. Valentine's was a week away. Frank was ready to present his paperwork and ask for the deposit. His life was on the line.

31
CUPIDS

On February 14th, the sun glared through Lewis's bedroom window and awoke him well before his alarm. He'd dreamed of Katrina half the night and envisioned her here in the morning light. In the shower, he remembered: it was St. Valentine's Day. Should he buy chocolates for Dorothea, flowers for Katrina, or both? He upped the cold water and told himself this had to stop. He was spending his days searching for Frank and his nights dreaming of filling the hole Frank had left in Katrina's bed. It was time to strap a harness on his pony, saddle up his Tennessee Walker, and set his sights on Dorothea; she was polished, single, and no further than the front desk.

Lewis arrived at the office with a beautiful bouquet of red roses, beginning to bud. The florist had tucked in a card, but he couldn't decide what to write. Was he so besotted with Katrina that an office romance was no longer in his bag of tricks? He stood at Dorothea's desk looking ambiguous until she settled the issue for them. "Thank you for brightening up the foyer, Lewis," she said.

It was a relief when the phone rang. Dorothea announced it was Pinzolo on the line, and Lewis retreated down the hall to take the call in Frank's office.

"Happy Anniversary," the detective chortled.

Right, the St. Valentine's Day Massacre. Lewis's mind had been on love, not murder.

"Still, no arrests, and the city has clammed up," Pinzolo continued. "No one's willing to snitch with the stench of reprisal hanging in the air. It's hard to hire a decent stool pigeon in this town."

Lewis wondered how he was ever going to find Frank if no one would talk.

"Meet me for a drink at Vinny's," Pinzolo said. "It's an Italian joint." No kidding, Lewis thought. "One block south of the crime lab. You can't see it from the street. It's down a flight of stairs. It'll be full of—"

"Brick agents?" Lewis had never heard the term.

"Yeah, guys who pound the pavement like me."

Betty Bureaus, brick agents, Hoover boys, rats, perps—Pinzolo had handles for everyone. He probably had pet names for his guns. Lewis groaned at the prospect of going to a bar with a dozen Pinzolos all in the same room.

Thirty minutes later, he was standing in front of the sign. Vincenzo's. He descended below the street into the dive. He was the only person in the joint who didn't look like he'd been born in Sicily, and Rosie was the only dog. Fifteen sets of agents' eyes pretended not to stare. The place smelled like Pinzolo: stewed tomatoes, stale sausage, and dried oregano. There were red-and-white-checkered tablecloths and wine bottles from a bygone era dripping with wax and dust, and the stench of potent liquor hung in the air. So, this was where the country's top law enforcement officers came to escape the mean streets of Chicago, thumbing their noses at the Prohibition laws they were mandated to enforce. It was the Drake, but for a different class of men.

Lewis perched on a barstool beside Pinzolo, and the agent introduced him to the pock-marked patron saint of the joint. While Vinnie poured medicinal-grade rum into their Cokes, Pinzolo said, "I hear you're smuggling the Black kid from the parking garage into the firm. Don't say I never warned you: Hector Ray is smart alright, but we have a file on him an inch thick. We're talking civil disobedience...organizing militant protests, writing articles for *The Chicago Defender*, and rabble-rousing from the pulpit at Olivet Baptist Church. Holy Toledo, imagine if Mr. D got wind of that."

Lewis decided he would not be drawn in: Pinzolo seemed to have a one-inch file on everyone and, no doubt, half the young Black men in Chicago. If Hector was agitating for better lives for Chicago's Black community, Lewis was inclined to applaud him.

"Is that why you asked me here?"

"Bobby's been talking to Frank."

"How so?"

"Call it intuition. I've seen a lot of men lose their best friends, but Bobby's not one of them. And he's not even pretending to be the head of an industry whose top gun just disappeared in a cloud of smoke. No, Bobby's covering for Frank. I've assigned an undercover operative. A lot of goodfellas are clamoring to get out of the city. Things get very risky in our business when you can't tell the gangsters from the cops. If Frank's alive, we'll find him."

Lewis took a sip. A twist of lemon might cut the taste of rubbing alcohol, but Vinnie didn't look like a man who kept fresh fruit under his bar. So, Pinzolo had assigned a desperate, loose-lipped informant to look for Frank. His search had veered off in a different direction, thinking his boss just needed a few days off. "Sounds like you've decided it was a mob hit after all," he said.

Pinzolo quickly disabused him of that. "Frank's a person of interest. The man's a financial whiz, and markets are bottoms-up. We'll be looking for racketeering, money laundering, tax fraud, and all the other ways a clever man like Frank might be making money in the shadows."

"I'm sure it's nothing quite so glamorous as all that," Lewis said. If Frank was now under investigation, Pinzolo could no longer be his ally in his search for Frank. So be it. Other than ogling Dorothea and fantasizing about Katrina, Lewis had nothing to hide.

"Undercover work takes time," the agent added. "We need to integrate our operatives into others' lives. I'll get back to you when I have some news."

Lewis stood to leave, but Pinzolo handed him something. "I've put Duttons down for a table," Pinzolo said. It was a book of tickets for a fundraising event—a children's shelter in South Side—and the cop wasn't asking; he was insisting. Was this a new charitable side of Pinzolo he hadn't seen before? Or was the agent putting the squeeze on the firm now that its head trader was under investigation for financial crimes? He strode out of Vincenzo's without so much as a nod. But walking back to the firm, he could hardly wait to stick the bill on Ricco's desk.

Would he ask Katrina as his date?

32
ST. VALENTINE

St. Valentine's got off to a very good start. It was an auspicious date to launch his thirty-day deal. Not only was the day dedicated to lovers, but it was the anniversary of the Chicago massacre, and still no charges had been laid. Frank wondered about the protocol. Should he congratulate his clients at this morning's drop? Wish them a happy anniversary? He went to the kitchen and helped Gabriella set the table and feed the kids. His mind was on fire. Will would be picking him up soon; today was the day he'd collect his deposit and present his paperwork to the mob.

But when Elzier entered the kitchen and found Frank helping his wife flip the eggs, all hell broke loose. "Are you expecting to live here month after month, eating my food, living in my shed, and fawning over my wife on St. Valentine's Day?"

Frank had learned the hard way that Elzier was, shall we say, mercurial; very little heat was required for the man to reach the boiling point. With his eyes fixed on the eggs, Frank tried to still those turbulent waters. "You are blessed with a beautiful wife, my friend. No red-blooded man could resist having a look." Then, to make his point, he looked directly at his host, "But I assure you, I've been as chaste as the fresh-fallen snow."

Elzier was not appeased. "You put in a few hours of work in the mornings, thanks to my friend Will. Then you idle around here all afternoon."

He gulped. He'd never been so busy in his life. "I've tried to pull my weight. I repair your fences, milk your cow, help your wife."

He'd done it again. Helping Elzier's wife was precisely the wrong thing to say. He tried putting the cork back in the bottle. "I'll..."

"You will leave, is what you will do." Elzier had reached full boil. The steam was pouring out of him. "Pack your things. And when Will picks you up, don't come back."

Kicked out. Frank felt humiliated and ashamed and couldn't stay one minute more. He collected his scribbler and the unsigned futures contract. He briefly considered taking the Hudson Bay blanket, but it was heavy and somehow felt like stealing. He snatched up his Chicago things and set out into the frigid February air. The thermometer was the last thing he saw as the door of the Durets' shed slammed shut—twenty-two below. He stomped off down the range road. The snow was blowing in drifts across the unbounded fields, and his breathing became labored, and his fingers turned a bloodless white. Why hadn't he brought the blanket? He couldn't possibly make it into town. Grain elevators dotted the horizon. He vowed to climb up to the headhouse of one of those prairie castles and stretch out on the bales of grain until he was warm again. But step after step, he was reminded that on a wide-open prairie, the horizon is a very long way.

His mind grew hazy and wandered back to happier times, combing the galleries on weekends with his wife. Katrina, so informed and discerning, was more beautiful than any of the items for sale on the walls. The road was silent except for the sound of whispering wheat. "Come lie in the fields and rest." It beckoned him like sirens luring sailors onto the rocks with their songs. Onward he went, his mouth parched, his lips chapped, the snow falling at a sharp, icy slant right into his eyes. In a lucid moment, he decided that his only hope was to turn back and head toward town. He would visit Dr. Fyfe in his stately Georgian with its flickering gas light. But when he reached the doctor's house, all he could think of was the man burying his infant grandson, and he was filled with remorse and trudged on.

The Dominion wasn't far. Were there beds upstairs in the abandoned hotel? Perhaps he was destined to stay there in the end. The chain was still in place, but around the back was a fire escape—the type on a hinge at an unmanageable height. Teetering on a garbage can, he reached the bottom rung, climbed the ladder, pushed open a window, and hauled himself through. The beds looked like they'd been rented by the minute. He collapsed, shivering and alone.

The hours passed, and St. Valentine's Day and Frank's thirty-day deal came to a close. He had missed them both—upstairs at the Dominion, stone cold.

IN THE MORNING, FRANK ENTERED the Dominion through the front door. His feet throbbed, and his fingers were a wreck. The time had come to ask Bobby to pick him up. Then, in walked Will.

"Heard you had a dust-up with Elzier. I've had a few of those myself over the years.

I got you a reprieve. You can go back to Elzier's place for thirty days. At that point, you'll have to move on."

Thirty days. Was it a coincidence? Did Will and Elzier know about his plan?

"Let's go," Will said. "It's time for our run."

AFTER DELIVERING THE WHISKY, FRANK met Shorty behind the Hup. He pulled out his contract and covered off the terms. Whacker hovered close by, although it was clear that numbers higher than ten fingers and toes were not the man's thing. Frank warned them there was no turning back once the paperwork was signed. "Investing is always a gamble; there are winners and losers," he said.

"Sure there are, Jimmie," Shorty replied. "So long as my guys win."

He had no inkling whether Shorty was a first name or a last, so he'd kept the signature line blank. His client printed "SHORTY" in block letters with his left hand while using his right to hold his gun. Franny and Robbie had better penmanship before they started school. Wally Whacker was the witness. Someone could have changed a tire in the time it took the man to write the same letter twice. But their efforts did the trick. The paperwork was signed. The moment of truth had arrived: it was time to collect the deposit.

"We agreed on a deposit of $20,000," Frank said, sticking out his hand. This man understood gestures better than words.

Shorty and Whacker reciprocated by opening the boot of the Hup. Out came cases of empty whisky bottles. Frank tentatively lifted a few of the dead soldiers, and there it was—glorious, crisp American cash.

The banknotes were new—laundered, one might say.

They were the new pint-size banknotes that Treasury launched last year, with Ulysses S. Grant on the fifties and Benjamin Franklin on the hundreds. Bemused, Frank commented on the irony that Treasury had accorded the former president less value than the publisher of *Poor Richard's Almanack*.

Silence.

Wrong audience, he reminded himself. He completed the count without saying another word.

ON THE DRIVE BACK TO Gainsborough, Frank asked Will to stop at the warehouse to drop off the empties. He was a familiar face there now, and they waltzed right in. Will chatted with workers, and Frank found a private place to handle the cash. He had a hunch that Will had never bought into his author alibi. Truth be told, he hadn't bought into it himself. But whatever the reason, Will never asked what he was up to that day.

Frank divided the cash into five bundles so he could spread the money around. You couldn't be too careful: bank closures had become an everyday thing. The first three bundles were destined for post office accounts in Anamoose, Gwinner, and Kulm. Will drove them from one town to the next as if they were on a pub crawl, although colas and lemonade were the only drinks on offer. In Anamoose and Gwinner, no one batted an eye at his substantial deposits. But in Kulm, the postmaster eyed his rope belt and broken-down boots and appeared poised to report him as a felon.

"Not to worry," Frank chortled. "In Chicago, a sum like this barely covers breakfast with the mayor."

The postmaster gave him a droll look. "Maybe so, but in Kulm, the mayor wouldn't be seen having breakfast with the likes of you." Then, the man deposited Frank's cash.

IN GAINSBOROUGH, FRANK EFFORTLESSLY PUT the fourth bundle into his bank account, and after Will dropped him off in front of the Duret's barn, he walked past the two horses, the pig, and the cow, and hid the fifth under the broken seat of Elzier's tractor. Then he retired, exhausted, to his shed.

Huddled under the Hudson Bay blanket for warmth, Frank took stock of his plan. There was only one step left to go: to wait for St. Patrick's Day and pray for good luck.

33
BORDER STATES

Lewis was catching up on international markets at Frank's desk when Pinzolo emerged in his office without so much as a knock. He stood on Frank's carpet, stomping the snow off his sodden black boots. How had the special agent managed to give Dorothea the slip? She hadn't even buzzed.

"We've found Frank," the agent said, with as much enthusiasm as a man who'd sworn off exclamation marks.

Lewis was flooded with relief and a pressing need to call Katrina. He excused himself and dashed for the stairs, descending them two at a time. He was mid-flight when Pinzolo barked at him from on high, "No phone calls." It was an order, not a request.

Lewis returned reluctantly to Frank's office, elated by the announcement but angry to be thwarted in sharing it with those who deserved to hear it most. Pinzolo and Rosie had clearly found common ground: the dog must have sniffed traces of Italian sausage and was licking the agent's fingers. Pinzolo was at the window with his back to Lewis. "I've got good news and bad," he said.

"Is he dead or alive?" Lewis pressed.

"Let's start with the good. Your guy is alive. Word came back from our field operative confirming proof of life."

"What's the bad?"

"Hold your horses. There's more good news. It's a mob matter, so the Bureau can stay on the case."

"I suppose that's good news. And the bad?" Lewis asked again.

"As I said, it's a mob matter. Frank Cork is selling whisky to the Chicago mob."

Lewis was aghast; Frank would never sell anything to the mob. There must be some mistake.

"What whisky? What mob?"

"He's selling Canadian whisky to some Capone apostles operating along the border states."

"Border states? There are a dozen of them. Which one?"

"We're not saying at this time. He's using an assumed name. And he's got a partner—a long-time bootlegger who's as tall as a tree. There's no rap sheet yet. But Frank's alive and wanted by the BOI."

"When can I talk to him?"

"We're keeping this quiet for now. To see how it plays out. Not a word to anyone—nothing to Bobby, Mr. D, or the wife."

Lewis didn't bat an eye.

Pinzolo reached inside his coat, pulled out a handle of whisky, and set it on Frank's desk. No wonder the agent's coats were so roomy: the man was carrying around the contents of a small still. "Show and tell," Pinzolo said.

He had a quick look at the label. Black with seven giant letters—WHISKY. It looked more like "Buyer Beware." Was Duttons' head trader really selling hooch along the US border?

"I gotta get back to the lab," Pinzolo said. "Come with me."

It was another order. Lewis imagined parading through Chicago's financial district with Pinzolo. He wondered which would be the bigger offense on LaSalle Street—being seen with a law enforcement officer or with a man in sodden leather boots? But wait, brick agent or not, Pinzolo was not a man who was likely to walk when he could drive.

Lewis followed the cop to his black Model T, which was illegally parked in front of the Board of Trade. He swiped the pizza debris off the passenger seat to clear a place to sit. Driving up Clark Street, Pinzolo chattered aimlessly about everything but the Frank Cork case. The agent complained about the weather—why had nobody warned him that Chicago was so much colder than New York?—and raved about the music, especially the jazz at the Green Mill. The competition for top singers was intense, and two years earlier, when an entertainer named Joe E. Lewis turned down a contract at the Green Mill for more money at a rival club, the Mill's owner, Machine Gun McGurn, had arranged for the man's throat to be slashed. Now, McGurn was the BOI's top suspect for masterminding the St. Valentine's Day Massacre, but no one had the gumption to arrest the man. Pinzolo suggested that Lewis join him for drinks there later tonight, but Lewis politely declined.

Then, out of the blue, as they drove past the Lincoln Park Zoo, Pinzolo announced: "Here's what we're gonna do. First, I'm going to tell CPD that Frank is no longer 'deemed dead.'"

He liked the agent's thinking. The death certificate would be revoked and the insurer would put a stop payment on its check to Mr. D.

"Second, I'm putting a tail on Frank. We're convinced that selling booze is a front. There are more likely ways for the whiz kid of LaSalle Street to earn his way back.

"You've got a vivid imagination, sir," Lewis said.

They arrived at the crime lab. Pinzolo parked beside three dozen cars that all looked the same. Lewis thanked the agent for his hard work and turned to leave.

"By the way," Pinzolo said, "the bottle of Frank's whisky was delivered to the Bureau by our field operative. It's backed by sworn testimony in support."

"What's the man's name?"

"Let's just say he's someone who blends in."

Walking back to the office along sidewalks thick with snow, Lewis decided Katrina deserved to know that her husband had been found. How could he possibly keep the news to himself? By the next block, he'd reconsidered. Katrina and Frank had already ridden the market up once, yet he still had a steep climb ahead from his cheesy flat. He'd netted a stern warning from Pinzolo for bringing Hector into the firm; was he about to defy a direct order from the BOI? There were only so many swords he was willing to cross with America's federal police.

Katrina would have to wait.

34
THIRTY DAYS

February may be the shortest month, but it was the longest four weeks Frank could remember. He'd never been so worried, never had so much on the line. On good days, he fancied himself as his hero, Fib, risking his life to save his family. On bad days, he felt like Fib's desperate descendants, doomed by famine and drought.

The autumn market crash was now a full-blown Depression. He could feel it taking hold at the Dominion and at the Durets. Savings were running low, and staying alive had become a relentless and uncertain task. Candles and kerosene cast half-lit shadows over everyday life. Hollywood may have moved to technicolor, but images of the Prairies were rendered in sepia.

Added to this potent mix was the new discomfort between Frank and Elzier. Ever since his blowout with Elzier on St. Valentine's Day, Frank had been retiring early and waking at dawn's first light to work through the many risks to his plan. Was he laundering the proceeds of heinous crimes? Was he aiding and abetting the mob? He could hardly claim innocence as to the source of his client's money: he had courted these men in dank tunnels and behind bulletproof cars. Their investment funds had been delivered in crates, hidden under bottles of illicitly traded drink. Images of broken knuckles, ripped-out fingernails, and chopped-off thumbs ran through his head. He filled his water jug, gripping the handle while he still could.

In the mornings, he tried to stay out of Gabriella's kitchen but was lured by her ribald stories and warm toast. She'd spent her first winter of married life living in a sodden army tent, pregnant, with a roof that sagged under the weight of snow. There could be no catalog home for the manager of Beaver Lumber. Frank marveled at her goodwill and the adjustments she'd made, this girl from London's West End. Her work never stopped: she hauled the water from the pump, made soap from lye, scrubbed the laundry by hand, knitted the family's scarves and sweaters, handstitched the samplers that adorned their walls, churned the butter, baked the bread, canned the vegetables, cooked three meals a day, and threw back her head when she laughed. On Sundays, she made *les pets de sœur*—Nuns' Farts. The rounds of buttery dough tasted better than their name.

Once a week, on Sunday afternoons after mass, when she'd cleared the luncheon dishes and Elzier was playing games with the boys, Gabriella wrote home. She'd taken to reading her letters out loud, appealing to her author-in-residence for support. Her subjects ranged from her boys to the delicate frost patterns on their windows, always sparing her parents any bad news. He complimented her on her writing, which was much better than his own. Then Elzier pulled out his accordion and led his family in a round of *chansons*. Gabriella hiked up her worn skirts, kicked up her heels, and belted out rollicking folksongs like "*Le Beau Whisky Blanc*." After a few stanzas, her longing for home had been quelled, and her spirits restored.

THE DAYS GREW LONGER AS February became March. Soon, the winter wheat would be pushing its way up to meet the sun. Frank's deal was animated by that promise and the implicit threat of more supply. He took to playing with Elzier and the boys in the yard: there's nothing like a game of cowboys and Indians to work out hostilities among friends. The Duret boys gunned each other down with pointed fingers, and Elzier shot imaginary arrows clean through Frank's heart. Any lingering jealousy was surely forgotten.

One Saturday night in early March, Elzier proposed they saddle up the beauties for a night on the town. Elzier introduced his horses, Lyon and Mackenzie, who he'd named after the Canadian prime minister, William Lyon Mackenzie King. From the rear of their stalls, Frank witnessed more beast than beauty.

Elzier also introduced his cow, Laurier, a tribute to an earlier PM, and his pig, who bore the name of a local politician who always had his snout in the trough.

Frank watched carefully as Elzier mounted his steed and did his best to follow suit. It was his first time on a horse. He'd never seen one in the financial district—even the Chicago police moved to automobiles years ago.

AFTER A GRUELING MARCH WITHOUT so much as a saddle between his manhood and Mackenzie's bulging back, the two arrived at the hitching post outside the Dominion and tied up. The bar was lined with the usual hard-drinking locals along the back, and up-front in the diner, several tables had been pushed together to seat a half-dozen rowdy men in suits. Having spent four months in and around the Dominion, including one freezing night in the vacated rooms upstairs, Frank instantly identified the men as out-of-towners.

Elzier plopped down at the only empty table, right beside the suits, and Frank took the last unoccupied chair in the entire place. They were close enough to overhear the loud banter from the next table.

"Whaddya think about all those Yankee traders losing their shirts in the Crash?"

"Serves 'em right."

"Give them a break. It's time for another round."

"Hey Dyachenko, does the Pool still have any money in the till?"

The name came whipping at him like a fastball at Wrigley Field. *Yuri Dyachenko from the Saskatchewan Wheat Pool?* He looked around for a quick escape. But Elzier had ordered the beer, and the waitress was on her way. They were stuck. He stole a glimpse at Dyachenko. The man looked harmless enough, with cloudy spectacles and a balding pate, as humorless as a house of sod. Hadn't he quashed this adversary and his baseless investigation? Was it a coincidence they were both here at the same time? He hoped so. If there was going to be a second round in their cross-border fight, the odds had changed; Frank Cork was now penniless on his opponent's turf.

Frank tried to keep an ear attuned to both conversations. In his right ear, Elzier was bragging about the "Canadian horse" being the best breed in the world and how the North won the American Civil War because they outfitted their cavalry with them. In Frank's left ear, Dyachenko was spewing invectives about traders and anyone else who made more money than him, which was just about everyone. When Frank couldn't stand the tension one second more, Elzier settled up for the drinks, and they left.

Outside, Elzier greeted his beauties with a barrage of kisses on the poor things' muzzles—left, right, and left again. It must be a French thing, Frank decided. He couldn't image a Pole or Irishman kissing an animal that way; they barely kissed their wives.

REELING FROM HIS SURPRISE ENCOUNTER with Dyachenko, Frank lay awake that night. Had he misread Elzier's show of friendship? Was his host still seething with jealousy? It could hardly be a coincidence that Dyachenko was at the Dominion the very night Elzier had invited him there. And what about Dyachenko? He tried to remember the dirt that Lewis had dug up on the man. He was a Ukrainian who had immigrated to Canada as a teen. He had received a quarter section of land for free—which was more than it was worth. He was declared an enemy of the state, his name recorded on some list of enemy aliens, branded for life, and subjected to military surveillance. My God, Frank would never feel sorry for himself again. But then—and Frank found this part simply unimaginable—Dyachenko was conscripted into the Canadian Army while still being treated as an enemy of the state. As for the man's time in the army, he was given some half-assed job in the commissary.

In the quiet of Elzier's shed, Frank cringed at how he'd exploited the man's hardships to serve his own ends. True, the fate of his family and industry had been on the line. For the first time, he realized that this was a man whose anger would know no bounds.

And Frank Cork felt deeply afraid.

35
SHAMROCKS

Lewis moved from Frank's desk to his couch, steering clear of the map of Pinzolo's arse. He plunked the bottle of bootleg whisky on the floor, cracked it open, and inhaled. Rotgut. It was not the kind of product he'd associate with Frank. He screwed the cap back on tight.

It was that sleepy time of day, and he wandered down to the pantry to paw through the fridge. Back at Frank's desk, he poured over the details of Pinzolo's report in his head. The whole thing was suspect. He hoped the part about Frank being alive was correct. But the rest? Bootleg whisky? A partner as tall as a tree? It all sounded ridiculous. And Pinzolo had produced nothing to back up his claims—no photographs, no location, not even an item of clothing. The agent's case relied on a bottle of knock-off whisky that could have been produced anywhere. Proof of life? Hardly. Thank God he hadn't told Katrina.

But he did owe her a call. He dialed her directly. Dorothea had been his date at Pinzolo's charity event and the belle of the ball, which is exactly what he'd whispered in her ear at the end of the night. He wouldn't humiliate her by asking her to place his calls to the other woman in his life.

Katrina was chomping at the bit. Everyone was imposing deadlines on her: the bank had served her with foreclosure documents and given her thirty days to pay. She was entitled to impose a deadline, too. "People look at me with pity—if they're willing to look at me at all. My bank account is almost empty, and shady men are lurking outside my door. I'm done, Lewis. If he's not home by St. Patrick's Day, that's it for me. I'll go to the police. I'll sue the firm."

He admired her inventiveness. He flipped open his daybook. It was St. Patrick's Day, March 17th. It would be his second St. Paddy's at the firm. Last year, Frank was on a float with the mayor and hosted an after-party of which any Irishman would be proud. But Katrina was right. If Frank didn't show up for that, it was a safe bet he wasn't ever coming home.

"St. Patrick's is a good date," he agreed and hung up. He'd already put lines in his Frank file through Suicide, Mistress, and Murder. He circled his final option. Hiding.

WHERE WOULD A MAN LIKE Frank hide? Pinzolo reported that Frank was making hootch in one of the border states. Lewis found a map of America on the eighth floor and counted thirteen states on the northern border alone. Some straddled Canada for hundreds of miles, including Minnesota, North Dakota, and Montana. According to the papers, all of them were awash with stills.

How to refine his search? The man loved art; maybe Frank was shacked up with an artist in one of the border states. And his boss was passionate about sailing; was he hiding out in a port city like Cape Town or Santa Barbara? Mostly, though, Frank liked speculating on wheat. And if Frank Cork were alive, Lewis decided, that's what he'd be doing.

The only place to trade wheat in Chicago was in the pit, nine floors below. True, during these past months, he'd sometimes felt Frank's presence, as if the venerable trader were working the back quarter of the room. But, no, the pit was like a tomb these days, not only in Chicago but in all the Big Six cities. And if Frank had so much as tried to poach clients in one of the wheat-trading capitals of the world, he'd have been thrown out on his arse.

Lewis wandered over to the window to rack his brain about second-tier markets—the smaller cities and towns where Frank might discreetly trade. The list was endless. If he was using an alias or a bucket shop, finding him was as likely as Hector being hired by the BOI.

Lewis moved back to the couch, stumped. He picked up one of the oversized arthouse books from Frank's pile. Cracking open the cover, Lewis sat bolt upright. On the inside page was a large photo of a snow-covered wheatfield stretching as far as the eye could see. He read the caption aloud. "The Canadian Prairies. The biggest wheatfield in the world."

Suddenly, it all made sense.

36
THE BONSPIEL

Loving the cold was key to surviving a prairie winter. It was early March, and the temperature had risen, but the fields were still crusted with ice and snow. Elzier had cleared the snow from a large rectangle on his frozen pond, added a bucket or two of water to make it sleek, and declared it a curling rink. Forty-four-pound polished granite rocks with brass handles had not made their way to Gainsborough, but Elzier had filled large jam tins with sand and water that, when frozen, turned as hard as concrete. He'd painted some yellow and some red, making a set for each team.

Katrina had taught Franny and Robbie to skate, but the closest Frank had come to an ice rink was a hockey game at the Chicago Coliseum. The Black Hawks versus St. Pats. He'd taken Lewis shortly after he joined the firm, but they'd left before the end of the 1st Period: the players were all Canadians, and the arena was too cold. After that, they'd stuck to baseball.

Elzier got home from work that day and announced: "That loud Russian from the Dominion came to visit me at the yard this morning. I asked him whether he curled, and—guess what—he's coming over this afternoon and bringing a team. I've invited a few of my men from the yard, and of course, you'll play, too." Elzier beamed. Frank blanched.

He hightailed it to the privacy of his shed and threw back a shot of Will's whisky. It tasted like someone had poured rubbing alcohol on your porridge. From his window, he saw Yuri Dyachenko pull into the yard in a royal-blue Model-A pickup truck with two in the cab and two on the side-rails smoking cigarettes—his team, Frank supposed.

By the time Frank gathered his wits and exited his shed, Dyachenko and his men were wielding yellow jam tins. He considered an emergency exit on Mackenzie the horse, but the temperature was fifteen below. Elzier had also assembled some robust, auburn-haired Scotsmen Frank had seen at the lumber yard. He hoped for Elzier's sake that they brought skills to their jobs other than curling. They certainly looked like they'd be adept at stewarding cans of cement down long stretches of a frozen pond. Out came the flasks. Elzier said that in Canada, whisky and curling went together like maple syrup and flapjacks.

Gabriella greeted her guests, then disappeared into the kitchen to make snacks. Elzier led the men in a round of introductions: "First name and the name of your rink," Elzier said. Frank was confused. Wasn't the rink the ice? Was it also the name of your team?

"Frank. Beavers," he said.

He glanced at Dyachenko. The man showed no sign of connecting his new curling rival to his old corporate foe. Nevertheless, Frank sought cover behind the red-headed Beavers. That didn't last long. Elzier boomed that tonight was the night that his American friend would learn to curl. There were hoots and hollers and the kinds of jokes men in locker rooms tell. Then, the bonspiel was underway: Beaver Lumber versus the Saskatchewan Wheat Pool.

The game did not go well. Frank was stunned by the weight of the can. His shots were so wildly off the mark they had to be removed from play while Elzier shouted, "Hogged," and "Right off," with obvious delight. When handed a broom, Frank was equally hopeless at brushing, chipping, cleaning, and sweeping. He couldn't help feeling he'd been set up again and imagined humiliating photos of himself in the Chicago press bearing a jam tin and a broom.

Elzier was, of course, masterful at the game. Everyone held their breath as his tins skirted around the others and bypassed the guard can. Soon enough, the Beavers had won, and Elzier invited everyone in for snacks. The players threw off their steamy coats and toques in the mudroom and gathered around the long wooden harvest table where Gabriella had laid out a spread of pork pies, French Canadian pea soup, and fried donuts. Elzier took up his accordion and, with his back to the fire, belted out rousing ballads by Mary Travers, the Queen of Canadian Folk, also known as La Bolduc. It was as much fun as a Broadway musical.

While Elzier played "If the Sausages could Talk" at full tilt, Frank saw Dyachenko move out of the living room and corner Gabriella in the kitchen. Frank inched closer, concerned for Gabriella and determined to hear what was said.

Dyachenko was loudly spelling out his last name with great indignation. Gabriella had probably asked him to spell it to ensure she got the pronunciation right. But the man was probably sick of the subject. Frank could relate. "Cork" often attracted unwanted attention, too—"Stick a cork in it, Frank," and so on.

"Why would I change my name just to fit it? It's my God-given name," Dyachenko fumed.

"It's a handsome name, and you should be proud of it," Gabriella replied, looking Dyachenko squarely in the eye. "Elzier tells me you have a very important job. And I suppose a wife and children, too?"

"No, you Prairie women are always looking for robust men. I grew up with nothing to eat. As for my job, yes, I used to lead the international desk at the Wheat Pool."

"Used to? Oh, I'm sorry," Gabriella said.

Elzier's accordion grew louder, Frank inched closer to the kitchen, and Dyachenko persisted. "Until I was demoted due to baseless rumors and treated like some kind of Russian spy. Believe me, I'm neither a Russian nor a spy. My people fought *against* the Russians." Dyachenko was virtually yelling now.

Elzier pumped his accordion harder, the men stamped their feet louder, and the children banged sandpaper blocks and spoons. Gabriella excused herself and rejoined the fun. She cranked up the gramophone and coaxed her husband to drop his instrument and dance. The teams formed a circle, and Elzier let his feet fly in ways that Frank had never seen before.

"Where d'you learn to dance like that?" he asked Elzier between songs while topping up their whisky glasses.

"Working the rocky fields of the Bas-Saint-Laurent as a boy with a hand-held plow. You guide the plow firmly with your hands while steering clear of the rocks with your legs. As for the music, it was all in my head. You Irishmen call it step-dancing. In Québec, we call it *le rigodon*."

Frank couldn't resist giving it a try. He reveled in the lighthearted freedom, stamping his feet and hollering out words in a language he didn't understand. Then, the music turned sultry, and Gabriella assumed center stage. A hush fell over the circle as she swirled and swayed with enough coquetry to stir every man in the room.

When the hijinks resumed, Frank slipped out to the porch where the coats were piled on a long wooden worktable. Which one was Dyachenko's? They all looked the same—

gray twill smeared with dust. He dug through the pockets but found nothing of interest.

He ventured outside to the man's truck. The cargo bed was spotless: not a single sheaf of wheat had despoiled that space. But the driver's door was unlocked, and Frank found a crumpled piece of paper tucked under the bench seat. There was just enough moonlight to make it out. A telegram from the Saskatchewan Wheat Pool: CORK FLED CHICAGO NIGHT OF CRASH STOP FORECLOSURE SIGN ON HOUSE STOP LIVING ON THE PRAIRIES STOP.

He read it one more time before returning it under the seat. So, Dyachenko knew who he was, knew he was the American trader who the Pool accused of manipulating wheat markets, knew he was the bastard who cheated him out of his job. This man was not only looking for him but had found him—here, a few steps away. His plan was clear: Yuri Dyachenko aimed to catch him in the act, selling wheat futures illegally in Canada and ensuring he never traded another wheat future again.

When Frank slipped back inside, the party was winding down. The Beavers had won the bonspiel, and Dyachenko had led his team to defeat.

But these were mere skirmishes. The battle lay ahead.

37
TWO ANTLERS

"The Canadian Prairies," Lewis exclaimed. After months of tireless searching in drydocks, hotels, and even the morgue, he'd concluded it was the only place that made sense. He waited in the lobby of the Board of Trade for the elevator to arrive and ran through what he knew about the vast region, which wasn't much. If only Frank had hidden in South Side; it would have been a snap to find him there.

What was that file he'd worked on before the Crash, the one about the Saskatchewan Wheat Pool and—Drabinsky? Davydenko? No, Yuri Dyachenko. The details were coming back. It was early March, almost five months since late October.

Back on his old floor, the eighth, Lewis was met by a chorus of grunts and greetings from his associates. Some simply looked up from their desks, and others stood and lavished Rosie with pats. Parking himself in front of his old filing cabinet, he began his search at the letter "S" for Saskatchewan. No luck. He looked briefly under "P" for Pool and wasted too much time under "W" for wheat. At last, he found the file—under "D" for Dyachenko.

Clipped to the cover was the closing memo he had written documenting the final exchange between Frank and the

SWP—the Saskatchewan Wheat Pool. "Frank advised SWP that Duttons would not succumb to meddling by foreigners," it read. "SWP confirmed that it had withdrawn its complaint, and Yuri Dyachenko had been re-assigned."

Wow. He'd forgotten that. The Chicago Board of Trade investigation never even got off the ground. Excellent work, Lewis, he congratulated himself. So, who was bamboozling Duttons into paying some trumped-up fine?

Lewis and Rosie went up to the ninth. Lewis scarfed down a fresh cupcake as they passed by the kitchen, then placed the file on Mr. D's desk. In Frank's office, he called the Saskatchewan Wheat Pool.

"Mr. Dyachenko, please."

"Who's calling, please?" the receptionist asked.

"I'm calling from Chicago."

"Chicago! I have an aunt who lives there—"

"Mr. Dyachenko, please," Lewis insisted.

"While I've got you, did you hear the one about the two farmers? The Yank says, 'Owning grain elevators is highly profitable. I'm going to make a *mill* this year.' The Canuck replies, 'Sounds like a *whisky* business to me.'"

The young woman erupted in laughter, and Lewis decided to share the moment. In his experience, there was much to be gleaned from being nice to the people at the front desk. He rallied with the only industry joke he knew. "Did you hear the one about the two traders?"

She squealed with delight at the mere prospect that he was reciprocating.

"The Yank brags, 'My firm specializes in grain futures.' The Canuck retorts, '*Barley* legal.'"

She guffawed, and he had no doubt the joke would soon be making the rounds at the Saskatchewan Wheat Pool. Who knows, maybe Canadians would even come to see that there was nothing quite so heinous about selling futures after all. He returned to his mission. "Is Mr. Dyachenko in?"

"He's out of the office for a few weeks. He's leading our new Grain Elevator Task Force."

"Oh. Whereabouts?" Abouts? Really? He must have been spending too much time with Mr. D.

"Your guess is as good as mine. We own six thousand silos. He'd probably start in the southeast, then fan out from there. That's what I'd do. Go there and ask around. Everybody knows when the Wheat Pool's in town."

Lewis buzzed Dorothea. "Have we received any calls from a Yuri Dyachenko or the Saskatchewan Wheat Pool?"

"Yes, quite a few, all of them asking for Mr. Cork. There was even one this week. I took the call myself. The number will be in the log."

"You were supposed to be forwarding Frank's calls to me." For the first time, he felt cross at Dorothea. He wasn't about to be hoodwinked by those pencil skirts and tucked-in blouses.

"I asked the caller to hold while I put him through to you," she said, "but he declined. He wanted to know whether Mr. Cork was back. He wasn't willing to speak to anyone else."

"Did you get the caller's name?"

"I asked, but he declined. I record all incoming calls in the log. Would you like me to find the entries for you?"

"I can take it from here. But if Dyachenko calls back, don't ask for his permission. Put him through."

Lewis reviewed the log at Dorothea's desk. There had been a dozen calls, and yes, even one this week. So, Dyachenko had been tracking Frank. If he'd known that, he wouldn't have wasted months asking barmen about mistresses. Yuri Dyachenko had beaten him to the punch with one simple question: Where would a trader go to squeeze one last buck out of his grain?

He reviewed his research on Yuri Dyachenko and his hard-luck life. This man had been constantly degraded for no reason other than his roots. Hadn't he left the old world to get away from all that? God, imagine being branded an enemy of your state, then being expected to serve in its army. Yet, in the face of all those obstacles, through perseverance and hard work, Dyachenko had still managed to build a brilliant career—until Frank appeared on the scene. With one call to the Pool, Frank had engineered Dyachenko's demotion from a leading executive to some make-work task force. He immediately regretted the part he'd played in Frank's actions and Dyachenko's demise. At the same time, he could also imagine the unplumbed depths of Yuri Dyachenko's rage.

LEWIS VENTURED BACK DOWN TO the associate floor to check out the maps. There was no sign of Hector. He checked his watch. It was noon, and Hector would be busy in the garage, jockeying cars. He reflected on Pinzolo's caution about this person he'd inveigled onto the firm's eighth floor. He'd dismissed the warning at the time—people were always inventing new reasons for holding back Blacks—but weighed it now. Seditious acts: that was one helluva serious charge. What was his new recruit really up to between his bouts of commodities research?

Hector's written work and his presentation skills were both top-rate. He wasn't sure whether Pinzolo's stories about Hector's extracurricular activities were true, but if so, they were of more value to Duttons than the night-school courses that were commonplace in the industry. Hector Ray was researching, writing, and publishing articles in *The Defender*; he was also pitching ideas from the pulpit of Olivet Baptist Church. Its congregation was bigger than Chicago's largest Catholic church. These days, the crowds outside Holy Name Cathedral were often as large as those inside, ever since Hymie Weiss of the North Side Gang was gunned down there on his way to pray. You could still see stray bullets in the cornerstones.

He picked up the phone. "Dorothea, order a subscription to *The Defender* for the firm." He'd better figure out what this young man was on about. Then, Lewis set about finding a map of Saskatchewan. On Duttons' eighth floor, there were dozens of fascinating federal maps, and several for each state, but only one of Canada. It was date-stamped 1890—forty years ago.

Nevertheless, he found Regina, the home of the Saskatchewan Wheat Pool. A note, in a lovely cursive script, stated that the city was once called "Pile of Bones," which seemed both ominous and ridiculous. Also, as of the date of the map, the city and the entire province were still in the Northwest Territories.

He scanned the sea of vacant land surrounding the city and, to his surprise, found two towns with the same name, only twenty miles apart—Antler, Northwest Territories, and Antler, North Dakota. The two Antlers. God, he loved maps.

But wait, Antler, NWT was in southeast corner of the province, just where the nice lady at the Wheat Pool lady had told him to start. He'd leave in the morning and ask for directions from there, just as she had suggested.

One of the interns yelled from down the hall, "Phone call for Lewis Montgomery."

"Anything new?" Pinzolo asked.

"Nothing. You?"

"Nothing," Pinzolo said. "Sticking around?"

"Sure," he said.

38
KINGDOMS

Frank decided to join Will for the ride, although he'd sworn off any contact with the mobsters during their thirty-day contract. Nothing good could come from talking to these men mid-wait. He'd planned to enjoy lunches with Will at the Dominion and drink too much whisky before bed. He had grown to like its brutal taste, and after the second shot, he felt like a Dickcissel flying home in the spring. But here he was, ten days after the post-office drops, sitting in the Buick while Will carried the crates to the border.

Shorty cornered him, "The boss wants to invest more."

Frank was so relieved he almost agreed before coming to his senses. These men must have troves of cash stashed under floorboards they wanted circulating in banks and post-office accounts. The Chicago press had reported on a string of laundries Capone had acquired to hide his illicit activities in the laundry's fake books. Ever since, LaSalle Street called it "money laundering." Frank wanted no part in it.

He thanked Shorty for his confidence in him and courteously declined. But Shorty was a traffic light with only one color—green. There were no cautions or stop signs in Shorty's world. Meanwhile, Whacker was unloading crates of money.

Frank declined again but tried a new tack. "Wheat markets are volatile. It's looking like your timing will be perfect, right down to the day. But another investment would not be prudent at this time." He lowered his voice to a menacing whisper. "I'm sure you don't want to be reporting losses up the line."

Shorty got the point and ordered Whacker to return the crates to the Hup. Will and Frank scooted to the Buick as Frank called out, "See you on St. Patrick's Day."

Driving to the Dominion, Frank said to Will, "My trips to the border have to end. We're even-steven on my room and board. I need a break. Gimme twenty days."

Will stuffed in a wad of tobacco, and his face grew sad. Frank felt the moisture gathering in the corners of his eyes—whether it was from fear or relief, he couldn't say. But he congratulated himself for sticking to the contract. It was his Goldilocks deal—not too big and not too small: it was just right.

THE NEXT DAY, WILL SHOWED up at the Durets at the usual time but with a different proposition in mind and not a hint of his usual insouciance. Instead, there was a whispered plea. "Laura-Jean's had a hard time since we lost the baby. The children need her; we all do."

"How can I help?" Frank asked, giving his friend a warm pat on his arm. He felt touched that Will was bringing this wrenching problem to him. Some days, he was wracked by guilt that he had used Will for his own ends, playing Iago to Will's Othello. He welcomed this opportunity to be helpful in his final days.

"She's stuck," Will continued. "She's spending her days in her nightgown in the rocking chair."

Will dropped off Frank at the farm, and the Howard children tackled him with warm hugs. Touched as he was by their affection, it triggered a deep longing for Franny and Robbie. He regained his composure and went to work, bundling the children into layers of warm clothes and sending them to play in the yard. Laura-Jean, still in her nightdress, was wan but managed a weak smile. She leaned on his arm as he guided her from her rocker to a chair. He made her a cup of tea and searched for a molasses cookie or date square, but the larder was almost bare. He hauled the metal washtub close to the woodstove, filled it with hot water from the reservoir, and threw in a handful of Epsom salts from under the sink. He helped her ease in her feet, turned his back, and encouraged her to enjoy a good soak. Then he joined the menage in the yard.

Outside, even the gophers were confused by the weather. The warm, dry days of early March had tricked them into coming out of hibernation, and the "flickertail rodents" were everywhere. The town was offering a bounty of a penny per tail, and Frank had overheard men at the Dominion admit that gopher money was the only thing keeping them alive. For Willard, gopher-hunting was a new adventure. He fashioned nooses from twine and set them gingerly on twigs crisscrossing the rodents' holes. When the critters popped up their heads, they were caught in Willard's make-shift gallows—another penny for the pot. Willard implored him to join in, but Frank was sickened by the thought. Was his own life about to meet a similar end?

He joined the girls, who were taking turns running anxiously to the window to check on their mom. They needed a distraction. He handed them pails according to their size and they marched back and forth between the pump and the woodstove. Frank pumped, helped them carry their pails, and dumped the water into the reservoir until it was full. Then he led them to the chicken coop, sending them hunting for eggs while he checked on Laura-Jean. He rapped lightly at the door and heard her call back weakly to come in. She was dressed and refreshed and listening to opera on CJGX. It was the first time he'd seen her simply sitting without doing a chore.

When the tenor wrapped up his aria with a tremolo, he let her win a spelling bee. He was reminded how much he enjoyed putting in a morning this way. He made more tea, and she told him more about her sister Maud, the one who'd died as a child from the Spanish Flu. Then she spoke of her stillborn son. He reached for her hand, and they cried.

The following morning, Will picked him up at Elzier's again. Will was right. Having a visitor had helped. Laura-Jean was dressed, her hair brushed, and she'd even made the beds. There was still much to be done. He split the wood into kindling, stoked the fire, drew more water, and entertained the children. He even did the laundry: grinding diapers against a washboard in a tub full of hot water and lye was the most exhausting thing he'd ever done. The youngest, baby June, would soon be out of diapers. He tried his hand at a loaf but burned the bread. At lunch, Will dropped by with sandwiches from the Dominion and a copy of the *Leader-Post*. He skimmed the front page, but now that his deal was locked in, he wanted nothing to do with grain news.

Frank flicked off the radio. In an effort to lead Laura-Jean to speak of her loss, he gave voice to feelings he'd spent a lifetime pushing from his mind. He told her about the hunger, insecurity, and sheer terror of his childhood years. As an adult, he said, the only role he'd ever understood was provider. Katrina had asked him to spread his wings, and he hadn't known how.

But in nurturing Laura-Jean back to health in the Howards' kitchen, Frank Cork had found other ways to be a man.

WILL AND FRANK'S NEW ROUTINE continued for several days. Will seemed untroubled by Frank's growing friendship with his wife, which was more than Frank could say about Elzier Duret. The man was prone to jealousy, yet no one enjoyed putting the cat among the pigeons more than Elzier's wife. Over dinner that evening, Gabriella said to her husband, "Isn't it wonderful, *mon amour,* to have our own Gary Cooper look-alike right here in our house?"

"You must have me confused with his horse," Frank said. Nevertheless, Elzier pouted.

Still, as Frank's deal with the mob ticked like a time bomb, he settled into a rhythm with the Durets, too. After dinner, he washed up the dishes while Gabriella and Elzier sipped tea and tried to engage their feisty boys in word games and discussions. He'd never had much luck with that with his own children, either. Elzier would step in with his dog-eared dictionary—the one he'd dragged from the monastery to the army and from the army to the camp—and the boys would work through another onion-skin page, ten words per night.

"Eh, *'tits Durs,"* Elzier would call them, which he pronounced "tee dur," and said it meant little tough ones in French. Then, he would ask what words they had for him that night.

Maurice went first: "Capability, capitalism, capitation—"

"What's capitation?" Gene asked.

"It's when I chop your head off," Maurice replied, taking a swing at his brother's head.

"No, Maurice, that's *de*capitation," Gabriella intervened. "Tell us about capitation, please."

Frank was impressed. He didn't have a clue what it meant and listened attentively as Gene read the complex definition aloud. When the boys finished their words, it was time to play chess with Uncle Frank. He had been teaching Robbie to play chess when he fled and struggled to stay positive as he showed them some classic openers and how to forecast three moves ahead. Victor, the youngest, had no patience for games or books, and certainly not chess, but his parents' passion for dance bubbled out of him. While his brothers studied the board, that wee prairie boy stretched his arms toward the sky. There, in his family's living room, young Victor would transform himself into the magical characters—sorcerers, cygnets, and sylphs—that emerged from his gifted mind. Oh, to be as free as young Victor, Frank thought.

Gabriella sat with her sewing kit on her lap, converting the remnants of her London wardrobe into clothing for her boys, setting aside the delicate floral prints for quilts. When the radio played Louis Armstrong trumpeting "West End Blues," she enticed her husband into a deep-dipping dance and squealed with mock indignation at his playful pats.

The kerosene lamps flickered then dimmed, signaling that their evening was coming to a close. Gabriella asked Frank to read from his book, and he announced Chapter Three.

"Nine hundred years after the fall of Cruithne's Kingdom, Fib set out for Saskatchewan. With a sack full of wheat seeds that could survive the cold, he would turn that vast flatland into fields of gold. He divided the plain a thousand ways for Cruithne's descendants and the come-from-aways. Some met the challenges with unrelenting grit; others were crushed by the cold and quit."

The Duret children chanted, "And the suffering spread all around, all around, the suffering spread all around."

Frank paused to think. The next part was bleak, for Fib felt the cruel winds blowing in his direction, and Frank foresaw a Great Depression. He skipped ahead to a happier time for Fib and the King.

"'Come join me, my son; the time has come. You've won my praise; you've earned my blessing. My blood, my heir, I name you King.'

"'Thank you, Father, but I shall stay. For my place is here, in the Kingdom of Céyh.'"

FRANK LOOKED AT THE CHILDREN, their faces alight with hope and optimism. He had no magic or special powers, but he could foresee the hardships that lay ahead. Should he stop when Fib's people arrive at their chosen land? Yes, he decided and skipped the last line. He closed his scribbler and, with all the authority he could muster, announced, "The End."

He had cast off his father's legacy and found his own voice.

His tale was done.

39
FLYING HIGH

The latest copy of *The Defender* and a stack of back copies sat in the center of Lewis's desk. One unplanned hour later, Lewis had read two thoughtful articles by Hector Ray on labor and housing reform. He had a flash of regret for extending a helping hand; his first recruit was likely to outperform him. Meanwhile, his search for Frank had come to a head. His only lead pointed to the border where, according to Pinzolo, Frank was selling contraband liquor along that great divide. It sounded like yet another kooky Pinzolo theory—although the agent's rundown on Hector had proven correct, and his own search hadn't uncovered a single lead. He couldn't act on it fast enough.

Would Dyachenko find Frank first? A border town on the Canadian Prairies was just the kind of place Frank might be. The storied trader could put his ear to the ground among the growers, gathering pricing data that urban trading houses didn't have. Then, he could slip across the border to trade. He admired Dyachenko's instincts. Why hadn't he been shrewd enough to think of that months ago?

But there were obstacles, too, including how to get to the two Antlers. A flight was an exhilarating idea. The country was enraptured by the launch of Transcontinental Air Transport's first passenger route to Los Angeles from New York. But the Antlers were nowhere close to either city, so Lewis quickly abandoned any thoughts of getting there by plane.

What about the train? An agent said there was a Soo Line from Chicago to Moose Jaw, five days a week. Really? A daily to Moose Jaw, Saskatchewan? The Friday, March 14th train had already departed, and he wasn't about to sit around for two days. If he borrowed one of the partner's cars, he could leave tomorrow, maybe even today. Now that was exciting: he'd never seen the American Midwest. His map suggested it was a thousand miles from Chicago to the Antlers—thirty hours, including an overnight break.

Traders start their days early, even when markets are dead. It was seven-thirty, and a few of the partners were in, if only to maintain some rhythm in their disrupted lives. Ricco hadn't arrived. Lewis poked his head in to see Mr. D.

"You're up at sparrow poop this morning," Mr. D said.

"I have a lead on Frank's whereabouts."

"You look as proud as a hound with two tails."

"I would like to borrow your car, sir."

"My car? Where are you going?"

"Canada, sir."

"You wanna drive my car to Canada?"

"Yes, sir."

"*Lawd*, that's clear up to the promised land!"

"I'm going to Saskatchewan, sir."

"Great glory, that place is so flat, if your dog runs away you can see him for three days. When are you going?"

"Now, sir."

"We'll need you in the office today and tomorrow, but you can leave Sunday. How long will it take?"

"Under two days, each way. If I leave early Sunday, I can be there by Monday afternoon."

"Faster than green grass through a goose. What's the urgency?"

"Frank's in trouble."

Mr. D looked skeptical, which wasn't surprising given the man had a hundred thousand dollars riding on Frank being dead. "What kinda' trouble?"

"Two kinds, sir. First, he's probably trading—outside the firm. Second, I suspect his margin account needs some paying down." They both grimaced. It may have been the understatement of the year.

"No one's gonna tan that boy's hide," Mr. D said.

"There's very little trading to be done here, sir. And he can hardly waltz into one of the Big Six. They'd shake his hand, then run him out of town. No, I figure he's looking for investors somewhere out of the way." Mr. D peered at him as if he'd lost his mind. The man had every major rural stockholder in America sewn up.

"It's a long shot, I know, sir. But I'm not quite ready to declare him dead. Are you?" It was a direct challenge. Just because he was here to borrow the man's car, he wasn't about to be pushed around.

"No, no. Certainly not. There's lots of cock-a-doodle-doo left in Frank. Who knows, Lewis, one day there might even be a Mr. C running this firm. But you said there were two kinds of trouble. What's the second?"

"They're not partial to futures traders in Canada, sir." They both smiled. Another understatement.

"So, what are you going to do? Ride in on my bronco and rescue Frank? You don't even know if he's there."

"I'm heeding your advice, sir: The secret to getting ahead is getting started." He could see that he'd landed his punch. "If I'm wrong, you can declare him dead. There will need to be financial support for his family. Then we can all move on."

"You've pursued this like a bull chasing a cow in heat," Mr. D said.

"Thank you, sir."

"No, thank *you*, Son. By the way, I enjoyed reading the file you dropped off." The managing partner said, "Take the Cord," and tossed his car keys across the table. Then, he opened his billfold and peeled two twenty-dollar bills off the top. "For expenses," he added. "Get back safely, Son. The last thing we need around here is another missing person. Oh... there's some protection in the glove compartment, in case you need it. Now shut the door as you leave, Son."

Lewis exited Mr. D's office, shoving the cash and keys into his pocket. He could all but see the managing partner picking up the phone as the door clicked shut—calling the insurer to demand they put a rush on his check.

RICCO WAS IN NOW, SO Lewis stopped by to settle the details of his trip. Ricco bubbled with a mix of jealousy and excitement, "I can't believe you got the keys to the Cord. It's the L-29—it makes the lobby bar in the Drake Hotel look plain. They're selling for $3,000 a pop."

"Three thousand dollars—you could buy five ordinary cars for that."

Ricco lowered his voice to a whisper and cupped his manicured hand beside his mouth. "Mr. D got it for free. It is manufactured by Mr. D's client. Errett Lobban Cord." Ricco said the man's name slowly as if each precious part was worth its weight in gold. "He's supposed to be showing it off among Chicago's monied set."

Lewis laughed. "Well, I can do one better. I'll drive it through the Dakotas with my dog."

Ricco flashed him a contorted look then resumed his tribute to the Cord. "She's got front-wheel drive and a three-speed transmission, and she handles like a well-broken mare. And there's a built-in radio."

He was as giddy as Ricco at the prospects of a radio in the car. The tunes were already crooning in his head.

"I'll let the parking garage know you'll be picking her up first thing Sunday."

The parking garage? Should he invite Hector to join him for the ride? He'd love some company, although getting out of the city in the Hudson had been fraught. Also, there were better ways to secure a place for Hector in the firm. Lewis needed to socialize the idea before springing an intern on Frank in Saskatchewan. Besides, whatever he had to say to Frank, three would be a crowd.

What about Katrina? He broke into a mile-wide smile at the thought of having her at his side, the rooftop down, and a trail of music blowing out behind. No, that scenario wasn't in the cards. Rosie was the only road trip companion he was going to get. But should he tell Katrina about the trip? He was feeling less confident about finding Frank after Mr. D's dismissive look. Why raise expectations? But he owed her a call. After all, Monday was her deadline—St. Patrick's Day.

"I HAVE A LEAD ON your husband's whereabouts," Lewis told Katrina. "But I'll need a few extra days. If my lead is useless, we'll declare the search over, and I will personally escort you to the police."

Katrina didn't say yes, nor did she say no.

"The movers are here," she said. "We have to be out in a week."

40
MARCH MADNESS

On Wednesday, March 12, 1930, with less than one week to go in Frank's thirty-day term, CJGX announced that America's Federal Farm Board had stepped in. The new agency had been given half a billion dollars to give the market a kick in the butt. Specifically, its mandate was to buy agricultural products at overblown prices.

Frank was in the Durets' kitchen when he heard the news. Holy Toledo, half a billion dollars was more than a bandage over the gushing wound. And what's more, the Farm Board had made its first purchase—six million bushels of wheat. It paid 60¢ a bushel, 15¢ above world prices, just as Frank had forecast.

But Frank was not in the clear, yet. Success required more than the right price: it had to be his price on his date. And there were still five days to go. Alas, the market had risen to his number five days early. Stated otherwise, the date he'd chosen was five days too late. Either way, for the next five days, he could only pray that the inflated price would hold.

MONDAY, MARCH 17TH, BEGAN AS a perfectly ordinary day. The sun rose earlier and set later every day, and the snow cover in the fields had grown sparse. Frank checked the thermometer

—thirty-four degrees, just above the freezing mark. A sure sign of a great day ahead.

In the kitchen, Frank was surprised that neither Gabriella nor Elzier made mention of St. Patrick's Day. There were no zucchini muffins or bits of green in his porridge. He'd never met a reasonable person who didn't celebrate the beloved event. Frank wished them a Happy St. Patrick's Day, and Elzier retorted that Canada's two founding nations, the French and British, had not always felt kindly toward the Irish—and not much had changed. It was the first hint that March 17th might not be the lucky date Frank was counting on. By the time he'd finished breakfast, he was second-guessing his entire plan.

Frank retrieved his stash from Elzier's barn. He found a pile of gunny sacks by the tractor—the type farmers use to take grain samples to the lab to test for weevils and rot. He gave them a shake: they were the best he could do.

In the workshop, he reclaimed his Chicago clothes from under his bed, buffed his cufflinks back into their former glory, and changed into his suit. Who was this man he'd almost forgotten about? He smoothed away the wrinkles from the luxurious fabric and admired the drape. Everything hung looser than he remembered; he tightened his buckle a notch.

He'd miss his rope belt. Somehow, it had helped him through his ordeal. People expect less from a man who holds up his trousers with a rope, he supposed.

Packing up took less than a minute flat. All his worldly possessions had been reduced to the contents of a burlap bag. He took one last look around. The Hudson Bay blanket was neatly folded at the foot of his bed. He brushed his hand slowly across its rough-hewn texture. He'd miss it—he'd miss everything. Still, he was heading home.

Pulling into the yard, Will was shocked to see him decked out in a suit. Frank hopped in the Buick for his final ride, then left the Durets' farm without saying goodbye. His deal was risky enough; he wasn't about to announce that he was off to collect his bags of cash. Besides, if the price dropped, he'd be back.

In town, there was no evidence of a pending parade, not even shamrocks or green beer at the Dominion. The barman growled, "Gainsborough was founded forty-five years ago, and there's never been an Irish parade. Nobody wants a bunch of Catholics tearing up our town."

"So, nothing special today," Frank pressed.

"Come back in July. The Orange Parade is a dignified affair."

Frank picked up the *Leader-Post* from the bar and flipped to the grain news. There it was on page one: "Wheat steady at 60¢." The price had held! He'd won his bet. Payday had arrived.

FRANK WALKED TO THE POST office to collect his cash. Suddenly, a man emerged from the shadows, scaring the bejesus out of him. Yuri Dyachenko was blocking his path.

"Business at the post office today?" Dyachenko sneered.

The man was as persistent as a crusty scab. Sweat was dripping from under Dyachenko's toque, and when he yanked it off, bits of lint stayed behind, pasted to his forehead like flies on a swatter. The man's eyeglasses were almost opaque with steam, as his hot breath collided with the cold air; behind the thick frames, Dyachenko's eyes were myopic and intense. When Frank side-stepped, the little man matched his every move. It was an embarrassing *pas de deux* on the front steps of the Gainsborough post office.

Dyachenko erupted in rage, "I know who you are, Frank

Cork. You and your free-market profiteering and picture-perfect—"

"Next time I see you, remind me not to talk to you," Frank said calmly, but it fell on deaf ears. Dyachenko was looking skyward like someone praying to God on high. Frank followed his gaze: Will Howard was towering over them.

"Can I help you?" Will said.

Dyachenko gawked like a bullpen pitcher watching Babe Ruth step up to bat.

"Will Howard, Gainsborough Police Force," Will said, forgetting to use the past tense. But it was clear to Frank that 'police' and 'force' in the same sentence had hit Yuri Dyachenko like a blow to the head. The one-time enemy alien disappeared into the shadows from whence he'd come.

Will tucked in a chaw and shuffled back to the Buick. With his path finally clear, Frank entered the post office, a dusty gunny sack paired with his pinstripe suit. Sure enough, the clearinghouse had wired the Farm Board money into his James Gordon Enterprise account.

"Arrived by Western Union this morning," the postmaster said.

Frank emptied the account but didn't close it: he liked his bucket shop. He struggled to look nonchalant while shoving the cash into his sack. He walked briskly past the shadows of the post office building and joined Will in the car. It was his moment of triumph, yet the incident revealed a plan that was far from perfect with crucial steps still to go. He sat on his hands in an effort not to scratch.

Will drove them around the now-familiar circuit—Anamoose, Gwinner, and Kulm. He loaded the gangsters' cash into sacks at each stop and closed his accounts.

Over lunch, Frank and Will talked about the weather

and how the Buick was getting long in the tooth. Neither mentioned the encounter with Yuri Dyachenko or the sacks of cash in the back.

41
THE CORD

At eight in the morning on Sunday, March 16th, Lewis presented himself at the parking garage with the keys to the Cord. There was no sign of Hector. Instead, there was a weekend manager who was twice Hector's age and half as nice. The man couldn't care less that Lewis had the keys; he was not handing over the Cord to a kid.

Lewis considered calling Mr. D but worried that, given the opportunity, the managing partner would renege. Instead, he gave the weekend manager a firm shove and dashed with Rosie to the Cord. By God, she was a wonder to behold—a crimson beauty with a long, tapered nose. Her fenders swooped upward, haughty and imperious, on a frame that couldn't have sat lower to the ground. Her winter hardtop was red, her leather upholstery white, and her mahogany trim was as fine as Frank's wet bar. He could only imagine what was under the hood. But there was no time for that.

Rosie bounded into the passenger seat while he slipped behind the wheel with the air of entitlement that car keys bestow. He gripped the gear shift by its polished knob and hit the gas. The Cord's powerplant responded with a deep-throated purr, and the weekend manager had no choice but to leap aside. As Lewis turned onto LaSalle Street, dammit, there was Pinzolo, stepping in front of his car. He resisted the urge to mow the man down.

"Going somewhere?" Pinzolo said as if he had nothing better to do.

"A Sunday drive."

Pinzolo parked his bulk in front of the Cord and toyed with the dazzling crystal ornament on her hood. The man was a menace. If Hector had been on duty, he would have been halfway out of the city by now. Instead, the weekend manager joined Pinzolo, looking sweaty and smug.

"Where to?" Pinzolo asked.

"Wouldn't you take this baby out for a spin if you had the chance?"

"The Bureau's cars may not be pretty, but I assure you they're twice as fast. Off to find Frank?"

"I'm just the intern. I do what I'm told."

"As my old man used to say, Lewis, there's a fine line between persistence and stupidity."

"I'll let you know if I'm planning to cross it, sir." Lewis nudged the car forward, and his two opponents had no choice but to step out of the way.

AT LAST, HE WAS ON the road. The Cord was attracting catcalls and lustful stares, and he wondered whether he could get out of town safely in this car. Murderers, armed robbers, pickpockets, and vandals had spread across the city like a social disease. He checked the glove compartment—a pistol! So that's what Mr. D meant by "protection." He'd thought the old man meant a box of sheaths. He slammed the compartment shut; there would be no Lewis Montgomery fingerprints on any gun.

Lewis pointed the car northwest, carving a hypotenuse across America's central plain. He cruised along highways, rumbled across rural roads, and sped down the main drags of small towns, the Cord's engine as smooth as an Old Fitz. Tractor trucks laden with produce passed him in southbound lanes, heading for Route 66. Everyone seemed oblivious to God's day of rest. As the miles whirred by, the L-29 became an intimate friend. She was a celebration of form over function with a propensity to slip out of gear at the most inopportune times. Rosie secured a spot for herself on the floor.

It was midnight when Lewis pulled into Fargo, ND. The Waldorf Hotel was on his right. In high school, he'd learned about Teddy Roosevelt's famous speech on race relations, after the former President won the Nobel Peace Prize. For some reason, it stuck in his memory that he'd delivered the speech from the balcony of this hotel. Lewis looked up and pictured the stateman imploring Americans with fiery rhetoric to cast their differences aside. Some twenty years later, Lewis wasn't convinced that any progress had been made. Perhaps Hector's circle of talented young people with fires in their bellies would move things forward at last.

Just down the street was a sign for The Donaldson. The sign said it was a truckers' hostel, although it looked more suited to place for prisoners en route to the state penitentiary from the county jail. The parking lot was full of long-haul trucks full of farm equipment, poultry, and grain; canvas tarps were the only thing separating the wares from thieves and the frosty night air. Some drivers were asleep, slumped behind the wheel, and others stood sentry hauling on smokes. Would the Cord be safe here overnight? And what about Rosie? It was too cold to leave her in the car. Lewis secured a room, smuggled in the dog, and slipped a roadie some money to watch the Cord, all of which was harder than you'd think.

After a fitful sleep, Lewis was relieved to find the Cord where he'd left it, gleaming in the morning sun. His map suggested a six-hour drive from Fargo to the Antlers. It was 7 a.m. now; he'd be there by 1 or 2 p.m.

At Grand Forks, ND, Lewis stopped for gas and to stretch his legs. Ambling around, waiting for Rosie to do what dogs do, he came across a historic plaque stating the town was so-called because it sat at the forks of two rivers: the Red River and the Red Lake River. He was struck by the lack of creativity among those who handed out names—two red rivers must be as confusing as two Antlers, twenty miles apart.

All gassed up, Lewis re-started his northwesterly trek toward Devil's Lake. He was barely underway when he spotted a muscular Model T idling on the side of the road. It pulled out suddenly when he passed, as if it had been waiting for him. Pinzolo's threatening words outside the parking garage sprang to mind: "Our cars aren't pretty, but they're twice as fast." Directly ahead was the widest-open stretch of flatland he'd ever seen. It was time to put the agent's claim to the test.

He stepped on the gas and shifted into third. The Cord took off. Ha! He should have known this car was built for speed: she'd been tripping over herself in low gear. But the Model T also upped its pace. Was it Pinzolo? Or roadies from the Donaldson issuing a challenge to the city boy in the spiffy car? He slowed to check it out in his rearview mirror, and the Model T slowed, too. Sure enough, it was Pinzolo in the passenger seat and another agent at the wheel.

Dammit, the Bureau could follow its own hunches. Lewis fiddled with the dial. Radio reception was spotty outside Devil's Lake, but Jelly Roll Morton and his ragtime piano broke through. He pumped up the "King Porter Stomp," and the Cord became an intoxicating mix of sound and speed.

But minutes later, the Model T was keeping pace. With his eyes peeled to his rearview mirror, Lewis almost slammed into the rear of a poultry truck. It swerved and sent a mess of chicken feathers into the air. He veered into the oncoming traffic in an ill-considered effort to get a clear view and narrowly avoided a car hurtling his way. Darting back into his lane, a half-dozen drivers laid on their horns, Rosie barked, and Jelly Roll Morton played on. What a cacophony. He hadn't had so much fun since he'd doglegged a Nash Quad four-wheeler through a patch of West Point mud.

By now, Lewis was sweating bullets in his business suit. He loosened his tie and floored it again, gunning that Cord until the Model T was nowhere to be seen. The transmission held firm in third. He sailed through Devil's Lake and didn't hit the brakes until the turn-off into Rugby, ND. There was a lineup of cars making the turn into town. He slowed, and the Model T reappeared out of nowhere, side-sweeping the line and pulling ahead.

Lewis saw red. Hell could freeze over before he would concede the lost ground: he would get to Frank first. Sure enough, by the time Ben Bernie and his orchestra were wailing "Sweet Georgia Brown," Lewis had left the Model T in the dust.

Up ahead, a sign read, "Welcome to Antler." Antler, ND, he supposed. Then, not long after, without so much as a road marker or a booth, Lewis crossed the border into Canada.

It was two in the afternoon on St. Patrick's Day, and Pinzolo was nowhere in sight.

42
WHACKED

In the Buick, the acrid smell of cheap tobacco and Laura-Jean's coffee hung in the air. Frank was tempted to roll down a window, but the temperature was hovering around freezing. They were due at the drop site at 2 p.m., and it was still more than a mile away. Given the shenanigans at the Gainsborough post office, they were running late.

How had Yuri Dyachenko known where to show on the very day that his deal with the mob came due? Had Dyachenko snuck into his shed during the bonspiel and read his plan? Had Elzier spilled the beans? Or the postmaster? It was easy to picture that small-town gossip bragging about his new business account to anyone who'd listen. Dyachenko could have put it together from there, matching the big new bank account with that American at the bonspiel.

Frank's plan now seemed as useless as a leaky umbrella. It was such a cliché—yet another Irishman begging for luck on St. Patrick's Day. Sure, his forecast had been correct, and he had a trunkful of cash to show for it. But closings either went smoothly or they didn't. And he'd had one giant setback already. Would these men really take their cash, wish him well, and be on their way? He was the witness in the green car and knew about their operations in Chicago, Moose Jaw, and the border, too. No, they were button men—killers for hire—and he was a loose end.

The closer Will got to the drop site the more Frank's trepidation grew. A litany of enemies paraded through his mind—federal agents, impulsive gangsters, and creepy Yuri Dyachenko. Even Cruithne, his imaginary king, took a turn on stage.

When they finally pulled up to the border, they were ten minutes late. It was collection day, and the gangsters had brought reinforcements—a convoy of eight black cars, waxed and gleaming, their chrome flourishes glinting in the afternoon sun. Frank and Will opened the doors of the Buick and moved cautiously toward the trunk. Without warning, Yuri Dyachenko's royal-blue pickup careened to a stop, spitting distance away. Dyachenko sprang from his truck and rushed toward the fleet of big black cars with the urgency of a firefighter arriving at an inferno.

"Stop!" Dyachenko shrieked. "I'm from the Saskatchewan Wheat Pool. This man"—Dyachenko was gesticulating wildly at him—"is Frank Cork. He's a crook."

So much for his months of work cultivating his Jimmie Gawdini alibi; Dyachenko had blown his cover in two seconds flat. But Yuri Dyachenko's hysteria was as useless as a curling rink in summer. These men couldn't care less if Frank was a crook. They liked crooks. They were crooks.

Instead, Wally Whacker fixed his gun on Dyachenko and barked a verbal warning: "Back off muthafucka."

Will unloaded the whisky without a flinch, and Frank weighed his choices. To the north, Yuri Dyachenko was screaming frantically, wielding the might of the biggest wheat pool in the world. To the south, Wally Whacker stood waiting with a convoy of bullet-proof cars and menacing men. Which direction to choose?

Frank reached into the trunk, hauled out the bulging gunny sacks, and took one large step south. Smiling wanly, he handed his client the cash.

Shorty gauged the cargo like a man who knew what a wad of money weighed. The full set of matching men poured out of their convoy and backed up Whacker while Shorty counted the cash, sack by sack. One thousand, two thousand, three. Time stood still. Then Shorty gave the nod.

The deal was done.

WITH HIS LEGS FEELING LIKE a couple of wet noodles, Frank made his way to the Buick. The engine was running, and the vehicle was pointed north. Frank jumped in, and as the car lurched forward, he swiveled his head for a final look at the drop. Yuri Dyachenko was fearlessly holding his ground: righteousness was his sword, and indignation his shield. Wally Whacker, who could smell a victim a mile away, opened fire. The rhythmic crackling of the mobster's gun never missed a beat, even as he leaped onto the sideboard of the Hup and his driver sped away. Yuri Dyachenko flew skyward, then landed spread-eagled in the dirt. Whacker had killed him, perhaps for no greater reason than he could. The convoy fell into line, slithering away from the crime scene like a snake in the grass.

Frank hollered, "Wait!" and Will jimmied the Buick into reverse. Back they crept until the rear of Will's car was almost touching Dyachenko's shot-up truck. Frank bent over the body. Yuri Dyachenko was dead, a single bullet to the head. Frank crossed himself and whispered a quick Hail Mary. He wanted to say something in Polish, hoping that the Slavic sounds might bring some comfort to Yuri Dyachenko's soul, but the only words he could remember were insults. *Dupek* and *glupek* were his mother's favorite, which meant bonehead and imbecile if you were being polite. While he was down there on his knees, he bid a silent farewell to Jimmie Gawdini, who died alongside Yuri Dyachenko on the prairie that day.

Hovering overhead, Will was taking in the scene. They eyed the truck, which was riddled with bullet holes. The pocks in the royal-blue metal tracked down and up, not once but twice—a W. Stepping around to the other side, there it was again. WW. Wally Whacker having a ball.

Will circled around the corpse, looked up to take stock of the sun's position in the sky, then declared the body, "Stateside." No one was going to find a slain body on the Canadian side of his whisky run, Will said. The partners pushed the bullet-riddled pickup into America beside Yuri Dyachenko. To Frank's surprise, Will retrieved two cartons of whisky from the Buick and set them in the cab of Dyachenko's truck.

"Just in case anyone wonders what a Wheat Pool functionary was doing at the border," Will announced.

They covered their tracks with prairie dust and snow.

And so, it was settled. Yuri Dyachenko had been killed transporting Canadian whisky into the United States.

43
THE BORDER

Lewis Montgomery arrived at 2 p.m. According to his map, he was in Antler, NWT. It was a simple frontier town with a train station, railway tracks, a post office, and a few stores. The trip had scared the bejesus out of him, and he wished for a moment that he'd taken the train. He would have stared out his window, sipped his bourbon, and settled into his book. But one look at the Cord and the train was forgotten.

Yet something was off. The sign on the station said Gainsborough, SK, not Antler, NWT. He double-checked his map. It looked like the wrong name but the right place—some twenty miles north of Antler, ND. He decided to park the car and check with the station master. He listened patiently as the man passed judgment on the weather and recounted how the town had changed, one name at a time. Finally, Lewis gleaned he was in the right place.

He decided to focus his search on Yuri Dyachenko; the locals were more likely to know the whereabouts of the Wheat Pool executive than the Chicago trader. Besides, Frank would be lying low, probably using another name. The station master directed him to the post office; it wasn't a long walk.

"Great day for a parade," Lewis chimed as he walked in.

The postmaster grumbled, "There are no parades here except on Dominion Day and the Queen's birthday."

The small talk had not gone well. Lewis went straight to his point. "I'm here to meet Yuri Dyachenko of the Saskatchewan Wheat Pool. I see that the hotel is closed. Could you point me to where he is staying?"

"Dyachenko? Yep. He's staying in the wheatfields, inspecting grain elevators or some damn fool thing. I heard he got chased out of one in Wapella."

Interesting as that was, he wasn't getting any closer to finding Dyachenko. He tried flattery instead. "It must be quite the load you carry here, managing the post office and the bank." He pushed out a whistle to show how truly impressed he was.

"You're right. I can hardly—"

"It's so kind of you to tell me where I might find Mr. Dyachenko."

"He was just here."

"How long ago?"

"Ten, maybe fifteen minutes. Never came in. He lurked outside half the morning until Will Howard scared him off. Nicest man in town. As tall as a tree."

As tall as a tree. Where had he heard that line before? "Mr. Dyachenko left in his truck?" It was a guess.

"Oh, you've seen it. It's hard to miss a blue pickup like that."

"And Mr. Howard? He was alone?"

"No, no. He was with Mr. Gordon—my client, James Gordon. Sadly, the man just cleared out his entire account. The most money I've ever seen. They went off together in Will's old Buick. Toward the border, no doubt."

Lewis said nothing. The postmaster was a man who couldn't let silence hang in the air.

"If you're going by Manitoba," the postmaster added, "be careful. They move their clocks around over there." Lewis headed for the door, and the postmaster bellowed, "Come back and open an account with us real soon."

Walking to the Cord through the slush and sludge, Lewis remembered who'd said it. Pinzolo. "Frank has a partner, a bootlegger, as tall as a tree."

A clear picture was emerging. Frank had opened a business bank account and found a way to fill it with the most money the Gainsborough postmaster had ever seen. According to Pinzolo, the money came from whisky sales, but Lewis thought it was more likely from operating a bucket shop. Either way, Frank was using an assumed name, James Gordon, and had a tall partner who now had a name. Will Howard, the postmaster had said. The two men were in an old Buick with a trunk full of cash, heading to the border via Manitoba, where the time was an hour ahead. And Yuri Dyachenko was giving chase in a snazzy, blue pickup. There was no time to lose.

Lewis knew the route to the border: he'd just driven from there. East toward Manitoba, a right turn on the 256 South, then a dozen miles due south. He was almost there when he spotted a decrepit black vehicle coming his way. Just off the road was a fancy blue pickup blasted full of holes. On the ground lay a man in a pool of blood. A corpse. He yanked on the steering wheel and slammed on the brakes. The Cord's gearbox complained loudly as it screeched to a stop, inches from the black car. It was a Buick. In the passenger seat sat Frank.

44
ST. PATRICK

Will was startled, to say the least. The gentle giant had narrowly escaped a barrage of bullets, inspected a stiff, and rearranged a crime scene. Now, he was being sideswiped by a remarkable red roadster, the likes of which he had never seen before.

Frank's first instinct was to leap out of the Buick and throw his arms around his protégé. But that could wait. From the moment he'd arrived on the Prairies, there had been one constant in his life—Will. The man had opened his home and heart to him. Yet here he was, leaving him with a corpse, a shot-up pickup truck, and a pack of lies. He owed the man some courtesies.

A game of musical chairs got underway. Will went straight for the Cord, Lewis stepped out to shake hands with Will, and Rosie leaped into the Buick, pinning Frank inside.

"Nice to meet you, Mr. Howard," Lewis said, beaming. "They told me at the post office that I might run into you on the 256 South. Nice-looking Buick you've got there."

"That's a mighty fine roadster you've got yourself, son," Will said, reaching for his pouch and inserting a wad. "I'm not sure I've seen one quite like that before." It was late afternoon, and the western sky, streaked with pinks and oranges, was changing the color of the Cord from burgundy to pinot noir.

"It's a Cord, sir. The 1930 two-seater L-29," Lewis said. "She's got a third gear and performs best at high speed. She's a bit petulant in second." He propelled himself around the car, grinning and gesturing as if he'd missed his calling as a used-car salesman. "You gotta love this," he said, pointing to the dash. "A built-in radio, right at your fingertips. You won't miss Frank's company one bit." He opened the driver's door and invited Will to get in.

Will couldn't have cared less about the radio but was delighted by the legroom.

"Take her for a spin," Lewis said. "A looker like this doesn't come along every day."

When Will took off in the Cord, Lewis slid into the Buick beside Frank as if it were the most natural thing in the world to be in a beat-up Buick with his boss on the 256 South. They traded boyish smacks, playful punches, and broad-beamed grins. Lewis kicked things into gear. "We only have a few minutes. The BOI has been on my tail since Chicago. A couple of agents are likely to be showing up any minute. There's a lot to cover. Let's get started. First, the stiff. Take it or leave it?"

"Leave it."

"Dyachenko, I presume?"

"Check."

"Second, the money. I assume that your time here, and this mess"—Lewis's sweeping gesture captured both the corpse and the truck—"was about money. Have you got what you came for?"

"Got it," Frank said. It was not the time to protest that his time on the Prairies had been about a lot more than money.

"Third, your partner, Will. Time to say goodbye?"

"Yup."

"Anything else?"

"Nope."

The Cord was back in sight, and not a moment too soon.

"By the way, am I supposed to call you James Gordon in front of your partner?"

"No, call me Frank."

Will pulled up beside the Buick, grinning like an oversized kid. Lewis got in beside him in the front seat of the Cord. "How'd you enjoy the drive?"

"Her front end's a bit bossy. And she's skittish when you shift gears."

Lewis was impressed. The car's flaws had eluded E.L. Cord and his world-class engineers, yet Will Howard had diagnosed them in five minutes flat.

"There's nothing that a twitch to the ears can't fix. Overall, she's a real treat. Thank you for letting me drive her, Son."

"Mr. Howard...may I call you Will?"

"Certainly, Son."

"Will, I propose you and I take a quick minute to settle our business. As soon as we're done, Frank and I will be on our way. No good can come from hanging around here any longer than required. Does that fit with your plans, sir?"

"Yes, Son. That'll be fine."

"First, the deceased. Do you need any help with the body?"

"No. We've done nothing wrong here. I was out for a ride with my author friend—" An

author? Lewis hid his surprise at that, "—when this fellow passes us at high speed in his fancy blue truck. By the time we arrived, the man was laid out on the ground. Shot. Frank and I never saw a thing. We checked his pulse—he was dead—and looked in the truck. Based on the whisky bottles in the back, it looked to me like the man was in the business of running rum."

Lewis guessed that Will had used his time in the Cord to great effect. He'd not only road-tested the car but the facts. Lewis nodded. Without anyone saying more, their story was set.

"Don't you worry, Son," Will added. "Everything'll be fine. The police sergeant in these parts is a friend of mine."

"Second, money." After his long and uncertain drive, Lewis was feeling as focused as a hound who'd finally caught the scent of the fox. "I assume Frank owes you a buck or two for incidentals," he said, opening the Cord's glove box. Will flinched when he saw the .38 caliber pistol. But Lewis reached past it for his billfold and handed Will his second twenty. He figured it was probably more than Will made in a month. "Does this cover everything that might be owing?"

"Yes, Son, it does."

Frank stepped up to the Cord and inserted himself into the closing remarks. "I'm all squared up with Elzier," he told Will, "but I left two gifts, one for each family. They're under Laura-Jean's blanket—I mean the Hudson Bay blanket—on my bed. You'll be glad to have it back, and please pass on my thanks again. I hope you find your gift sufficient. It's meant to cover the cost of replacing your shed...and more.

"Laura-Jean will appreciate that. And the rest of us, too."

"We seem to be done here," Lewis said, wrapping it up.

"One last thing," Frank added. "The Buick's getting mighty tired. She's a 1911, as I recall. Would you like to keep the Cord?" It was the least he could do: the man had saved his life.

"You betcha," Will said.

Lewis was shocked by Frank's offer but readied the cars for the exchange. From the Cord, he took his billfold, leaving the gun. "It came with the car. They're a matched set," he said. Then he looked in the cargo space of the Buick to check for anything belonging to Will. Before Frank could intervene, Lewis was staring at sacks of cash.

"This car trade is looking fairer for you by the minute," Lewis said. "Will gets the Cord, and you get the Buick and the cash."

Frank grinned. The kid cottoned on fast.

Lewis took the seat behind the wheel and put the old clunker into gear as Frank and Will said their awkward goodbyes.

"Let's drive through the night," Frank said. "It's time to get home to Katrina and the kids."

It may have been the fatigue from his cross-country adventure, or it may have been the way Katrina's name had dripped from Frank's lips with yearning and desire, but Lewis snapped: "It's time? Are you kidding me?"

PART THREE

THE WIZARD OF WHEAT

One day, in retrospect, the years of struggle will strike you as the most beautiful.
SIGMUND FREUD

45
THE BUICK

Frank had never seen Lewis like this.

"You didn't even have the decency to call me," Lewis howled, "let alone your wife. You've been away five months, and now you want to drive all night?"

The Buick was as out of control as Lewis.

"Stop the car," Frank yelled. "I didn't spend the entire winter holed up in a shed to end up dead in a ditch on my way home."

But the Buick showed no signs of slowing, and Lewis almost bawled: "We thought you were dead. Did you consider what that was like for her? Did you even think about Katrina?"

It was primal the way Lewis hurled his wife's name at him. A mother bear standing over its wounded cub couldn't have conveyed more anger or pain. He glanced sideways. Lewis's hands were shaking on the wheel. With every ounce of authority he could muster, Frank tried again: "STOP THIS CAR NOW."

It worked. Lewis pulled over, got out, and stomped to the passenger side. Frank took the helm, and stone-cold silence settled over the car. They gained an hour when they crossed the border from Manitoba into North Dakota and were in Fargo by sundown. All the way to Minneapolis, jealousy raged through Frank's body like the flames that had devoured the Howards' shed. The green-eyed monster had taken hold. His mouth became rigid, his spine stiff, and his white knuckles gripped the wheel. What had passed between them, his wife and this well-built Lothario beside him? Was the crush one-way, or did his wife feel the same about Lewis? How had he stayed away so long? Would she even take him back?

Frank had to admit that in his made-to-measure suit with a trunk full of cash, he must look to Lewis the same as the day he'd left. The kid knew nothing about his months of hardship to save his family from financial ruin—the lonely nights, worn-out boots, drafty sheds, and numbing cold. But as invisible as it might be to others, Frank knew he'd grown; he'd confronted his worst fears and survived.

By the time they reached Milwaukee, Frank had acknowledged that his intern, too, had grown. He'd grown from a boy to a man. Admittedly, he'd hardly thought about Lewis these past months. Yet, who had been fielding his phone calls, stick-handling his clients, and running circles around Mr. D? And the kid had made a two-thousand-mile road trip, punctuated by a corpse. He owed Lewis a great debt.

WHEN ROAD SIGNS FOR CHICAGO appeared on the horizon, Frank broke the silence. He was going home to Katrina, and Lewis was not. Whatever had passed between his wife and his intern was over. It had been a moment in time, a calamity, yet another fallout from the Crash. He had done what was required of him as a husband and father, even if no one else understood. And Lewis? All the boy deserved was unfettered praise.

"It's been quite the trip," Frank said.

Lewis turned his head sideways to look at him, his face softening with relief. "Thanks for doing the driving," Lewis said.

Lewis told Frank about Teddy Roosevelt's famous speech at the Waldorf in Fargo, and Frank confessed he'd been thinking about helping the man's cousin, Franklin Roosevelt, who was rumored to be running for president in '32. "It would be my first time working for a Democrat," Frank said. "I learned many things during my time on the Prairies, but one was that governments can play an important role in people's lives during calamitous economic times."

Lewis pretended to be taken aback by the radical ideas his boss had acquired in Canada. "Given your new political bent, it sounds like you might want to give up your head trader role and hand it over to me," Lewis teased him like old times. "Will I see you in the office this aft?"

"Gimme a day. And take one for yourself, too. It's on me." They both let down their guard and smiled, almost laughed, as Frank pulled up in front of the young man's flat. It was morning, and newspaper hawkers and fruit vendors were readying their wares for the day. Lewis patted Rosie goodbye, and then the head trader and his intern exited the Buick and stood together on the sidewalk.

The last thing Frank wanted was another round of awkward goodbyes. "Some things," he proffered, "are better left unsaid. My problem is that I always realize it too late. I'm sorry if I've hurt you in any way." He put his hand on Lewis's shoulder, then threw his arms around him in a heartfelt embrace. "Thank you. For everything."

"It's good to have you back, sir," Lewis said to Frank. It was not the time to tell him about Hector.

WHEN FRANK PULLED INTO THE driveway of his home, the first thing he noticed was the "Foreclosed" sign jammed into his lawn. The single word stared at him in bold print above the snow. Katrina opened the front door for a look at the black jalopy parked out front. For the love of God, how had he ever left? Her hair was in long, loose curls, still wet from the shower, and he could almost smell the scent of her fresh shampoo.

Time stopped. They were locked in their places, Frank and Katrina, each taking the other in. What would come next? She advanced toward him in a winter jacket over her robe and slippers, her face moving from shock to disbelief, then anger. He stepped out of the car and reached to touch her; she recoiled as if he were a snake lashing out at her from behind a rock.

He followed her inside. The foyer was full of boxes, and his family in the throes of a move. In the kitchen, he saw her easel in the corner, laden with sketches and paint. He reached for her—he couldn't resist—but she rebuffed him again.

The clean, modern setting made him conscious that he'd been in the closed-body Buick for hours on end; he probably smelled like Will. And not so many hours ago, he'd been kneeling over a bloodied corpse. Heading upstairs, he briefly wondered if his personal things had been hurled out the door. Relieved to find things pretty much as he'd left them, he soaked up his first hot shower in months. Wrapped in his white terry-towel robe, he ventured back downstairs. But still, there was no embrace. Whether he was dirty or clean was clearly of no consequence to Katrina.

He returned to their bedroom and pulled on some weekend clothes—he'd forgotten how the luxurious velvet slippers felt. And talking about luxury, his study felt like Heaven itself. He felt a need to touch his things—the framed photos of his family, his favorite books, and the one he was reading when he'd left, still lying open on his desk. It must have been difficult for her to have left this room untouched. Had she expected him back? Or been too angry or distraught to even enter his space.

He settled into his high back chair and tended to some long-overdue chores—most of which required writing some very large checks. By late afternoon, Franny and Robbie arrived home and threw themselves into his open arms. My God, how they'd changed in five months. He lined them up against the doorframe in his study, and while they stood on tippytoes, he memorialized their new heights with a pencil. Minutes later, they were scurrying outside to play with Rosie in the yard. Had they even missed him? Or noticed that he'd been gone? Whatever the answer, the fault lay entirely with him. Over the past months, he had spent more time playing with other families' children than he'd ever spent with his own.

On the Prairies, he had charmed the Howard and Duret children with his made-up stories. He had trapped gophers and played cowboys with them in the yard and found fresh eggs with them in the hen house. He'd washed up their dishes, filled up their buckets at the pump, and watched them dance. He had done none of those things with Franny and Robbie—not even once. He vowed to do better now that he was home.

In the kitchen, Katrina set up dinner for the children, then poured whisky fizzes in the living room. It was a sure sign of a thaw. The maid had been cut with the budget, and they took turns tucking the children into bed. Their evening was spent speaking of practical things: no, they wouldn't be moving; yes, he'd unpack every box himself; and yes, he was here to stay. The tension in her face lifted, and the life returned to her eyes. They made decisions on other practicalities, too. The children would stay at their new public school for now, and Frank would arrange for some repairs to the Buick and give it to Lewis. The young man deserved a car.

By the time Katrina announced she was heading for bed, Frank understood that restoring their relationship and rebuilding trust would be a complicated thing. She'd avoided his touch, his yearning looks, and all talk of his time away. When he eyed the set of sheets she'd placed on the couch, he acquiesced. For almost five months, he'd searched for a path back to Katrina. Now, it would take time to find a way forward together.

IN THE MORNING, HE WANDERED into the kitchen in his robe. He'd slept in. The kids had left for school, and Katrina was sipping coffee and reading the Tribune. The paperboy had dropped one off even though the subscription must have expired months ago. He added the chore to his list, topped up their mugs, and sat down across from his wife.

"You never even called," she almost spat.

"I would welcome an opportunity to explain my decisions. I'm not sure I fully understand them myself, but I'd like to try."

He took her silence as a yes. "In the first days after the Crash, I was in shock. It's as if the market crashed, and I did too. We lost everything, Katrina. And not just that, I was in trouble on other fronts, too. You may find it hard to believe—and I take responsibility for that—but the one true thing I can say is that everything I did was for you. To save our family and our home, to keep you safe, and to get back to you. I will tell you anything you want to know. But for now—"

"For now?" she snapped, her emotions at the fore. He saw anger, hurt, and relief cross her face in a flash until she dropped her head and cried. He surprised them both when he wept too—deeply, loudly, with blubbering gasps and animal sounds. The last time he'd wept was with Will, in the Buick, for the Howards' stillborn son. The thought of it made him cry harder still. Could she ever forgive him? Had he lost her, too?

Katrina reached across the table to take his hand. The shadow of her cleavage beckoned like a stretch of highway to a distant place where he desperately wanted to go. He imagined her breasts swelling under her robe, the areolae darkening, the nipples growing erect and engorged. The children were playing in the yard, not far from the kitchen window. He took her hand, leading her down the hall and guiding her into his study—a place once as verboten to her as her easel was to him.

He shut the door, covering the fresh markings he'd made of the children, and embraced her as if he would never let go again. He pressed his lips to her mouth and kissed her, roving her down her neck to her collarbone as she kissed him back and entwined her fingers in his hair. Wedged between his desk and the fire, they clung to each other until the warmth overtook them and every stitch of their clothing lay on the floor.

"I will never leave you again," he whispered urgently, passionately.

They tumbled onto the pile of silk robes and plush slippers, and five months of fear and anxiety erupted in front of the fire.

46
GLENCOE

Throughout his first full day home, Frank didn't venture further than the bank. And in the stillness of their bed that night, he told Katrina in hushed tones about his time away. His story began with Yuri Dyachenko.

"Sometimes I despised that little man," he said, "but I never intended for him to end up dead."

"Dead?" Katrina inhaled sharply.

"He used me. He was investigating me for transgressions against a country I'd never so much as visited at the time. He treated me like some pawn in a cross-border trade dispute—threatening my industry and our livelihood. Lewis helped me develop a plan to shut Dyachenko down."

"Lewis?"

He was taken aback by the way she repeated his name. Or was it her tone? Had she sounded too personal, as if he, Lewis, were her close friend—or her lover? Or had she simply been shocked that her husband's intern knew all this when she had not? They both let it dangle, and she moved back to Dyachenko.

"How did the Russian guy end up dead?"

"He wasn't Russian. He was Canadian with Ukrainian roots. It was a mob hit."

She gasped.

He rolled toward her and made an effort to kiss her, but she would not be deterred mid-story.

"Markets need men like Yuri Dyachenko to rail against the excesses of capitalism," he said with a sigh. "But the poor bastard had a half-crazed belief that it was his God-given role to mete out punishment on anyone who thrived. He died fighting for his cause. He was a martyr, if only in his own mind's eye."

"Are you a suspect?" Katrina asked. For murder?"

"The police are looking into it—the Bureau of Investigation because it's a cross-border thing. They will be banging on my office door the minute they hear I'm back. Listen, I did not kill Yuri Dyachenko or anyone else, but I made a lot of mistakes."

He kissed her, then smiled. "Now that I'm home, I promise that I'll only make better mistakes."

She rolled her eyes as if to say she wasn't going to be waylaid by one of his smart-ass quips. "Who killed him?" she asked, still fixated on the murder.

"My client, Wally Whacker."

"You have a client named Wally Whacker!"

"Yes, he's one of the mobsters—"

"Your clients were mobsters?"

"Whacker killed Dyachenko with a single bullet to the head while I stood a stone's throw away," he said. Saying it aloud brought those terrifying moments rushing back.

Katrina went silent, tabulating for the first time the risks he'd taken to insulate their family from the Crash. "I was so worried, Frank. I kept having this nightmare of you...wading into Lake Michigan on the night of the Crash. I stood on the shore...I was calling your name and watching as you... were pulled further and further from shore. You were trying so hard...but you couldn't make it back." She got out the last part, then burst into tears.

"I'm here, sweetheart," he said, caressing her back.

"You are. But you weren't...for five long months, Frank. And while you were busy fleeing mobsters, I was alone, caring for our children through every possible stress. You had an epic adventure, but I paid the price. History casts the lives of women and children in the shadows of men, but I promise you this, Frank Cork, that was the last time I will pull the blinds and wait by the window for you like some pitiable operatic wench."

He caressed her back and thought she must be imagining herself as Puccini's Floria from Tosca, who stabs Scarpia to death then hurls herself off the castle's parapets. He'd come to know the opera surprisingly well on the Howard farm.

"I understand," he said.

"I won't lie to you: I found my own ways of coping. And I plan to make some better mistakes myself over the coming months."

He felt her body relax as if she'd finally let go of the tension she'd been carrying for months. She draped her arm across his chest, wrapped her leg around his thigh, and drew their faces together in a web of warm breath. Their passion had never burned hotter or brighter.

THE NEXT DAY, FRANK VISITED his mother at Chicago State. Her sanity had all but disappeared while he was gone. There were moments of lucidity and recognition, but mostly, she didn't seem to know him at all. When he left, he decided to search for his father. It was time to determine whether Conor Cork was even alive. He walked for hours around the familiar streets of South Side and made inquiries at the bars. If he was alive, he was nowhere to be found. Both of them, his father and his mother, were essentially lost.

LATE THAT AFTERNOON, GRIEVING HIS losses in the wing chair in his study, he imagined Laura-Jean sitting in her rocker on the Howard farm. That was who he really missed—Will, Laura-Jean, the children, even Queenie the cow. He would write a letter to Laura-Jean.

He moved to his desk but found the surface too sleek and his page too clean. He looked out the window for inspiration but missed the long line where the wheatfields meet the sky. He dug through the small sack of his Saskatchewan things and retrieved his scribbler—the smell of whisky and cedar rose from the page. Using Willard's stolid pencil, the words began to fly.

He began with an apology for leaving so abruptly without saying goodbye. He had much to learn about working through hardships, he wrote. He thanked Laura-Jean for listening to his stories when his pretenses of being an author had clearly been lies. He also thanked her for encouraging him to let his mind explore the great beyond like Gip the Backward Pig and Magpie, his barnyard friend. He ended his letter with a proposal. Forecasting the price of wheat required many insights from multiple sources. Would she be willing to share her findings for a regular fee? After all, he wrote, she had a view of the wheatfields from her window, she listened to the grain news every day, and she could report on whether the drought was getting better or worse as she walked in her yard.

It would take weeks, if not months, for his letter to arrive in Gainsborough and for him to receive her reply. Still, he poked at the fire and imagined what it might say. She would start, he guessed, by telling him she was at her kitchen table, that the sun was out, and the winter wheat was beginning to head. She would tell him that Will had decided to keep the Cord—there were not a lot of buyers in Gainsborough these days. Then, she would update him on the sergeant's findings that Yuri Dyachenko's corpse was on the US side, the whisky was contraband, and the cause of death was a territorial dispute with the mob. She would comment that not even the undertaker was sorry to see the man go: his death, like his life, was a cautionary tale.

He felt certain she would add a note about Will's clients and how he continues to tell them Jimmie Gawdini thinks the futures market will be too risky for many years. Then, she would accept his retainer and tuck in some clippings from the Regina Leader-Post. One might report that the new US tariffs on agricultural exports from Canada were devastating wheat farmers and would soon destroy the Pool. She might let it slip that she and Will would be voting with other western farmers in favor of retaliatory tariffs and throwing William Lyon Mackenzie King out of office. Frank would remind himself that she meant the Canadian prime minister and not Elzier's horse.

Her letter would be everything he'd hoped for; he would write back, tuck in a money order, and fleetingly wish he was in the Howard kitchen with the radio on, eating warm cobbler with a dollop of Queenie's cream.

THAT EVENING AFTER DINNER, KATRINA asked about the letter she'd found on the kitchen counter addressed to—was it Lorna? Or Laura? And why he was writing to her the moment he was back.

Frank spoke for quite a long time about Laura-Jean. Katrina listened intently, and when he was done, she said: "I am grateful to this stranger for housing my husband during a difficult time. However, I resent how someone with a husband and family of her own hid you away for so long without so much as a thought about the consequences for me. And now, here you are, barely through the front door and corresponding with this...this Lorna-Jean."

"Yes, it is an unconventional friendship," he said, looking away and feeling a bit sheepish. "However, I assure you it is no threat to our marriage."

Katrina did not reply.

IN BED THAT NIGHT, WHEN he was almost asleep, Katrina tapped his shoulder and said, "I'm sorry for being cross about your friend. I'll try to be more understanding."

Then she turned away and whispered in the dark, "I, too, developed a special friendship while you were away."

She paused and lowered her voice until he barely heard it.

"With Lewis," she said.

47
THE BUREAU

Frank's second morning at home started with a hot shower, a clean shave, real coffee, and the Tribune. When Katrina slipped his cufflinks into place, he felt for a moment that he'd never been away. He remastered the demands of a buckle belt, and the skin on his neck was healing for the first time in months. The drive downtown with Rosie in the Hudson was as smooth as an Old Fitz. And there was Hector at the parking garage, welcoming back the only two-tone Hudson in town.

He owed money to the Soo Line for his train fare dating back to the day of the Crash. Retracing his steps to Grand Central Station, he took stock of how crazed he had been. But he'd not been the only one, and promised to give himself some slack. He handed the fare to the manager, "Sorry, sir, it's five months overdue."

He couldn't wait to resume his daily visits with Bobby, but what he had to say to his friend merited a longer visit than their morning splash. Upstairs, Dorothea greeted him as if it were any other day. He popped into the offices of partners and associates, casually saying hello. Everyone registered abject shock as if he'd risen from the dead, then broke into smiles. The word spread quickly: Frank was back.

As for Mr. D, the man can come looking for me, he thought. He stepped into his office and looked about. It was the size that struck him most, as big as the Howards' house. But something was different: it smelled like Lewis.

He called Katrina simply because he could. Wait, what was that greasy atrocity on his couch? Had Lewis been entertaining after-hours? He put down the receiver and cautiously approached the stain. When Frank looked up, a figure in a punched-in hat and oversized trench coat was standing at his door. The man was a dead-ringer for Shorty, but bigger. Here he was in his own office, as anxious as he'd been in the Moose Jaw tunnel when the door slammed shut.

"Special Agent Joe Pinzolo," the man said, sinking into Frank's couch. The mystery of the stain was solved.

"I'll take your things," Frank insisted, but the agent didn't budge. He called Dorothea. "Come get the agent's coat and hat and hang them at reception, please."

"Don't trouble yourself," Pinzolo said, waving him off.

"I see you've been here before," Frank said, gesturing at his couch. The agent had won their first showdown, but Frank vowed to win the next. "What can I do for you?" he asked, still standing.

"I wanted to be among the first to welcome you home," Pinzolo said. "Maybe even share a glass of that fine Canadian whisky you've been illegally selling into the United States."

His mind raced: Who was the snitch? If it were Whacker, he'd have drawn the line at killing anyone, and Dyachenko would still be alive. And it certainly wasn't Will, whose life depended on this work. My God, it must have been Shorty. He could see it clearly now: Shorty was the pied piper who'd lured the rats to the river to drown.

Dorothea rapped at the door.

"Thank you, Dorothea, but Special Agent Pinzolo will be leaving shortly. Please call me in fifteen minutes when my appointment arrives."

Frank turned back to the agent. "You're mistaken, sir. I have never sold liquor in America. Any liquor I consumed or handled in any way was in Canada, as the laws of that country allow. Will that be all?"

"You made a lot of back and forths to the border with a trunk full of liquor for a man who's not in sales," Pinzolo said.

"Asked and answered," Frank said.

"We both know you were on the Canadian Prairies to pay down your trading account."

"I specialize in wheat-related securities. Last fall, wheat suffered its worst price drop in the history of the grain. Except for a few days when the Farm Board intervened, there has been no rebound. I've chosen to spend some time with growers, trying to understand the problem and possible paths back for my industry and clients."

"Cleaning mobsters' money, you mean."

"Feel free to call my clients what you may. They are investors, not soulmates."

"Ha. That was no soulmate you left dead beside the road. Did you see him take the bullet to the head?"

"No. I had left my meeting and was traveling home."

"Did you see your clients draw their guns?"

"No, the guns were drawn when I arrived. It's not how we do business here at the firm. But it was North Dakota, sir. Each to their own."

"How many shots were fired?"

An image of Wally Whacker's initials sprawled across Dyachenko's pickup truck popped into his mind. "I don't know. I didn't count," he said.

"Were you in possession of a gun?"

"No."

"Yet we found a gun in the glove compartment of the Cord."

Poor Will, having to contend with federal agents snooping through his new car. "I do not own the Cord and have never been in the Cord."

"And why was the deceased at this meeting between you and your clients?"

"I didn't invite him. I assume he had business of his own."

"Who is he?"

"I don't know the man. I met him twice—at a curling bonspiel and at the Gainsborough post office."

"Mr. Cork, you're blowing smoke," Pinzolo said, taking a long haul on his cigar.

Frank thought the visual effects meant the agent must be hard-pressed, resorting to cheap tricks. But Pinzolo came back with a new line of attack. "Did your friend Will Howard know the deceased?"

"Will Howard is a retired police officer. Ask him yourself whether he knew the deceased."

"What time was the shooting?"

"It was 3:25 p.m. in North Dakota and Manitoba and 2:25 in Saskatchewan." He watched the federal agent start writing it up, pause, then strike it out, confused. Will was right. Changing the clocks was befuddling to not only the cows but a cop. It was time to show Pinzolo the door.

He looked pointedly at his clock, picked up his daybook as if a meeting beckoned, and the buzzer shrieked. "Your next appointment is here," Dorothea said. God, she was good.

"I'm sorry I can't be of any help," he said, moving toward the door. Then he paused and looked his guest squarely in the eye. "I'm a forecaster, Agent Pinzolo. Like federal agents, we search in the corners for clues that others don't see. But sometimes, it behooves us to admit that there is nothing there." He reached for the special agent's hand, but Pinzolo didn't budge from the couch.

"Funny you should say that because I don't think we're one ounce alike," Pinzolo said. "What I find interesting is that your wife cottoned on to your intern before she'd had time to change the bedsheets after you left. And Mr. D, too, was more interested in finding you dead than alive." The agent stood and showed himself out.

Frank had pledged to be a better person when he got home, but Pinzolo could put any man to the test.

48
MR. C

It was turning into a busy first morning back. Agent Pinzolo had scarcely left Frank's office when Lewis showed up.

"C'mon in," Frank said as if Lewis were the one who'd been away.

Lewis was all business. "Here's your daily briefing binder, sir. After a short-term rally last week, wheat is at an all-time low."

Frank skimmed the page. The Farm Board intervention had driven the price up for only six precious days. He'd been lucky, alright. If he'd set his closing date a week earlier or later, his deal would have failed. He'd be gasping for his last breath in the trunk of the Hup instead of cuddling with Katrina at home. Frank looked up. "I suppose the word has gone around that I'm back. What are you hearing?"

"The office is abuzz," Lewis dodged the question.

"Good or bad?" Frank insisted.

"I'm hearing that you were on the Prairies assessing the long-term prospects for wheat. Miraculously, you managed to make money while the entire industry was surviving on fumes. You've paid off your trading account and are back in the game. In your spare time, you stared down the mayor and staved off an investigation that could have destroyed us all. Your status has never been higher."

"I should get away more often."

Lewis cast his eyes around the room. "Sorry about your couch, sir."

"Not to worry. I'll have it cleaned. I don't think Agent Pinzolo will be back anytime soon."

Frank moved toward his intern and gripped his hand. "Thank you, Lewis, for everything you've done. I will never understand the half of it, I'm sure. But let's turn to the matters at hand. First—you. Have you settled back in on the eighth?"

"Yes, sir. I'm looking forward to getting back to work."

"You've certainly earned a position in this firm. You'll be upstairs among the partners soon enough," Frank said. "Second, the Cord. You owe Mr. D a car and a set of keys. He won't want the Buick, and the Cord is staying in Saskatchewan. Tell him it's a limp-geared machine that wasn't fit to drive. If he protests, remind him that he got his top intern and head trader back but no car. Besides, he never paid a cent for the Cord. If you have any difficulty, let me know. I suspect there might be a few speeding tickets to pay." They both cracked a smile.

"I'll cover those," Frank said and returned to his list. "Third, insurance. Did that come up?"

"There's a copy of the Key Man policy in your top drawer, sir."

"Interesting. Who knows about it?"

"Everyone."

"How did you learn about it?"

"I asked myself why Mr. D had assigned me, the lowly intern, to find the firm's top trader. Did he really want you back? I wondered if there might be other financial stakes in play. So, I asked Ricco for copies of any insurance, and sure enough, there was a policy I practically needed a wheelbarrow to carry down the hall. That was the good news. The bad news was that I chased my tail in circles for months while Mr. D stealthily filed his claim."

Frank nodded as if to say it was hardly a surprise. "And Pinzolo?"

"The agent had a theory a day. According to Pinzolo, Mr. D became fixated on the insurance money and would stop at nothing to get it. At one point, Pinzolo had even convinced himself that Mr. D had hired a hitman to knock you off. The agent has a vivid imagination and a knack for seeing the worst in all of us. Maybe that goes with being a cop. We market men are optimists: we wake up every morning thinking today's the day the bear will become a bull."

It felt good to be back. He'd missed the shop talk. And for a flash, he almost felt sorry for Mr. D. The man had gone to great lengths to save the firm. Wouldn't he have done the same? "What happened next?" he asked Lewis.

"Like all of Pinzolo's theories, it went up in smoke. How could anyone have killed you when you weren't even dead? Pinzolo was the first to uncover that you were alive...other than Bobby, who'd known it all along. Of course, Pinzolo had a whole friggin' crime lab at his disposal and a suite of operatives in the field. The only support I had was your goddam dog."

Lewis stooped to give Rosie a pat, and Frank remembered that the kid had spent five months taking care of Rosie while also driving halfway across the continent and back.

"Looks like she's as much yours as mine. You'll be seeing her at the office. By the way, where was Bobby in all this?" Frank braced for the worst.

"Pinzolo had a vile theory about Bobby, too. He accused Bobby of lining his pockets and telling Mr. D that he'd shut down the investigation in return for a wad of cash. But I knew you'd already shut it down. Besides, the notion that you were driving up wheat prices looked foolish after the Crash: wheat has never been lower."

Lewis firmed up his stance and took a deep breath. "Which brings me to corn, sir. The associates have been feeling it might be a good time to diversify, and corn would be a good place to start. It's been around for seven thousand years and it's not going away. As you know, the Board authorized trading in corn futures some five years ago, and we've never given New York and New Orleans a run for their money. I took some action while you were away. You know Hector Ray. I understand you saw him this morning in the parking garage. He knows a lot about corn, literally from the ground up. He's been helping out these past months and has all the markings of a great trader. He could usher the firm into corn. What do you think?"

"I like it. Let's make it happen."

There was a long pause. They'd covered off their business, assessing the scrapes while avoiding the wounds. They looked at each other tentatively; the time until the morning gong was ticking loudly in both their minds. Would either say more?

It was Lewis who broke the silence. "At some point, everyone in the city seemed to know you were alive—Pinzolo, Bobby, everyone except me and Katrina." Lewis's voice cracked with emotion. "Why, Frank?"

Frank paced. "You said it yourself. I needed some time. I'm not sure there's anything more I can add. Speaking of which,"—he glanced at his watch—"time's up." With his hand on the small of Lewis's back, Frank guided his intern out the door. Opening up at home with Katrina was one thing, but getting weepy at the office with Lewis was another. Besides, there was unfinished business between them. Katrina's soft words—I came to care about Lewis—were seared into his head.

In the corridor, Frank called over his shoulder, "Oh, I almost forgot." Then he turned and looked Lewis right in the eye. "How's Dorothea?"

Lewis flinched. They both understood that Frank's question wasn't really about Duttons' receptionist. In fact, it wasn't a question at all. It was a declaration that Lewis's journey to the ninth floor had come to an end. His trips to Frank's home and any feelings he'd harbored for Katrina were behind them.

"I still have some wild oats to sow, sir," Lewis said, and they set off on their rounds.

BY 10 A.M., FRANK AND Lewis were in the pit. The room looked more like a tomb than a trading floor. Frank greeted old friends and watched the trades as they were posted on the board. Tomorrow, he'd reach out to clients. Today, there were other matters to tend to.

By noon, Frank was upstairs making his first call—to his insurer.

"Welcome back, Mr. Cork," the broker said, as cool as a cucumber. Did the man have a large check made out to Mr. D sitting on his desk? Was it already in the mail?

"I'm calling to let you know I'm back. I've been out of town gathering insights from farmers on wheat markets."

When Frank hung up, he beamed broadly to himself, envisioning the man drawing an X through the middle of the check and marking it VOID.

AFTER WALKING ALONGSIDE WHEATFIELDS AND crossing international borders, Frank found the distance to Mr. D's office very short. He'd bypassed it on this morning's rounds, having decided the man could manage his own orders for one more day. But now, he had other business to take up with Mr. D. There had been no need to rehearse; he knew exactly what he was going to say.

Ricco looked up in shock when Frank Cork extended a hand. The young man's handshake had as much vigor as those flowers—morning glories—that were limp by mid-day. Frank stepped into the office of Mr. D.

"You've had quite the adventure. Lots of borderline behavior, I hear." The managing partner laughed at his own wit, then launched in. "What is it you always like to say—good things come in threes? So, I get a rogue trader, your hotsy-totsy wife, and the Bureau of Investigation. Nice work, Frank."

He'd promised himself that he wouldn't rise to the bait. Yet, how could he leave the affront alone? "I wasn't the only trader to disappear after the Crash. Half the partners in this firm took up residence in the bars along LaSalle Street, and the other half didn't bother coming downtown at all. I cost the firm nothing while I was away. Instead, I visited wheatfields, spoke to growers, and returned a better trader."

"Horsefeathers. You upset clients."

"There were no clients."

"Balderdash. You wasted Lewis's time."

"Are you going to pretend that you care one iota about Lewis? Or any of us? I met strangers on the prairie who cared more about me than you ever did. Did you even look for me? Never mind. We both know the answer to that."

He was getting emotional. Time to rein it in and turn the tables on the double-dealing Mr. D. "We've all had enough of your chicanery. You're part of the old guard of this city, the men who thrive on bare-knuckled power—like the governor and the mayor. It's time for a new generation to usher in the future of this firm. Young people like Lewis. And Hector. Why wouldn't we give a kid like that a chance?"

He stepped closer, cornering Mr. D behind his desk. "You siphon off one-third of every dollar earned by this firm. That's money we'll need to survive as this economy becomes a full-blown Depression."

"Who licked the red off your candy, Frank?"

"There's not enough room for both of us. Here's my offer. Take it or leave it."

"You're making me an offer?" Mr. D was all business now.

"Step aside, and your name stays on the masthead for two years. During that time, you'll get 20 percent of the firm's earnings instead of one-third. But you will not show your face around here, not even once. You will have no office, you will make no decisions, and the money stops in two years. That's option one."

"You're all hat and no cattle, Frank."

"Here's option two. I will leave. I'll take Lewis, Hector, and any partner who prefers to work with us rather than you. We both know how that will shake down. You'll have a new rival down the street, and you'll never get another cent from me or anyone who comes with me."

"That makes about as much sense as tits on a bull." Mr. D was up and pacing now, weighing his options. Frank waited. It was a good offer all around. There were troubled times ahead, and Frank felt ready to lead the firm with the courage and compassion it would require. At the same time, two years of income for doing nothing was a fair transition for Mr. D.

"Perhaps you're right," the managing partner finally said. "It may be time to make way for Frank Cork—make way for

Mr. C. No more riding two to a mule. Put your first option in writing, and I'll give you my answer by the end of this week."

FRANK'S NEXT STOP WAS BOBBY. The last time he'd been in the Board of Trade office, no one would even say hello. This time, the receptionist smiled broadly at him, checked with her boss, and waved him in. He and Bobby shook hands, slapped backs, and grinned.

"You've managed things expertly," Frank said. "The investigation, the insurance monkey business, and revealing Mr. D for the snake that he is."

"That just about sums it up," Bobby said.

"No, there's something else. You kept your promise to me, even under questioning from the BOI. And you watched out for my family. None of that was easy, I'm sure."

"What's next for you, Frank?"

"Mr. D has opted to retire. We'll have the deal firmed up by the end of this week. I'll be taking over. You're a proven manager, Bobby. Me, I'm a trader. This market looks like a hundred miles of lousy road ahead. I'll need someone to get the partners back to work and to help me rebuild this firm."

"I'm listening."

"You'd report to me. I'll set the broad strokes, but otherwise, you get free rein. Bad market or not, your starting salary will be double what you make here, and we'll review it at the end of year three."

"I am confident that we'd work well together, Frank. We always have."

49
THE KINGDOM OF CÉYH

Frank and Katrina ambled along the lakefront, hand in hand. It was late March, and the snow glories were in bloom as blue as the sky. She asked him to tell her more about his time on the Prairies—about the people he'd met and what he'd learned from each. There was a picnic table nearby, and he steered her there.

"Will Howard," he said, "spent his entire life roaming the center of the continent, changing roles as required. He was a card shark, a farmer, a bootlegger, a cab driver, and even a cop. The man was an expert at reimagining himself."

"Is that what you did? Reimagine yourself?"

He reached across the table for her hand. "On LaSalle Street, I learned how to trade, make money, and buy a lot of things. I had a great run. But as my world crashed down around me, I had no skills beyond trading, and I couldn't cope. I had no idea how to save our family from the violent men in this city, let alone from financial ruin."

She looked at him with compassion, nodding and encouraging him to continue.

"James Gordon helped me navigate the world of bucket shops, rural post office accounts, and making money when there wasn't a cent to be found. Jimmie Gawdini taught me how to stare down men who work in tunnels, carry guns, and drive terrifying cars."

"And now? Who are you now?"

"I accept that my choices wreaked havoc on our lives, and I am profoundly sorry for that. And yet the Prairies were a place to stretch and grow—instinct and imagination were my only guides. Now, I'm ready to confront the economic hardships ahead of us and the powerful men that have frightened me for too long—my father, Mr. D, the mayor, and these mafia men."

He was excited to tell her about the plans he had for the firm, but her mind was still on Laura-Jean. Katrina had listened with interest to his stories about Will Howard and the made-up men, but it was this woman who had cared for him who aroused her curiosity most.

"Laura-Jean's family moved to the Prairies looking for adventure, but she got a pandemic and poverty instead. She taught herself how to treasure simple things—a worn blanket, a speckled egg. And she taught me how to sit at a table talking—like this."

He looked steadily into his wife's green eyes. What did he see there? Anger? Jealousy? How could Katrina be jealous of Laura-Jean? Did she understand how bleak life could be on the Prairies? He decided to tell her about Gabriella and Elzier instead.

"I can't muster up a single memory of my parents loving each other or even sharing a laugh, but Gabriella and Elzier... they were masters. Elzier's childhood was as cold as stone, yet he grew into the big-hearted head of a family and a manager of men. I watched him turn a stretch of frozen land into hours of carefree fun. Gabriella crossed the Atlantic to be with him, guided by passion as her northern star."

He stooped to pick a snow glory and tucked it in Katrina's hair. "I want to be a better husband and father. Since the first time I saw you across the pews at St. Stanislaus church, you have helped me grow and become a better person. You have loved me when I didn't feel very lovable, nurtured our two exceptional children, and taken me back when I wronged you in the most profound way. And once again, you are right. It is time for a new vision for our marriage—one in which we can both be better prepared for the hardships ahead."

"We'll discuss that in time," she said, staring into the distance across the lake. "But tell me, what comes next for these people?"

He recognized this Katrina, cool, analytical, an artist preparing her canvas before dipping in her brush to paint. He reached for her hand, stroked her long fingers, and twisted her wedding ring until the diamond sparked in the sun. She looked into the distance across the lake, then turned to him. At last, the trust had returned to her eyes.

"The Prairies are a promise as much as a place," he said. "The promise has eluded many, but I feel certain that its people will prosper over time."

She stood and held out her hand.

"Let's go home," she said.

WALKING ALONG THE LAKESHORE TOWARD home, Katrina decided it was her time to open up. "I also learned a few things when you were away. While you were talking to Laura-Jean about faded blankets and speckled eggs, I was here...with two children, no income, and a house I couldn't pay for. And leering policemen trolling outside my front door."

She ripped her hand from his, almost gasping for breath.

"What I learned was that people who love you leave. And

you're not sure you can ever trust them again—or want to."

She was crying now. He yearned to take her in his arms and comfort her, but he could see there was more she desperately wanted to say. "What else did you learn?"

"I learned that depending on others for your wherewithal is a trap that springs without warning, leaving you crippled and caught. Above all, I learned to reimagine myself as someone other than Katrina Cork."

She bent and picked up a pebble from the shore, and he waited as she brushed off the sand and admired its smooth shape.

"I'm not bitter," she said. "I have chosen not to invest in that. But I will never be the person I once was. I require more information and more say. I need to know I can survive, if I have to, on my own. Will you commit to that?"

"I do," he said.

THEY WALKED IN SILENCE UNTIL they arrived at the children's park not far from home. His thoughts turned to spring. Soon, he'd be taking the hardtop off the Hudson, putting the sailboat in the water, and opening up the pool. Katrina lowered herself onto a swing—two worn ropes supporting a wooden board—and he pushed her gently in the breeze. In a burst of what he could only hope was forgiveness, she pumped her legs until her feet sailed high and her hair fell back and swept the ground.

IN THE KITCHEN THAT EVENING, Frank helped with the evening dishes. He told Katrina a bit sheepishly that he'd taken to making up children's stories to pass the time when he was away. He took a deep breath and confessed he'd even made an effort to write one down.

"Interesting. Why don't you go get it and read it to me while we finish up here."

He fetched his tale but, feeling a bit foolish, didn't get past the title. How had he read it so effortlessly on the Prairies but couldn't recite three words to his wife?

She suggested he read it at the kitchen table to Franny and Robbie, and she would listen at her easel and sketch as he read. He tried again and it worked. He read until their bedtime—well into Chapter Three—and he was encouraged that they made him promise to read the ending soon.

A FEW DAYS LATER, KATRINA presented him with a surprise. It reminded him of the homemade card the children gave her on her birthday, the day before he left. But this one was both childlike and professional, with decorative script and soft watercolor drawings of golden wheatfields and a king with kind green eyes like her own. It was his tale, written on crisp linen paper and bound with a strand of wool.

"I sent a proposal to a publisher of children's books," she said. "I am delighted to report that they are very enthusiastic."

Frank felt, well...what did he feel? Exposed, taken aback, maybe even betrayed. The words he'd strung together as a private gift to his children had been pushed into the world without his consent.

She was staring at him, expecting him to be overjoyed.

How could he disappoint her again? Wasn't she, with this gesture, launching them in a new direction? Living out the more collaborative vision they had discussed? She was adding to his creative work and leading on the business side, softening the boundaries between their roles.

"That was good of you," he said. "Thank you. Let's work together on next steps."

THAT EVENING, AFTER THE CHILDREN were in bed, and he and Katrina were settling into the living room for the evening news, she said quietly, "There's one more thing."

"Oh?"

"I'm pregnant."

Frank's mind raced. How far along was she? Was he a cuckold or the father? Was this their baby? Should he ask?

He looked at her tentatively from arm's length on the couch; he had reached the brink. He'd fled to the Prairies bereft and promised to return a better man. Now was the time, his first test. He must cast off his doubts and embrace her.

"What joyful news so soon after my return. And a harbinger of good things to come."

He snuggled in beside her, and they giggled and bubbled over with talk of a sister or brother for Franny and Robbie. Then they gamboled upstairs and celebrated her news.

IT WAS A SATURDAY MORNING when weekend papers carried book reviews, and there it was, The Kingdom of Céyh, written and illustrated by Francis and Katrina Cork. His publisher billed it as a tour de force, and the Daily News praised it as a parable about man's search for the promised land. The Tribune further elevated it, calling it a coming-of-age story about forefathers, absent fathers, and heavenly fathers on high. From Saskatchewan, the Star-Phoenix embraced it as a short history of wheat, and the Regina Leader-Post commented on Katrina's engaging artwork, and celebrated the book as an important contribution to the history of the settlement of the Prairies. A critic writing for the New York Children's Literature Review called it an apologue about child abuse, which sent Frank scurrying to his dictionary.

Apologue, a pleasant vehicle for conveying a useful lesson without stating it explicitly. Interesting, he thought; the children's critic had got it right. Perhaps that was why he'd called his hero Fib.

Given all these opinions, it was amusing that no one had thought to ask his. Just as well.

He would never have told them that what began as a bedtime story for his children had become a new path forward with his wife.

FRANNY AND ROBBIE FLUNG OPEN the door and plunged into his study. Katrina was one step behind, carrying something small. She looked at Frank with her sparkling eyes, her smile as warm as the sun. Her hands lingered on his as she passed him her gift: their book. It was magnificent—artful and colorful, with Katrina's portrait of Cruithne the King on the cover.

The children knew the story inside out, but they clambered onto Frank's knee and begged him to read it again. "Daddy, please...please...The Kingdom of Céyh."

"First, your mother and I have some very special news," he began. Then he changed his mind: "Well, it's not so much news as a story."

He moved to the couch in front of the fire, and his family gathered around. He glanced at Katrina, and she winked, anxious to hear him spin the news of the baby into a story.

"Once upon a time," he began, "on the shores of a saltless sea lived two charming children, a she and a he."

Robbie giggled, and Franny groaned. Slowly, he rolled out the story. "How long will it take to have an actual sister or brother?" Franny piped up.

It was a very good question, he thought. Had Lewis given the baby a head start?

"Soon enough," he said.

Then he cracked the cover and read the dedication aloud: "To Jimmie Gawdini, who showed me the path home."

They asked, as they always did, "Who's Jimmie Gawdini?" And he told them again: "He was a friend I met when I was away." One day, he would tell them more about Jimmie Gawdini, but not today.

"Once upon a time," he began, then turned to where he had left off—the final page of Chapter Three, when Fib decides to stay on the prairie with his people instead of becoming king.

"Fib tried to see into the future...but his magic was gone. He called on his father to restore his powers, but all he could hear was silence. All he could see was dust. Alone and afraid, Fib gathered his loved ones around him."

Frank drew the children and Katrina closer under the cozy woolen throw.

"'We have faced pestilence and plague and bone-chilling cold,' said Fib with a heavy sigh.

"Then, on the breath of an angel, Fib heard his father's voice: 'Fear not, all is not lost. Our fields will flourish, and our people will prosper again. Now, for the very last time, I implore you to take my place as king.'

"Fib reached into his sack and cast a handful of seeds onto the plain.

"'Thank you, Father, but I will stay.'"

FRANK CLOSED THE BOOK, AND Katrina took the children up to bed. When she returned, she asked, "So, what's next for Frank and Fib?"

"We're home," he said, swiping away a tear. "And you?"

She rubbed her hands slowly over her belly and the new life inside.

"You're home," she said, "and we are, too."

THE END

GRATEFUL ACKNOWLEDGEMENTS TO
Dr. Bill Waiser, University of Saskatchewan; Robert Rotenberg, author; Dr. William Kaplan, arbitrator; Victor Duret, Michel Lucas, Gerda Hnatyshyn, Guy Djandi, Marguarite Keeley, Linda Kirk, Kevin O'Farrell, Thomas McMurtry, the Maureen Moyer Burt book club, my agent Michael Levine, my publisher Matt Joudrey, and my family, for their stories and support.

TERRY KIRK is a lawyer and writer living in downtown Toronto. She studied journalism and English literature and holds a Juris Doctor (Law), and Masters' degree focused on digital transformation. Widely recognized as an innovator in the finance and fintech sector, *Pitfall,* her historical novel about day trading in Chicago's leading brokerage firm in 1929, is her debut novel.

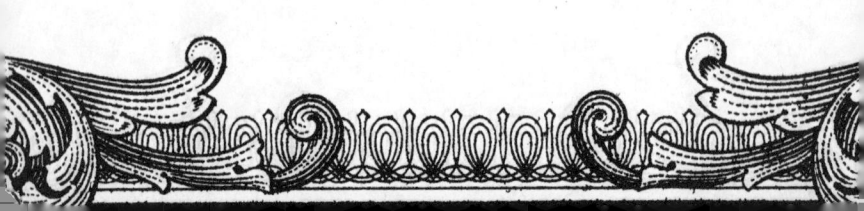

OUR AT BAY PRESS ARTISTIC COMMUNITY

Publisher
MATT JOUDREY

Managing Editor
ALANA BROOKER

Substantive Editor
KAREN CLAVELLE

Copy and Proof Editor
COURTNEY BILL

Graphic Designer
LUCAS C PAULS

Layout
LUCAS C PAULS AND MATT JOUDREY

Publicity and Marketing
SAVITA SINGH

Thanks for purchasing this book
and for supporting authors and artists.

As a token of gratitude,
please scan the QR code for
exclusive content from this title.